Simon Mason was born footballer father and a sex Sheffield and at Lady Margaret Hall, Oxford, he now works as a senior editor with the Oxford University Press. He lives in Oxford with his wife Eluned and son Gwilym. His first novel *The Great English Nude* won a Betty Trask Award. *Death of a Fantasist* is his second novel.

PRAISE FOR SIMON MASON

The Great English Nude

'One of the year's best first novelists. For intelligence and grace he is a resounding discovery'
Mail on Sunday

'A vivid variation on a classic theme ... Excellent black comedy'
Guardian

Death of a Fantasist

'He has unusually fine control over his material ... often very funny and sometimes deeply unnerving'
Independent

'His account of their adventures in New York combines slapstick, caricature and exhuberant description in an appealing and refreshing way'
Sunday Telegraph

Also by Simon Mason

THE GREAT ENGLISH NUDE

DEATH OF A FANTASIST

Simon Mason

An *Abacus* Book

First published in Great Britain by Constable 1994
This edition published by Abacus 1995

Copyright © Simon Mason 1994

The moral right of the author has been asserted.

A CIP catalogue record for this book
is available from the British Library.

ISBN 0 349 10627 4

Printed and bound in Great Britain by
Clays Ltd, St Ives plc

Abacus
A Division of
Little, Brown and Company (UK)
Brettenham House
Lancaster Place
London WC2E 7EN

For Eluned

His right arm too jingled with bells whenever he thrust or swung it. This was to give music to his sword-play, for he was hot in pursuit of fame! Such was the style the great prince rode in, magnificently caparisoned.

Wolfram Von Eschenbach

and if I fall asleep in your arms
please wake me up in my dream

Tom Waits

1

It was high summer in Oxford, mild and damp. Dawn came out of fog over the water meadows and showed the mouldering city to itself, the spires, the gatehouses, the shopping arcades, the multi-storey car-park.

Two hours later, in a Victorian terrace cottage built too close to the river, Bethanay Beaumont rose with a cursory yawn and made the short automatic trip to the bathroom. On Sunday mornings it was her habit to slip out of bed while Dudley lay dreaming, and clean her teeth preparatory to sex. Some years earlier he had intimated that he could not bear kissing her with the fetor of sleep on her breath. But habits can be broken, and besides it was not Sunday.

Dudley's dreams confused not only the days of the week but most other aspects of reality; so while his wife got ready for work this Friday he lay kissing the duvet, by now wet, relishing such small shifts of weight he believed took him closer, jolt by jolt, fantasy on fantasy, towards a weekly comfort.

Above the bed the curtain was snagged on a small plaster bust of Napoleon which kept vigil over Dudley's dreams, and some grey light was let in. The room was small the way lives are small; it contained a clothes-rail, a dresser and a fake Moroccan rug, like a summary of something better.

There was not much Dudley to be seen: a single nostril, the bump of a closed eye, a tuft of blond hair. Every night what was left of his hair attempted to escape *en masse* over his right ear. The rest of him was hidden beneath a cataleptic duvet imprinted with a floral motif of primrose yellow and baby blue:

an enigma in sleep as he would have liked to be in life. Blessed are the simple for theirs are the dreams of God.

From the bathroom door came the slap-slap of water in a basin, brief snippets of naked arms groping for a towel, long, wet hair twisted into a turban, and some yellow dressing-gown flapping free of a knee. Dudley dreamed on regardless.

Over the years his dreams of fame had become remarkably comprehensive. He was able to play in his head, word by word, whole hours' worth of dialogue with Nobel Prize winners and film stars and chat-show hosts, friends of his, with whom he sparred in conversation for the benefit of world-wide television audiences, describing to them amusing anecdotes of his early days before he was famous.

Soliloquizing in a perfect voice, he felt his legs crossing and uncrossing on creaky studio leather and saw a hand recognizable as his own waving in front of him, conducting the whole affair and wrapping it up with a flourish. Inexplicably he always forgot what he was famous for, but it didn't matter, what mattered were these consummating public performances, the fripperies of expression which laughingly acknowledged or disdained the idolatry of fabulous women, the friendship of powerful men and – somewhere in the background, beyond the television cameras' snouts and winking lights – the whole world laughing with him, not against him as formerly.

The cistern roared, a lid slammed, footsteps rocked the bed in passing, and a draught slid across Dudley's face. His wife stepped out of her night-knickers, drop-kicked them in the direction of the laundry basket, and began to dress. Knock-kneed, she pulled on a new pair of black lace french knickers advertised in a magazine as 'Lingerie funwear for those magical moments'. Arms akimbo, she coaxed her breasts into her de luxe lace bra guaranteed to give her the allure of love goddesses of old or her money back. Bending, she drew on a garter, black lace trimmed with red gauze flowers. Then she squinted in the dust-flowered mirror above the dresser and saw the familiar stranger looking back at her, a face still crumpled by sleep but wearier than that, and above all sad.

Dudley and Bethanay had been married for five years. They met when he was twenty and she was nineteen. He was an undergraduate studying history; she worked in a wine bar. One day she was invited to a party in college rooms, and there, through the hot, smoky crush and rainbow flicker of hired disco lights, she first saw him, a tall, ugly boy, talking loudly to someone about books. Later he talked to her. Although the subject of his conversation was neither here nor there, the extremity of his manner impressed her; it was both lyrical and strenuous, as if at any moment his words might inscribe a visible pattern on the air, sentences spooling out of him like the iridescent bands of red, blue, green and yellow from the light machine. Later still she found herself standing with him half-way up a spiral staircase in an older part of the building. Like the architecture it seemed a moment sealed in time. Bathed in orange light from a lamp in an alcove he stood four strategic steps below her, and her face was on a level with the top of his head. His hair was blond and fluffy, his face fleshy, his eyes small, his nose short, pert and misaligned. He was talking about Napoleon, about the Frenchman's physiognomy, dietary preferences and sexual habits. He had very little eyebrow, but what he had he made the most of. To call him ugly seemed to her uninteresting and off the point. For a year she had lived in Oxford just to see her friends at the university and to be introduced to their clever, wealthy associates, and now, for her pains, she had met someone completely different, and this, she realized, was what she had been waiting for.

Under the bed Bethanay's mongrel Sykes broke wind with a rasp. His unblinking eyes glistened in the shadows from a position he seemed to have occupied without respite since Dudley and Bethanay had met. That first Michaelmas term (weather dismal, youth triumphant) when Bethanay moved into Dudley's rooms, the dog had at once established itself. Sullen, vicious, foul-breathed, it had tyrannized them. Now, after five years of marriage, it was the same vigilant presence sourly intruding itself at the most awkward of moments. Dudley had been through several phases of reaction: tolerance, outrage, bitterness, revenge, lassitude and finally acquiescence. Nowadays he often took Sykes with him to the office while Bethanay looked after her shop in Banbury. At home the mongrel slept in a fitful stink under the bed, periodically farting to draw his inventive abuse. But, being of a literary bent, he also revered the mongrel as a symbol of his marriage: the animal discontent at its heart.

Bethanay put her toes into a concertina of black stocking, unfurled it up her leg to within an inch of her knicker line and snapped the clips shut. In full Playmate regalia, she stared grumpily at Dudley in the mirror, watching his head shift on the pillow, blond hair springing upright like the bristles of a broom. Hairstyle – like dress – was of extreme importance to Dudley. 'Dress to kill, but, if you can't, dress to maim or cripple' was one of his maxims. At present he gelled his hair back from his forehead in long, wet loops, but it would not last, he was insatiable for new styles, soon he would develop a fringe or be razored for a flat-top. In a single year he had run through a quiff, a cowlick, a wedge and a crew-cut. It was madness, he would never grow up.

Bethanay's reflection bit its lower lip, the dark hair swung, tedious and severe. She could not take her eyes off her husband; even in sleep he demanded her attention. His head was revolving again, the face turning, the hair stiffly following.

Slowly she buttoned her blouse, silk hanging sheer like water from the suspended animation of her breasts. On tiptoe, looking away from her reflection, she pulled on her tightest and shortest and most scarlet skirt.

It was nearly time to go, not to work in her shop in Banbury but to a rendezvous with James, a man who was a perfect blank, duller and handsomer than Dudley. She would give herself to James as she never had to Dudley. Her mood was depressed and careless and vindictive. She pressed her mouth with a stick of Luscious Hot Crimson and briefly buttoned her lips. Shaky smoker's fingers drew smudged outlines of kohl round her eyes and attached two dangly silver spirals to her ears. Her pale, loose face was stark under the bright colours.

Dudley was trying to break into her thoughts again, shifting and murmuring in the bed behind her, but she hardened her heart against him, gave a quick functional smile like a mechanic testing machinery, and cleaned a tooth of Hot Crimson. Stalking past him in her high heels, she went down the stairs. Soft, carpeted thumps gave way to a hollow clop-clop across the bare floorboards of the hallway, and then, after an empty pause, came the window-rattling slam of the front door.

Dudley sat bolt upright in bed, his hair bolt upright on his head. 'What now?' he said loudly.

From the bedside table his glasses, propped on top of a notebook marked *Pensées*, frowned at him. Consciousness slowly regained him like light leaking under a blindfold, and he suffered the ordinary confusion, disappointment, vacancy and detumescence. Punch's nose.

It was not Sunday.

Still snagged in pleasurable dream-memories, he began to masturbate. Shutting his eyes tight, he dissociated himself from his hand. The hand belonged to a girl from the slums of Rio de Janeiro, it was dextrous and indiscriminate, it had no time for ceremony or pranks, it took hold of him as it might a kitten or a hen (such things roamed freely about the slums) and caressed him roughly. The girl's ragged vest fell off, her skin was brown and dusty, smelling of stale coffee. She was speaking in a guttural language he did not know. The grunting he recognized as his own.

His eyes still half-closed, his hand supporting the fragile moment, he kicked off the duvet and slid awkwardly off the bed, landing on Sykes, who, after waiting so many years for just such an opportunity, bit him deeply in the ankle.

11

2

By mid-morning there was a warm drizzle of rain, and the offices of the Learned Press were unbearably humid. Down the long corridor that Dudley had christened Death Row two dozen doors were propped open with piles of books — *Selections from Pyrrho of Elis*, *Flora and Fauna of the Balearic Islands*, *Gender in Chaucer*, *The Sexuality of Meat*. They had never enjoyed such general use, but the ventilation they facilitated was negligible. Instead, through the open doors came the unintelligible hum of conversation.

At one end of Death Row the elevator opened with a sigh and Austin Ord, the Managing Director of Academic Monographs, recently promoted and already feeling the strain, ran out. With the huge build and squashed features of an ex-boxer, he was still capable of giving his staff a fright as he jogged along the corridors in pent-up fury, his big hands dangling at his sides and his close-cropped head jerking left and right, ever-vigilant for only he knew what. He was never completely at rest. When required to stand still he would rock anxiously backwards and forwards on the balls of his size eleven feet, dripping with perspiration, while his forehead puckered and throbbed. For such an outsize man his voice was surprisingly quiet, but it was the kind of repressed whisper that trembled on the verge of a scream. 'Well now,' he would say, so softly that he could hardly be heard, 'that's a very, very, very ... *silly* question.' And his knuckles would crack like glass. He didn't like Dudley. Dudley's reputation as a gossip, idler, raconteur and dilettante prejudiced him. Dudley's casual, showy way of doing things, or not doing them, made him very anxious. Dudley accelerated his heartbeat, metabolic rate, and the frequency of his tics and spasms.

Austin Ord jogged up Death Row and stopped at the one

12

door that was still shut. On it was the name G. *Dudley*, an inoffensive name, a name without pretension or style. Ord's left cheek twitched. He licked his lips and hustled inside.

The light was off, the window shut, the blind rolled down. Nothing stirred in the airless gloom, not even Ord who had encountered the desk. He despatched the blind with a shrug of his big shoulders, struggled titanically with the tiny clasp of the window, and in the sudden light and air hunched over Dudley's desk, his knuckles resting on the mountain of paper that covered it, rhino eyes aswivel.

In daylight, the claustrophobic walls, once white, now aged to magnolia, closed round him. Overloaded bookshelves pressed forward with their weight. Posters of Renaissance masterpieces crowded him.

One corner of the room was taken up with the impressive fossil of a long-dead, unidentifiable plant, and in another a smudgy, glass-topped table bore a selection of liqueurs and half a dozen tumblers with different sized pigs etched in pink up their sides. The desk, situated beneath the window, facing the door, was a mass of letters, books, polystyrene coffee cups, files, folders, socks, magazines, scrap paper, tubes of hair gel, stationery and typescripts, on top of which were stacked two wire trays marked IN and OUT containing nothing but a crumpled packet of Gitanes cigarettes and a desk-lamp rearing blindly from the coil of its own unplugged flex. Such is the almost fabulous debris of the materially idle.

Ord inhaled deeply, suddenly held his breath and thought, 'Dog?' He lifted his nose, lowered it, and found on the carpet under the desk a thick coating of dog hairs and the saliva-encrusted remains of something rubber-stamped 'Priority' in red print.

Along the corridor in another office two secretaries were talking in low voices while they typed, their eyes glued to their screens, their fingers in sonata across the keyboards, their questions and comments addressed to their machines.

13

'Is he in yet?'

'Who?'

'Cuddly.'

One stopped typing and flipped a page in a loose-leaf folder. She said, 'Haven't seen him. More to the point, haven't *heard* him.' The other hummed, long-suffering. The first paused to scratch her nose.

'Austin's looking for him.'

'Austin Rover?'

'Just went past, nose to the ground.'

A telephone placed between them began to beep.

'Amazing, really,' one said. 'How he gets away with it.' The telephone's measured peals continued with her hand resting on it.

'There is talk,' the other said, 'of an Employees Evaluation Committee Meeting.'

'Hello. Yes, it is. From where? The hospital.' Pinning the receiver between ear and shoulder she reached hunchback for a pink transmittal form and wrote on it in large, slow letters. 'Has he? I'll tell him when he gets here.' She replaced the receiver, and began to type again, her eyes on the screen.

'A Jeremiah Dudley has left his golfing umbrella in Emergency Out-Patients.'

'Why he won't stick to his real name . . .'

'He had an accident on the way to work.'

'The way he rides that bicycle of his. You know he knocked Austin down last week?'

'Apparently he was attacked in the street by a rabid dog.'

For a moment there was nothing but the tapping of their keyboards, then both sighed again.

At eleven o'clock, Dudley, briefly Jeremiah, broke the stagnant calm of the morning. Junior editor of Humanities monographs, late of the Emergency Out-Patients Department of the John Radcliffe Hospital, he scorned the lift, wished he hadn't, and clawed himself up the spiral stairs on his aluminium crutch, grunting like a tennis pro at every step. Finally he came to rest against those lift doors which had shut only a minute earlier on the departing Austin Ord. Knowing nothing of his Managing Director's visit, he leaned on his crutch and recalled the past hour.

At the hospital he had asked for two crutches and had been given only one, and that grudgingly. His view of this was clear. White-smocked, anally-repressed, Crippenesque hospital officials hoarded stockpiles of these playful, mollusc-footed things for no other reason than the irresponsible expression of corrupt power; their denials were the po-faced edicts of tyranny which he was well used to in other forms and against which he had voided some wit, the last resort of the liberal mind, to no effect. He had come away with a crutch and a limp, no more and no less, as if he had not the sense of theatre to carry off more of both.

'War criminals,' he said loudly, and the editor in the nearest office to the lift kicked aside his copy of *Meaning and Beyond* to let the door swing shut.

A second crutch from On Stage, the theatre costumiers, had tempted him, an enormous piratical oak wishbone tipped with brass, but expense did not permit it. It is true that the greatest theatrical effects can be managed with minimum props but the minimum in anything usually requires the maximum effort. Perhaps (he theorized) he preferred to struggle.

Blinking down the corridor he adjusted his cravat, aware that the yellow and magenta silk struck an unpleasant contrast with his flushed features. After his hairstyle, his clothes were his greatest preoccupation.

Tucking the cravat into the V of his baize-green pullover, pulling down the rim of his fedora to shield the glare of his face from bystanders, he shook his good leg to align the pleats of his Oxford bags, and limped down the corridor with ostentatious fortitude.

Several people nodded to him from their offices.

'Morning,' his secretary called as he toiled past her open door. He paused and silently looked in on her, lifting his thickly

15

bandaged foot, gesturing with a stab of his pert nose for her to see and admire, and toiling on tragically in a flurry of elbows.

His tragedy was this – despite the slight drama of his ankle, despite his hair and clothes, the day was like any other, a composition of second-hand hours and third-rate evasions. He saw himself sitting at his overloaded desk, nose to his unending and uninteresting correspondence, a hack with pretensions. Little wonder that he would take any opportunity to enliven the day's wait. Even biting served a purpose. It was very depressing.

His secretary gave him fifteen minutes to settle, then took him a cup of coffee. He was sitting behind his desk, a long shred of *pain au chocolat* in one hand and an unlit small cigar in the other, his injured foot stuck high in a vacant slot on one of the bookshelves. With difficulty he was reading a note left for him by Austin Ord. His head with its blond slick of hair was as picturesquely still as his fedora which hung like a *trompe-l'oeil* from a peg on the back of the door.

'This man is an illiterate,' he said, without looking up. 'Don't you agree?' He handed over the note. 'Do you think you might translate? I'm presuming it's from our querimonious leader. His Ku-Klux-Klan-like logo is at the bottom.'

His secretary took the note and spoke in a fluent matter-of-fact tone. 'Urgent, exclamation mark, where are you, question mark, annual publications meeting, dash, eleven thirty, full stop, need retrospective figures, comma, sales, comma, number of titles commissioned last year, full stop.' She handed back the note to Dudley. 'Could that be it?'

'It *could* be,' he said. 'We mustn't discount it.' He looked at his watch: eleven twenty. 'But I've missed it anyway,' he said. 'Thank God. I haven't finished my breakfast yet.'

His secretary put the coffee on top of the litter on his desk, and her eyes, narrowing, went to the fat ball of bandages on his foot.

16

'I stopped a motorcycle in St Giles,' he said, chewing. 'But you should see the motorcycle.'

'I heard it was a dog.'

'There was a dog involved, one of those dogs you see around. Nasty, wiry, vulgar, halitosic, peripheral dogs. But it was squashed flat.'

'The hospital phoned to say you'd left your umbrella behind.'

Surprised, he frowned. 'Did I have an umbrella? I doubt it. Still, it might be worth having. Would you phone to ask them to drop it round later? Better check first that it's good quality. Oh, and I'm having lunch with Professor Dix; would you also book a table at Pinks for one o'clock?'

As she backed out a telephone began to ring somewhere in his office.

'I reconnected you to the switchboard,' she said as the door was closing. 'You can take calls direct. If you can find your phone.'

Alert but immobile amidst the rubbish of his room, pastry in one hand, cigar in the other, he sat staring at the closed door. He was silent for a moment, listening to the ringing of the phone, then he sighed. For several years he had fantasized about his secretary. She was not beautiful, she was short and graceless and she had red hair, but there was something in her walk or the movement of her hands or the revelatory looseness of her starched blouses which excited him. There were few escapades with his secretary which he had not imagined, few scenes of primal instinct which they had not shared. In some ways he felt closer to her than to his wife.

The telephone was still ringing and he found himself still staring at the closed door. The concept of the closed door suddenly interested him. It defines a room as a cell, its occupant as an inmate. In captivity the animal of intelligence develops abnormal characteristics, its behaviour becomes perverse. Often it chews its fur with yellow stumps of teeth, creating pink bald patches around the rump. It does not stalk up and down in front of the bars ferociously swishing its tail but droops in the corner, thinking and chewing *pain au chocolat*. Its expressions are melodramatic, its breath bad, its powers of concentration nil. Often it appears to be deaf. What is left of its hair is always changing. A ringing telephone fails to elicit a response.

On the other hand the closing of doors marks the beginning of the performance, the lights going down, a hush descending on the auditorium, the orchestra in the pit striking an evocative chord, a spotlight coming up on stage. A man appears in a funny hat.

The phone stopped ringing and his interest in the concept of closed doors vanished. He took out his *Pensées* which he carried with him at all times and wrote in it.

> 218. *Comic characters, unlike tragic characters, need a play, a world, to inhabit.*

3

He stood gazing out of the window, trying to remember what he had been about to do. Nothing occurred to him. The most difficult part of a day in the office was deciding where to begin; sometimes he didn't decide until it was time for him to leave.

The familiar scene through the window mocked him, the grey road, the plastic bollards, the swart green leaves of sycamores, the Georgian townhouses stuccoed pink and cream, the pale lampposts. They receded in order down St Giles towards that Gothic spire at the end of the avenue – the Martyrs' Memorial, rigid with piety, crowded with foreign language students and darkened with drizzle.

He gave a sudden shove to the window and gulped in the toxic air. In Oxford the weather is never one thing or another but both at once or neither; it is always just about to rain, or the sun is just about to disappear. He longed for baking blue droughts and torrid storms. On the fabulous journeys he dreamed of the scene was always exotic, the trees stretched in canopies over his head, the road ran like an imperative across the orange desert, the natives clustered round him with their dogs and old, wise women told his inscrutable future in the lucky creases of his outstretched palm. Space and freedom and destiny: these were the themes of his travel fantasies.

Here, he was imprisoned. He was imprisoned in his cluttered office. He was imprisoned in his tiny terrace-house. Imprisoned in Oxford with its medieval streets and medieval weather, and in England, crammed with people, suburbs and motorways. The weight of the whole island seemed to bear down on him. He was the martyr pinned beneath the lot, crushed like the correspondence at the bottom of the piles on his desk.

Finally he settled himself and took up a book. Above his shoulders was a poster of Dürer's *Melencolia 1* of 1514. Furrowed brow, keen eyes, stubborn mouth: details of compelling introspection. Turning back to the book, he tried to emulate such concentration.

Sexuality in the Myth of the Holy Grail by Professor Maximilian Dix, first published in 1953, was possibly a classic work worthy of enterprising reissue, but the opening chapter – 'Various Techniques: The Long and the Short' – was turgid by modern standards. Within five minutes Dudley was gazing vacantly at Melancholy, absorbed by the intricacies of other techniques – for instance, the control of his back muscles should he lie outstretched on his untidy desk and his secretary, naked to the waist, sit athwart him, rearing up and plunging forward like an actress in a scene of classical mourning, seeking the rhythm (strenuous) and facial expression (Maenad-eyed and Monroe-mouthed) which would release them.

The book fell from his lap and so vivid was the intrusion that he was suddenly overwhelmed by guilt and immediately picked up his telephone to dial the number of Bethanay's shop. He thought he would tell her what an awful day he was having. After a little while he began to count the ringing tones, and

19

when he had counted to three hundred he reluctantly put the phone down. It instantly rang, making him jump and snatch it up. 'Who's that?' he said.

'I thought your call would never finish,' his secretary said. 'Austin rang you. Can you ring him back? I've a feeling your phone has been put through to me again. I'll reconnect you to the switchboard.'

'Many thanks,' Dudley said and putting down the phone he at once tapped in the command to divert all his calls back to his secretary. Then he dialled Bethanay's number again. 'Where is she?' he said. This time he let it ring for fifteen minutes, doodling on what was near to hand, mainly important correspondence, before remembering, with an immediate sense of pressure at the temples, that he had to return Austin Ord's call.

There was a knock on his door. 'But soft, who comes?' he said, and in ran Austin Ord, a minor figure of vengeance, biblical in spirit, damp and florid in his bulging double-breasted suit. There was a sudden shift in Dudley's feelings of guilt.

'I was just phoning you,' Dudley said. 'No wonder there's no answer.' He proffered the phone as evidence. 'About your message. I wondered if our chat might wait till this afternoon.' He glanced at his watch and winced elaborately. 'I have a lunch appointment with Maximilian Dix quite soon. You know, author of *Sexuality in the Myth of the Holy Grail*. Fabulous book, I've just been rereading it. He's an extremely old Freudian and will need plenty of time to be walked to the restaurant. I don't think it would do to have him killed on the busy roads of Oxford because of undue haste on our part. By the way, did I tell you what happened to me on the way to work this morning?' Ord appeared not to hear him but paced up to the bookshelves, and after a moment violently rearranging a few titles, turned to face him.

'Tell me, Geoffrey, how would you define your job?'

Dudley looked blank. 'Define my job?'

'You remember. It's what we pay you for.'

'I think I'd be loath to define it at all, the simplest definitions can be so insufficient.' Ord took hold of his knuckles. 'But if

20

you insist. Let's see. A publisher's editor. I think of myself as . . . as what? Well now. Yes. As a sort of literary midwife. Yes. I deliver authors of their difficult books. Actually, to develop – to *deepen* – the metaphor, I might add that in commissioning an author I actually plant the seed of a book. Commission, emission: interesting chime. I like that. To conclude, I conduct a sort of literary artificial insemination service.'

Austin Ord was shaking his head.

'Do you think that's a little strong?'

'No, no, no,' Ord said quietly. 'You misunderstand me. How is your job defined on your Job Definition Form? How many books will you *commission* this year?'

'Oh, I see what you're driving at,' Dudley said. 'I thought you were after something more all-encompassing. I think it's around fifty. Or eighty. Something like that.'

'And how many have you commissioned so far?'

'When you say "commissioned", do you mean . . .'

'Five? Ten?'

'Oh, I don't think it's that many.'

The room was quiet. Austin Ord cracked a knuckle and startled himself. 'I have to ask these questions,' he said quietly. 'I'm Managing Director after all.' His voice was a compressed whisper, as if a loud noise had been squeezed into a very small space.

'Of course,' Dudley said. 'It comes to us all, Austin.'

'Let me ask you another question, Geoffrey. What do you think you're best at?'

Dudley thought for a moment. 'Lunches. I'm good at lunches.'

The phone began to ring, gently, from its nest of unanswered letters.

'Excuse me.' He picked up the phone. 'Hello.'

'Have you phoned Austin yet?' his secretary said.

'Ah, Professor Dix,' Dudley replied. 'Very well, and how are you?' He mouthed mutely *Get back to you* at Ord, who was mopping his brow with a handkerchief, distracted by Melancholy. Dudley glimpsed a struggle of wills. 'Directions, Profes-

21

sor Dix?' he said loudly, 'Yes, of course. Let me see. Don't come down the Woodstock Road, I was knocked down in it by a double-decker bus only this morning. Thank you, I can manage with a crutch. Come along the Banbury Road as far as North Parade.'

'Have you got Austin with you now?' his secretary asked.

'Yes, you've got it. Then cut through to Leckford Road. Pause to remark the dreadful Victorian Gothic church on your right.'

Austin Ord stood with one big hand on the doorknob, chewing the thumbnail of his other hand.

'Yes, you've got it, Professor Dix. Ah, do you? Hold on, I've got the file here.' Dudley clasped the receiver to his pullover and hissed, 'Sorry, Dix is a bit of a chatterbox. Why don't we talk this afternoon?' Ord looked at him, turned, and after a second apparently trying to alter the alignment of the door, exited.

Dudley stood theatrically at his desk, phone held aloft. 'Many thanks,' he said into it after a moment's reflection. 'Wonderful interruptus. See you after lunch.'

The drizzle had stopped and fitful sunlight steamed through the window, creeping over Dudley, who sat at his desk, head bowed, avoiding Melancholy. Unmoved by his exchange with Austin Ord, but saddened by everything else that had ever happened to him, and by everything that had never happened to him, he took up his phone and slowly dialled his home number. His own recorded voice answered, inappropriately glib, and he replied curtly, 'Tried to call you at work. No answer. Getting drunk with Martin tonight. Don't wait up.'

4

A mile away in his curtained bedsit Martin Prout lay on the bed thinking about Dudley. The bedsit was one of those rooms lived in so long by different people that it had developed the air of being unoccupied. Nothing could enliven the foam sofa and collapsible chair, the Baby Belling cooker and sink missing its cupboard doors, the dim, patterned square of carpet and prison-style bed.

Martin lay on his back, smoking and staring at the ceiling, intent on the naked light bulb which hung on a direct trajectory above his right eye, as if this association might, with effort, tell him something. He had been awake for hours, waiting for the day to claim him, resisting it, and now it was nearly one o'clock and he was too tired to resist any more. Abruptly he heaved himself up and hunched forward, his head in his hands, a wedge of stiff black hair canted upward like a horn.

Shavings of cigarette ash tumbled between his knees and landed on his yellow feet. Mornings were difficult. Afternoons too.

A few more minutes passed, the ash drifted down. Lumps of it already lay, like delicate scabs, on his skin.

Outside, one of the famous Oxford clocks chimed remotely, and he slid off the bed and limped to the sink. When the nausea had passed, he leaned over and spat into it, and watched his spittle gasp on the plughole. Then he stood on the books put there for that purpose and his face appeared in the mirror, a long, thin face made beautiful by cupid's-bow lips and dark eyes. Slowly he began to shave, scrutinizing himself with such concentration it could not be out of vanity but as if to discover something he had previously missed: the origin of the fault which had caused everything in his life to go wrong.

He believed there was a tiny fault which lay in his past,

23

embedded in his memories. He spent his days examining his childhood, his schooldays, college life and aborted adulthood in the hope of finding it, that hairline fracture, that damaged cell which had caused the rest to crumble. His analysts used to try to get him to talk about his mother, his father, growing up an only child, his first girlfriend; but he did not think these analysts were on the right track at all: the fault was in him, in his own life, not in the lives of others – the only problem was to discover it.

He was twenty-seven years old, white, heterosexual, five feet two. Since leaving drama college he had been involved theoretically in the theatre and media. 'Theoretically' because his college had not provided him with an Equity card, and so he existed in that twilight world of fringe performances in garages and schools, and of budget voice-overs and one-line appearances for fly-by-night film agencies operating from addresses in Rotherhithe and Tooting Bec. For a while he performed with a youth theatre company called Spring Chicken which put on pantomimes at primary schools. But one afternoon, when another actor made an entrance, he turned and walked off stage (Bobo the rabbit spurning Coco the clown) and never went back. Later he was used in a few adverts and some voice-overs in radio commercials. His mimicry was superb and these had been a success; he even had an agent who loved and despaired of him.

Before Spring Chicken, he had studied at Erlington Drama School, but he had not completed the course. All he remembered of the period was his training in solo performance: for him nothing compared to the feeling of walking on an empty stage, that first impression of its spaciousness as if it ran like a river beyond the theatre walls, its preliminary silence, the softness of his footfalls, the lonely, gaseous spotlight in which he might transform himself, in which he floated as if it were water, dissolving like a drop of paint, spreading out until he could imagine himself anything.

Shaving methodically, he stared at himself. Tiny bubbles of blood appeared along the line of his jaw.

He knew he was ill: he had been told, he possessed medical certificates and the testimonies of doctors and specialists. In 1990 he voluntarily entered the Warnford clinic in Oxford as a day patient and began a course of lithium. After London, Oxford seemed human-sized and believable. No more nights walking round the concrete tracts under Westway reading the graffiti of football hooligans and sex maniacs on the walls, smelling diesel and the river, the ground always wet whatever the weather. In Oxford he sat in creaky old pubs, listening to people talk, locals and students and tourists, their conversations disintegrating towards closing time, melding into a single, sociable babble. Voices surrounded him like promises.

When he had finished shaving, he pulled on a pair of black denims and laceless tennis shoes, and limped out to the front door of the block of bedsits where the mail collected on a russet bristle-and-mange doormat.

Back in his room, he opened his letter and read the first two sentences. *Dear Martin, I hope you got my previous letter telling you the wonderful news about your award nomination. My American associate Ed Slezinger tells me he has tried to get in touch with you to organize your trip, but he appears to have had no success as yet . . .*

Peculiarities always occurred like this, in formal style, on headed notepaper or some equivalent. He stuffed the letter with the others into an army-navy kitbag he kept behind the sofa and, putting on his Walkman and lighting another cigarette, he searched in the bag until he found a packet of photographs.

Here was a creased memory in black and white, a group of schoolboys in a playground tiered on benches above a notice which said: *Jude House, Shammings Senior, 1981*. Shammings sat behind, a squat brick model. Seven rows of boys of various ages stared from these ranks into the future. It was a bright day but a cold wind froze them, sweeping hair and ties across scrunched-up faces. At the end of the back row was that undersized, moody-faced fourth-former, himself, but he didn't look at him, he looked, as usual, at Proctor.

Proctor sat in the penultimate row, an innocuous position,

but that was his genius, to mimic the ordinary. He had a lisp and big hands and empty eyes. He would wait for Martin everywhere – by the labs, outside the gym, in the toilets, over the football pitch – perfectly composed, almost careless, knowing he would come. He always came. They were made for each other. In his first term Proctor broke two of his fingers. In his second he used a compass to tattoo Martin's arm with a cross which became infected. By the fourth form he had dislocated Martin's jaw several times, destroyed one of his toes (leaving him with a permanent limp), burned his nipple with a cigarette, ruptured one of his kidneys, cracked a rib and almost perforated his eardrum with melted plastic. He was not a bully, he was a psychopath, not a psychopath who runs amuck with a hatchet, but one who applies the rules of human behaviour without recourse to morals. He could do nothing without a victim, and for four years of his life Martin was that victim. When Proctor was expelled Martin's first depressions began.

In the photograph Proctor had a paw up to his snout, sunlight illuminating his knuckles. Martin lit another cigarette, ash dropped on Proctor and he reverently wiped it off. Beatings had not done him any harm; they had toughened him up, they had enabled him to survive and justified his bitterness.

His finger rubbed clean the front row of boys as well. In the middle of the row was an ugly, lanky sixth-former with thick blond hair, Head Boy of Jude. Two months ago he would not have remembered his name; his nickname was Stuff and he was one of those boys who at the age of sixteen discover in themselves the aptitude to adopt an adult and affected personality. They are invariably exposed and humiliated as poseurs. Stuff was. At Shammings he wore a worsted jacket and wool trousers and carried a briefcase. His voice was loose: the baggy vowels and weak consonants that ran on in endless sentences were an invitation to impersonation. He was Head of Jude, Secretary of the Drama Society, Secretary of the Debating Society, Secretary of the Sixth-Form Dining Club, Secretary of the Schools Committee and Secretary and sole member of something called the Arts League. One Christmas he performed

26

the part of Falstaff in the sixth-form production of *Henry IV Part One*. Padded with mattresses and drunk on the sound of poetry in his own mouth, he reeled off the stage at the end of the third act ('Hostess, my breakfast, come!') and plunged into the audience, crushing the Headmaster's youngest daughter Jemima.

Martin put the photograph back in the packet, put the packet in the kitbag and slung it behind the sofa.

Two months earlier he had received a phone call from someone calling himself Geoffrey Dudley. Standing on linoleum in the crook of the hallway outside his room, looking at the lists of taxi numbers on cards on the wall, he heard the loose, affected voice in the receiver. This Dudley was interested in a television advertisement that Martin had 'starred in'. He added that as an old boy of Shammings Senior of Poole Martin might remember him. He did not remember Martin, he had heard about Martin by chance.

'I was Head Boy of one of those silly houses for a while. Was it Diggory Venn? Can't remember.'

Martin read the taxi listings. ABC Taxis. 001. Cavalier Cars. He read them to himself in a loose, affected voice.

'Hello? Have we been disconnected?'

'Stuff,' Martin said.

'Well, yes, that was my *nom de guerre*. But I don't think there's any need to carry on such formalities.'

When they met, Dudley was unrecognizable; he had become plump and lost much of his hair. His face sagged on to his chin. But when he began to talk – and he talked for an hour about their 'shared past' – his mannerisms turned him back into Stuff and Martin recognized him as one of the weak whose self-importance blinds them to the indulgence they demand.

'I want to know about this TV thing you've got going. I expect to break into television myself quite soon, so your contacts could be useful. Think of me as an initiate.' He was still arrogant and affected and implausibly untroubled. They met several times over the next few weeks. Television, Stuff said, had brought them together.

At first he wanted only the opportunity to put him down. But their meetings were complicated by something more than this; they produced in him a faint imitation of those feelings of resentment and need he had suffered with Proctor years earlier. Brooding on this, as he brooded on everything, he came to believe that Dudley had been given to him for some purpose. He thought that he would like to hurt Dudley in some way if he could.

Outside, unseen behind curtains, Oxford endured the midday, distant voices drowned by more distant traffic as the tourist coaches steamed into the centre. The weather was cloudy but warm, damp rising into the heavy air. Today a freak had happened: he had been nominated for the American Advertising Council's Award for the Best Advertising Actor of the Year, for his 'performance' in an advertisement for a soft drink, and he was assured by a man in his agency's New York office that his career was made. Advertising actors were the biggest stars in the world these days, having taken over from film stars who were not seen so frequently or in such striking sequences. They commanded the highest fees, their faces filled the celebrities pages of the chic magazines. At first he had assumed the nomination was a practical joke, but he knew no practical jokers, and today it had been confirmed.

He lay down on the bed and stared up at the light bulb hanging on its noose above him and thought some more about Dudley.

5

Under the muted lights of Pinks restaurant, Dudley was preparing to speak. Professor Dix had committed the tactical error
of asking him his opinion. Settling back, he crossed his legs,
rested an elbow on his crutch, and looked round the restaurant
while Professor Dix finished recounting an anecdote from his
early life, vaguely sexual, which he was comparing to an
episode in the Arthurian cycle.

Conversation reached them from the other tables, a murmuring of the same *soigné* quality as the décor. Pinks Wine Bar had
been decorated entirely in types of pink. There was maroon
upholstery, cinnamon table-cloths, rose lampshades, coral
carpet, salmon walls, nipple-pink curtains and on each table a
magenta vase with a carnation in it. Everything was tasteful,
restful and uneventful. The part-time models who staffed the
restaurant posed behind the bar, their perfect profiles multiplied
in wall mirrors between the racks of liqueurs and the television
clamped above the swing doors which led to the kitchen.

Dudley's reflection appeared from time to time from behind
those of the waitresses. Slicked hair showed dark above a pale
forehead which wrinkled enquiringly as he sought himself out.
(Frowning, he put a hand to his head.)

'Yes,' he said arbitrarily, brushing his shoulder. 'Yes, quite.'

The voice he used for entertaining authors was rich and
slightly arch, as if a college don were being imitated by a drag
queen. Academics in particular were soothed by it. Glancing at
the pastel portraits of the immortal dead on the wall (Monroe,
Lennon, Chaplin, Garland), his thoughts tended to his future
and the tumultuous years of his fame.

Professor Dix, he realized, had at last fallen silent and was
looking at him. For a moment, forgetting himself, he simply
looked back. Dix was a stooped octogenarian with a wrinkled,

freckled face and a habit of running trembling fingers through what was left of his white-with-a-hint-of-nicotine hair. He had taken off his jacket and rolled up his shirt-sleeves, revealing ropy, chicken-flesh forearms. His eyes appeared enormous when he had his glasses on and tiny when he took them off, and – disconcertingly – he was always taking them off and putting them on again.

'Would you like a brandy?' Dudley asked eventually. 'I always have one about this time.' He pulled a long-suffering face. 'I have this cognac habit.'

Professor Dix nodded sympathetically, and Dudley, waving towards the bar, began to talk, at last (and rather loudly), of Quest Literature of the Medieval Age.

'I hadn't realized until I read your book,' he said, 'that Morgan le Fay has a complex named after her.'

'Not a complex, an anima.'

'So many useful terms to remember. I must say, though, that I'm still rather puzzled as to what you think these quests are all about.'

Professor Dix removed his glasses. 'The mysteries of ages,' he said.

'Do you think so? My own reading is more simplistic. They were following an ideal. Perhaps they didn't know what it was but they followed it anyway. In my view, that's the only thing that makes them believable, that makes them human.'

Dix nodded sympathetically again. 'A superficial view,' he said. 'I've come across it before. Superficial.'

'Dare I say that it is better than no view at all?'

'Oh, if you want a simple view I can give you one.'

'Please.'

'Self-knowledge. That's what quests are about.'

Dudley looked very disappointed.

'Really? Is that all? Honesty compels me to say that as obsessions go, the pursuit of self-knowledge has always seemed to me overrated and dull. I am conscious of running counter to the age in which I live.'

'You find self-knowledge boring? You think it is merely

something Americans pay their analysts to dispense? You must read the quests again. Self-knowledge is something the questers literally die for; it kills them, they are destroyed by it. Self-knowledge banishes them from the world. It always does, you know.'

Dudley looked into his lap and Professor Dix put his glasses back on and blinked like a cartoon cat. He added, 'Of course, Freud said, "The only motive is honour, power, wealth, and the love of women."'

'I like that,' Dudley said.

'He was wrong, I'm afraid.'

'A pity.'

'The only motive is self-knowledge.'

They both fell silent and in this hush their brandies were placed in front of them.

Images chopped and changed on the silent television screen above the bar, adverts plying their messages over and over, superimposing them on cities, cars, women, pets. Soon Dudley was absorbed in their glamour. Often he could not tell what they were advertising, but he lost himself in the pictures, like a tourist walking in a foreign city that holds no meaning for him, only splendour.

'Do you mind if I smoke?' Professor Dix repeated.

'I would love you to. Have one of mine.' He offered a cigarillo. 'You might find it rather Afro-Gallic at first but it's worth persevering.'

Professor Dix took one and had it lit for him. He sucked on it hard, eyes closed.

'Nipple complex,' he murmured, smiling sadly and blinking. He sighed, self-absorbed, and Dudley turned back to the television.

He might have been alerted to the advert sooner had the television's sound been turned up. The crackly version of Ella Fitzgerald singing 'It's Too Darn Hot' was the perfect tag for the visual sequence. Half of it was already over, the first sight of the young man with a ponytail sitting in a wicker chair, hands in his lap, gazing moodily out of french windows over a

31

moonlit scene of rooftops. Close-up of his face: marksman's eyes, cupid's-bow lips. Close-up of the plain wall with its sweating barometer and corner of rumpled bed. Now a silhouette formed behind him and hands not his own (polished fingernails, long, bare arms) slid round his neck and began to undo the buttons on his shirt. ('According to the Kinsey Report,' Ella would be singing.) The man's face went through the many changes of expression promoted by the Method School as her unbuttoning fingers descended. Close-up of his widening eyes and flaring nostrils. Close-up of his damp chest heaving out of his shirt. Close-up of sweat tracking down his puckered forehead. ('Prefers his lovey-dovey to court when the temperature is low.') The woman's hands were held out above the man's, wanting. Give me. They descended into the man's lap, and pulled out . . . a canned drink beaded with condensation and labelled *Quench*. There was a moment of mutual anticipation, then the man lost self-control and (despite the heat) reached upwards with both his arms to embrace or throttle the unseen but imaginably stunning woman behind him; she gripped the ring-pull, and a long spurt of spray drenched his chest and face. Close-up of Martin's face filling the screen, frozen in astonishment, obscured by the slogan *Live it Up – Cool it Down*, as Ella was singing 'Too darn hot . . .' and the saxophone was fading.

'Advertisements are pseudo-parables,' Dudley said. 'It's really quite interesting. In our time they have become the paradigm of all other discourse. But terrible without the music.'

'Quite agree,' Professor Dix said, removing his glasses and rubbing his tortoise eyes. 'Adolescent lust should never be without it.'

'He's twenty something. Old by today's standards.'

'Retarded emotional development. He looks much younger.'

'A good friend of mine, actually.'

'Tell him I said so.'

Dudley stubbed out his cigarillo and waved for the bill.

Dix said, 'Pretty boy, your friend. But isn't he on the short side?'

32

'Your train of thought eludes me.'

'He would benefit from music. Who wouldn't?'

Professor Dix's face had become very pink; it matched the table-cloths. His mouth was loose. Belatedly Dudley read the situation and said with an air of suddenness, 'Goodness, is that the time?' Dispensing with the usual glance at the watch (it was a quarter to four), he waved again at the waitresses.

'What extraordinarily good brandy. I feel like living it up. I don't suppose . . .'

'Alas, duty calls.'

'So soon? And I've told you so little about myself.'

'I've a board meeting scheduled.'

Dudley attached himself to his crutch, and, wincing slightly, rose to babywalk his guest out of the restaurant.

'Professor Dix,' he said. 'It has been a great pleasure.'

'Tell me, what will you be discussing this afternoon?'

'Discussing?'

'In your meeting.'

'Oh, the usual. Company policy mainly.'

'How marvellously well you can move on these modern crutches. Remember now: self-knowledge.'

'Yes, self-knowledge.'

'That's the thing. Usually fatal. Goodbye.'

'Goodbye.'

For a moment he watched Professor Dix sway slowly up the street, then, as if seized by sudden energy, he swung urgently in the opposite direction, his flight giving him the appearance of someone in pursuit of something as yet ill defined and obscure.

6

But his flight was meaningless, there was no quest or desire or need, and eventually realizing this he stopped. His ears were buzzing, confounding him; he shook his head from side to side, and the street – dirty, crowded and floral – jigged in front of him. No amount of good cognac could disguise the fact that he was drunk.

Slipping free of his crutch, and mopping his brow with the end of his cravat, he leaned against the window of a Lebanese restaurant and tried to regain his composure. Someone on the inside tapped against the glass but he stayed where he was, eyes glazed, enveloped in a mongrel aroma of lavender, coffee and garbage.

In Oxford the drift out of town begins early. Already the tourists and shoppers had been joined in the streets by people leaving work and mothers collecting children from school. Traffic slowed towards the daily jam, cars extruded in meandering single file as if by slow peristalsis through streets not designed for them, going in a manner that was at once firm, polite and bored past the colleges and libraries, slowly into the Victorian suburbs and interwar estates, and beyond the ring road to desirable villages on the outskirts. Compared to the cars, the cyclists were free spirits, pedalling by, each with the same large and comical gait. The drizzle had stopped and the sun was dull and fierce, throwing shafts of light and shadow across buildings and roads, enchaining them in heavy patterns. The city sulked, gloomy with flashes of brilliance.

Dudley rested his full weight against the restaurant window, inert and indecisive. Wiping his damp forehead with the back of his hand, he straightened up, as if posture had something to do with it. He swayed slightly and lifted his eyes.

Baskets of flowers were hung at regular intervals along the street. Shop roofs formed a perfunctory outline of tear-stained concrete which hid the low-lying city skyline behind, the density of small towers and spires jammed into the ancient centre round Radcliffe Square, history in perfect immobility.

Then he was off again, hobbling with as much style as he could muster, up Little Clarendon Street, as if, caught between the heaviness of his lunch and the rich stillness of the city, he only could exist in sudden activity. Down St Giles he lurched past the Learned Press, and went on towards the Martyrs'

Memorial and the muddled church of Mary Magdalen (appearing behind it through sun-crowned chestnut trees), ignoring everyone: the tramp who solicited him, the tattooed youth with a dog who hawked and spat, the man in a gaberdine who shouted of Jesus from the traffic island by Balliol. Through the crowds he persevered, head down, until he came to the junction of Beaumont Street and St Giles, and there for the first time he paused, breathing heavily, to wait for the traffic lights to change.

He looked up. A mother carrying a baby against her shoulder crossed in front of him and, as he swung after, the baby scrutinized him with a stare of such devastating clairvoyance – wide eyes of a new, superior blue not to be taken in by a silk cravat and a tin crutch – that with a start he woke up to his surroundings, turned away and stared intently at the dull façade of the ABC Cinema where his reflection was staring back at him, horrified.

'No escape, no escape,' he murmured. With redoubled effort he crossed the road into the shadow of Balliol's ugly south façade and forged along Broad Street. The pavement was packed with tourists who stood, as if stupefied, in front of the plaque which commemorate the burning of Latimer, Ridley and Cranmer on a spot in the middle of the road under a stationary Ford transit. Dudley skirted round and hurried on to Trinity where a thousand bicycles were piled against the wrought-iron gates like idle parts of a vast machine. Veering into the road again he ploughed the cobbled gutter with his crutch, and a cyclist coming up quickly behind shouted as he whirred past, sending him back on to the pavement. Undeterred, he crossed the road without looking, swung past the stained north front of the Old Ashmolean and finally stopped.

In the shadow of the huge stone heads of Roman emperors which guard the Sheldonian, he rested on his crutch, panting.

The Sheldonian Theatre, like much in Oxford human and architectural, is ostentatious and odd. For one thing it is built back to front. To Broad Street it shows its plain, rounded rear, while its grandiose and eccentric front façade is displayed to a cramped, unvisited corner of the Divinity School. Here matriculating undergraduates take possession of the university, and here, a few years later, they receive their degrees in a ceremony rendered unintelligible to most by being conducted in Latin, and depart, entitled for the rest of their lives to talk of Oxford as their own.

Dudley paid a man in a cap and went up the wooden stairs, carrying his crutch over his shoulder like the lance of legend. On his way through the attic, he paused to stare at Christopher Wren's timber rafters, a mathematical marvel, then mounted the steps to the lantern, feeling for the first time that day that he was at last where he was meant to be.

Oxford lay below, the colleges, libraries and churches, a solid history of architecture, of crenellations, buttresses, oriels, spires and towers. Damp stone, dense and dazzling. The crooked back streets and alleyways unchanged since the Middle Ages were hidden. His vantage point gave him a sense of privilege, as if he had inherited it all, a gift, an idea to toy with, but immediately he felt dispossessed: he had no claim in Oxford, no claim in general; he was a bystander, a face in a crowd, a reader of newspaper headlines.

Silence prevailed over everything, and he was alone in the glass-sealed lantern. Nothing reached him from Broad Street or Catte Street where foreshortened figures traced ant-patterns round candy-coloured links of parked cars.

Quite suddenly, the day with all its routines and disappointments and persecutions fell away from him, and taking *Pensées* from his blazer pocket he folded it open and wrote:

219. *Change my life.*

Through the window he saw himself surrounded by the works of Great Men. In a niche in the Clarendon Building next door, below the figures of the Muses with their trumpets and masks of comedy and tragedy, a statue of Edwardvs Comes Clarendiae struck a Thespian pose. He seemed to be offering Dudley something, a book or a picture or stone tablets bearing secret

36

laws. But, straining to see the detail, Dudley saw no more than bird lime and the litter of feathers. He knew his history, he knew this Great Man with his ripe nose and silly wig, Clarendon the Chancellor, Clarendon the exile sopping up wine and pâté in France, Clarendon the sot. Naturally he identified with him. It was no effort to imagine himself in France, making Paris his own. He had actually been there once, on a school trip when he was thirteen, but his parents had not been able to afford to send him again. All their savings went to pay for his extra books, his classical records, his trips to Covent Garden and Stratford and the British Museum. For a moment he couldn't help thinking of home, of what used to be home. Dudley's father had been a draughtsman with the Royal National Lifeboat Institute until his disability pension came through. Dudley's mother was a secretary at the Midland Bank. Theirs was a totally placid marriage, silent in fact, in a silent house, a bungalow in a row of bungalows in a quiet suburb of Poole. Only the murmur of television or the apologetic slop of washing-up compromised that silence, and nothing disturbed its neatness, its spotless furniture and knick-knacks: Parker Knolls, grandmother's doilies, framed prints of sad-eyed spaniels, china animals on the mantelpiece. Pink pebble-dash and a miniature front garden ornamented with gnomes and crazy paving shut out the world which Dudley longed to escape into. But how many times since had he forced an entry into a new world only to find it the same old world viewed from a different angle?

Below him figures were crossing the quadrangle behind the Clarendon Building. Others emerged under the Bridge of Sighs, couples trailing a single shadow into the sunlit end of Catte Street, sauntering among cyclists and workmen. One couple in particular caught his attention: a young woman walking quickly with a man in a turquoise jacket. He suddenly craned forward with his nose pressed to the window-pane. The woman had Bethanay's hair and Bethanay's walk. She seemed also to be wearing Bethanay's scarlet skirt.

He stood on tiptoe, squinting as the woman disappeared

round the corner of the Clarendon Building, and his view was blocked by Edwardvs Comes Clarendiae who looked back at him smugly, still pretending to offer something, concealing far more, until Dudley wished he were that pigeon balancing on his wig, not the victim of his disapproving appraisal.

Five thirty struck as he descended from the lantern, and he decided to drop in at the Learned Press before finishing for the day. His crutch clicking like a knitting needle – knit one, purl one – he set off along storm-shadowed, yellowing Broad Street, sighing and groaning every few minutes.

He attracted little attention at the Learned Press for turning up at a time when most people were beginning to leave: his oddities were common knowledge. 'Got to get on,' he said. 'Ignite the midnight oil,' he said. 'I am a slave in the house of literature.' The cleaning ladies smiled to see him.

In his office he collected his hat and prepared to leave for the pub. But as he checked his overcrowded desk for messages from Bethanay he found a recent note from Austin Ord. It was written on an unusually large sheet of paper in small, spiky handwriting which showed signs of strain.

Be in my office at 5 p.m. We must talk. ARO

'The man is a bundle of nerves,' Dudley said out loud. 'I must remember to see him tomorrow.'

The telephone was ringing again, and he took the oppportunity of making an exit.

7

The Three Feathers, originally a poky Victorian terrace cottage in one of the side streets off the Banbury Road, was now a poky pub full of Victoriana. Sooty portraits of muttonchop-whiskered aristocracy, peacocks' feathers in vases, ormolu clocks, framed mottoes from the Bible and bits of coloured glass filled its small rooms. The landlord's appearance and manner, and his moustache in particular, recalled a type of a shabby minor character in the early Sherlock Holmes stories. Considering this his charm, he encouraged the comparison.

The Snug was the smallest of the rooms; it had a low wax-yellow ceiling, japanned floorboards, wooden chairs and tables and a wrought-iron fireplace. Lop-sided daguerreotypes of victorious college crews of the 1890s (striped jackets, louche expressions) combined aspects of the faded glamour and homey clutter cherished by the semi-social Englishman.

At 6 p.m. the Snug was comfortably filled by two elderly men sitting on either side of the fireplace reading newspapers. Their zippered cardigans belonged to an earlier age and bestowed on them an air of mild permanence, as if they had been installed in the room at the same time as the antique furniture and fireplace. They displayed no more animation than those articles, imperturbable behind their *Oxford Times* and lacquered by the glow of evening light.

Seated on the end of a bench opposite, his gaze fixed on his pint of lager, Martin sat gnawing his thumbnail, half-drunk and bad-tempered, waiting for Dudley who was late. His face was a study of violent concentration, his thoughts apparently intolerable, as if he were asking himself not only the small questions concerning Dudley's lateness and his own surprising willingness to wait, but also the large, alarming ones querying his place in the last decade of the twentieth century.

At half-past six the hush was broken by sounds of flying metal. There was a clatter in the hallway, and a short cry, and Dudley appeared. He lurched part-way into the room and stood swaying on his dented crutch, his cravat ragged.

'No facilities', he said, breathing heavily, 'for the disabled.'

Turning and meeting the landlord's sarcastic eyes, he ordered a pint of lager and a glass of red wine.

'Of what vintage is your *vin rouge*?' he asked.

'Hirondelle.'

'Make it a small glass, will you?'

After the fuss of divesting himself of his crutch, he sat at the narrow wooden table with Martin and immediately began to talk. Sipping his wine with careful rodent-like movements of the mouth, he pronounced it muck. For a while he talked about the viniculture of France, Italy, Spain and the late Roman Empire, and speculated on the decline of English taste, periodically holding up his glass to the dim light and interspersing his monologue with noises of bewilderment and outrage.

Martin said nothing. He seemed scarcely to have lifted his head since Dudley came in.

'Muck,' Dudley said. 'Characterless ·muck. Muck unenlivened by any trace of personality of any sort. Why is it that a merely passable *vin ordinaire* seems entirely beyond the imagination of the average English publican? One would think that there would be some drinkers of discrimination left in this country.' Critical and righteous, his gaze fell on the two cardiganed old men, both drinking the local best bitter. 'Perhaps not,' he said. 'Perhaps I am the last.' He talked for several minutes about this possibility, then finally fell silent, the pub falling silent with him.

A newspaper rustled.

Martin swore at the top of his voice.

Dudley stared.

'What the fuck,' Martin said, rising. He swore again.

'Too quiet for you?' Dudley asked in a quiet, shocked voice, glancing round.

'I'll tell you one thing.'

'Wait.'

'I can't believe I've waited here all this fucking time.'

'I'll just finish my . . .'

Martin was half-way out of the pub already, and Dudley, gulping down his Hirondelle, hobbled at speed after him.

In a rush they went down a narrow alleyway towards the Woodstock Road, Martin leading, Dudley propelling himself after. 'Sorry I'm late, by the way,' he called.

Dying sunlight flung their shadows into the gutter, creating another chase. The air was amber above the powerful, squat

40

church of St Philip and St James, weathered Victorian Gothic sheathed in coloured stone like a dinosaur in its armour-plating, standing rooted in a past age, watching them without concern. Here Martin stopped abruptly and asked Dudley for a cigarette, and to his renewed disgust Dudley offered him a French-Moroccan cigarillo, lighting it for him like an attentive movie hero, cupping his hands above the pavement plastered with rose petals, small and pink as confetti and heavy-scented.

Both of them breathing hard, they stood there, as if over-powered by the scent.

'Forgive me for mentioning it,' Dudley said, 'but you seem drunk and ill-tempered.'

Martin looked at the ground.

'Anything in particular? Anything I can do?'

Martin looked up from the pavement as far as Dudley's bandages. 'What have you done to your foot?'

'My foot? Which foot? This foot? This foot here? Nothing, nothing worth mentioning. Hardly anything. A multiple fracture or something.'

'You're joking.'

'There was a pile-up in the Banbury Road. An infirm Professor of Psychology had a seizure at the wheel of his car and drove it up the pavement. I was quite lucky, there were several fatalities. Where are we going, by the way?'

'You're bullshitting.'

'Not entirely.' He shifted his weight on his crutch and let out a long sigh. 'Though mostly.'

'Does it hurt?'

He waved a hand. 'It's only pain.'

Westward down Plantation Road they went more slowly side by side, Martin with his short, bitter limp, Dudley loping with a clunk, until they came to Walton Street.

Dudley said, 'Have you ever visited San Sepulchre's Cemetery?'

'Never heard of it.'

'The graves are very comforting.'

They crossed the road, passed the betting shop and the

41

bicycle repair place, and turned down a narrow gravel lane. Under the arch of the old stone gatehouse a blistered sign read: *Flowers, plants, trees and shrubs are not to be taken away without the knowledge of the cemetery keeper.* There was no injunction against the despoilment of the graves.

Following the earth path between scattered yews they reached a grassy space and lay down. Tombstones surrounded them: plain slabs, tall Victorian crosses, miniature mausoleums and classical urns, all the crowded, appearance-conscious, middle-class deaths of the 1870s and '80s. They were tilted at every angle and blackened with soot from the factory next door. High brick walls, grimy windows, drainpipes, flues and smokestacks loomed at them from another era, history as remote as the memorials they sat among.

'In the midst of life there is death,' Dudley said as they settled. 'Do you think of death much?'

'No.'

'Really? You surprise me.'

The grass around them was darkened with shadow from a huge chestnut tree which should not be removed without permission. Faintly spectral in this shade, Martin sat with his knees hugged to his chest, as statuesque and terse as a gravestone, and Dudley glanced at him apprehensively as he propped his crutch against Charlotte Anne Beeley, Dearly Beloved.

'What did you want to talk about?' Martin asked.

Dudley took a hip-flask from his jacket pocket and offered it. 'Nothing in particular,' he said. 'One or two general things about television, I've a few ideas I'd like to discuss. But there's no urgency. Have a swig. Rather a good cognac.'

As Martin drank Dudley began to talk about the terrific coincidence that they had been at the same school at the same time – the usual prelude to his enquiries about Martin's later career. Although he frankly admitted that he could not remember Martin ('terrible thing a good memory – cramps the style') it did not prevent him musing lengthily on the tantalizing vision of their semi-shared boyhoods. To hear him talk no one would have guessed that when he was at Shammings he longed to leave it.

'I hated that fucking school,' Martin said, interrupting.

Dudley paused. 'Dreadful in many ways, wasn't it?' he said. 'A ridiculous school in many ways.'

'I think about it a lot.'

'Violent too. The beatings that used to go on, the bullying, the *torture* – I can hardly believe it when I look back.'

There was a pause.

'What do you mean, beatings?'

'Lots of beatings. Perhaps you weren't aware of them as I was, being head of house and so on, but the bullying was endemic, really.'

'Nothing wrong with beatings.'

Dudley was silent.

'I can't stand people who decide what's right and wrong, interfering with everything, musn't do this, must do that, always pretending to be shocked when they hear about something. They don't know what life is like. I was beaten up, it didn't do me any harm, it taught me things, important things.'

Dudley considered this. 'Who beat you up?' he asked eventually.

'You'll have forgotten.'

'I can remember some of the bullies. Not that I particularly want to, but they stick in the mind.'

Martin was silent for a while. 'Called Proctor,' he said at last.

'Proctor? I remember him very well, I had him expelled. There was a gang of them but he was the worst. He was in my house and the Head came to me and asked what did I think about this and I said get rid of the lot of them, and he did. Best thing. I mean, regardless of what you think about beatings, he was inhuman, he was a beast. I'm being unkind to beasts.'

'Proctor wasn't the worst, there were others. People who ignored you, weak people.'

They were silent for a while. Grey smoke rose slowly through gold light and blended with grey shadow.

43

'I wish I could remember you from school,' Dudley began again, jaunty after these false starts. 'We have all this in common, but I can't recall it. You're younger than me, of course.'

'I remember you.'

'Do you? I suppose I was quite prominent in a way.'

'We talked. At one time we used to talk.'

'Did we?' Dudley was so surprised he paused with his flask half-way to his mouth.

'You've forgotten. It doesn't matter. It might have done, but it doesn't.'

'Well. My memory *is* terrible.'

'Forget it.'

There was an embarrassing silence as they looked around the graveyard, watching the light change from gold to green and shadows lengthen over the chiselled debris of the dead and forgotten. Moss and soot softened everything to the smudgy delicacy of a charcoal drawing.

It was one of Dudley's peculiarities to consider a poor memory a virtue, no more and no less than the prerogative of those intuitive characters who transform recollections into a cinematic art, and life into vividly lit and melodramatic footage. Unfortunately his own memory was crystal clear. He knew with absolute certainty that he had never exchanged a word with Martin at school. What Martin said troubled him but mainly moved him to pity, and he consigned himself, as he had done so often, to act out the charade of forgetfulness.

They talked for several minutes about nothing while Dudley worked round to an opening for his theme of television. Soon he was telling Martin that he had seen his advert again. Martin grunted as he lit another of Dudley's cigarillos.

'You're embarrassed by it,' Dudley said, 'which is inevitable, I suppose, given its commercial aspect. But I don't think it's that bad. It has a certain moody charm, a certain *jeu d'esprit*. It's fairly sophisticated, in fact. It wouldn't be going too far to call it radical. I mean, it neatly reverses the traditional sexual roles; it begs important questions about gender; it mimics female rape – a highly exciting and underdeveloped cultural phenomenon. It's iconographic. It's inconoclastic. It's a paradox for our time.'

'It's crap.'

Dudley nodded. 'You may be right.' He would say nothing to upset Martin. As he talked he watched him. Hunched against a tombstone he appeared as inward and unrelenting as the figure of Melancholy which decorated Dudley's office wall and haunted the margins of his favourite Renaissance art. Something about him suggested a creature from a past age, a fallen angel, alone and in torment.

Martin shifted slightly and looked up. 'It's been nominated for an award,' he said.

'The drink.'

'The ad.'

'The ad? They give awards to *adverts*?'

'The American Advertising Council.'

Dudley was astonished. 'What for? Increase in sales?'

'For the acting.'

'What do you mean, acting?'

'For my performance. They're like the Oscars, for ads.'

'Extraordinary. They give Oscars for *acting* in *adverts*?' He was overcome with admiration. 'The Americans are so much more advanced than us. So you're on a short-list?'

Martin nodded. 'I have to go to New York.'

'I love New York. A wonderful city.'

'You've been?'

'I've heard a good deal about it. Listen, when you say these awards are like the Oscars, does that mean there'll be something in the way of publicity?'

'The ceremony's televised. There's interviews, chat shows, that sort of crap.'

Dudley unsprawled himself. 'Martin, this is serious. This is the big time.' He became animated and his voice grew louder as he told Martin about the spin-offs, the opportunities for film work and the merchandising possibilities. His hip-flask jerked in the air and a spurt of brandy stigmatized his pullover sleeve.

45

'I can see it all. You win the award. You are hailed as the premier advertising actor of your generation, of any generation. You join the Actors' Union. You run it. You enter politics. You get a Governorship – California, say. There are precedents, Martin. Who knows where this might end?'

Martin was more like Melancholy than ever, moodily contemplating the alien nature of good fortune.

'When do you go, Martin?'

'I'm not going.'

There was silence as Dudley considered this problem. 'Isn't that going to be awkward, the ceremony and suchlike being over there?'

'I'm not going. I don't want to go.'

The air was cool and the graveyard was getting dark. Shadowed gravestones blurred together until they formed one long memorial.

Martin said, 'You want to go. You go and pretend you're me.'

'Don't you think someone might spot the switch?'

'You could carry it off.'

'I'm not skilled in mass hypnosis.'

'I'm not going alone.' After a while he added, 'Come with me if you like. My agent'll pay.'

Embarrassed, Dudley laughed. 'What, as your minder? I'd have to have my forearms tatooed with pictures of motorcycles and poisonous reptiles, I'd have to fight off hordes of teenage American girls. I can see it, I'm struggling against them, I'm bloodied but unbowed.'

'I'm serious.'

He wanted to shriek at the thought, a symptom of fear. He was shaking his head. 'No, I can't,' he said. 'I couldn't.'

They rose into the shadow of the chestnut tree and began to make their way out of the graveyard. Dudley wanted suddenly to tell Martin about all the absorbing delicacies of his marriage, put into words the images that came to him, Bethanay crying, Bethanay shouting, Bethanay justly accusing him of every lapse, all these images complicit with his own love and guilt. It was the wrong time to leave her, even for a week, he couldn't go without a long prelude of anxiety and an endless postscript of recrimination. And there was the possibility that if he once left he would never return.

They were back at the gatehouse, an arched shadow which let them through like a veil.

'I'm sorry. It's my wife. I have to think of my wife.' This sounded lame, and he added, 'She's just miscarried. It's a difficult time.'

'You don't have to lie to me,' Martin said.

It was eight thirty. Woodstock Road curved towards the town centre through blue dusk, quiet and familiar. Victorian villas with their jutting turrets and crenellations and towers of scaffolding touched pale rags of clouds. The only sound was of the occasional car sliding past on shushing rubber.

They parted in town, at the Martyrs' Memorial.

'I must be getting home,' Dudley said. 'Beth will be waiting.' He stood watching as Martin walked away down Beaumont Street towards Worcester College, jerking one foot as he always did, head down, hands in pockets, hugging the high wall of the Ashmolean Museum until he practically dissolved in its shadow. Then he turned homeward.

Broad Street was silent. A few laughing students crossed the road from Exeter College and went into the White Horse. Passing under the Bridge of Sighs Dudley remembered looking down from the Sheldonian and seeing a woman who resembled his wife. Day-dreaming of running away, he thought that in different circumstances, or at another time, he could have used Martin Prout to launch himself into a new life. What contacts in the world of the New York media were to be had simply by hanging round with that deranged boy-actor? Images of himself fantastically altered paraded themselves before him. Fame wreathed him.

He stumped on.

Deep in New College Lane he was cut off from the rest of

the city. Tall rubble walls of New College and All Souls hemmed him in, occluding everything except the inky sky. Max Beerbohm had called the lane a 'grim ravine'. Dudley called his whole life a grim ravine.

He groaned as he went, and as he groaned he lifted his head, and as he lifted his head he saw in a high niche above New College gatehouse a weather-melted Virgin and Angel carved in stone, a last streak of grey light showing him their misshapen, divine bodies. He had seen them before, but now they were transformed by the dusk, they seemed to be bestowing on him an inscrutable benediction. And at that moment he saw in them the figure of Melancholy locked on to the forms of another world, and he felt himself blessed not by the Virgin and Angel, but by Martin Prout, improbable and terrifying. This came to him in a flash and vanished. Hastily he set his good foot towards home and fixed his guilty heart on his wife, and in a minute or so he emerged into the sunset of the High, and the city claimed him again.

8

It was nine o'clock – much earlier than expected – when Dudley got home. He stopped by the gate and looked at his watch, resting on his crutch. Anxiety had given way to calm, calm to irony, and irony to guilt. Whenever he went home, in fact, whatever idealized thoughts of domestic life he had contrived tended to vanish and he remembered that of all the women he longed for none was his wife.

Retracing his steps he went back along the street until he came to a house with a well-stocked garden and there he picked himself a small bouquet of dusty flowers. Glancing up once from his labour of love he thought he saw a bedroom curtain in his own house twitch, and he wondered if Bethanay was already going to bed. It was a depressing thought. She would have a headache. When he went in she would be lying awake in the dark, her pale face on the pillow reproachful, her questions unanswerable, her breath bad. She would want to know why their lives were so miserable and how they had become strangers and what he had been thinking about. He would tell her about Sykes's attack on him, his hospitalization and the battle for his life.

A door slammed down the street. Straightening his back with a sigh, he admired his posy: two roses, a cluster of sweet-peas and a large, strangled daisy. Not for nothing is *Say it with flowers* a famous slogan. Turning homeward again, he saw a figure retreating quickly away from him beyond his house and the image linked itself to the idea of arguments and their consequences, part of the visual sequence in which the man bursts from the house with an oath and a suitcase and storms towards the bus station, the door slamming behind him and the whole street echoing like an empty bucket.

In his hallway he stopped at the mirror to examine the other man with the flowers who had apparently just come in to pay his last respects. He was annoyed: if he could not regain his calm at least he could attempt irony. Running his fingers through his hair he opened the door into the living-room and to his surprise found Bethanay waiting for him bright and edgy on the sofa. She was wearing a T-shirt from the laundry basket and a scarlet skirt she was too fat for.

'You're early,' she said. Her smile ended in a silly twitch.

Murmuring, he raised his bouquet and, stepping forward on his crutch, he saw the turquoise jacket lying promiscuously on the carpet where the dog usually sat. He remembered the couple in town and the slammed door and the rapidly retreating figure and without a second's respite of ignorance saw everything as clearly as if he had been in the bedroom with them, witnessing even the post-coital *tristesse*, the argument about some petty adulterous detail, the panic as they glimpsed the returning patriarch from the upstairs window and the hilarious dressing in Charlie Chaplin speeded-up time. It was his habit to make inspired guesses, and usually they were wrong, but this time he was unlucky and he was absolutely right. Nothing had ever been more obvious to him. Like the actor who falls through the stage trap-door, precipitated out of the safely invented world into dusty piles of props and joists, he saw how worn and mucky the things are that hold reality in place.

Sykes entered the room, stopped, lowered his head, turned and went out again, leaving a smell behind.

'What have you done to your foot?' Bethanay asked.

Dudley stared at her.

'Why have you got a crutch?'

He looked down at it as if he hadn't noticed it before, raised his head and moaned.

'What happened to your foot?' she said again like a child who is justly ignored.

'Fell down the stairs,' he said loudly. 'Or was I pushed? Can't remember. It's all a dark plot, isn't it?'

Bethanay flushed. 'What do you mean? Why are you shouting?'

'Who is he?' Dudley said. 'Do I know him?'

'Who?'

'The man I saw you with in town, the man who just ran down the street, the man who has left his jacket behind. Him. That man.'

For a second she was absolutely still, then she sobbed, jumped to her feet and ran past him out of the room.

Some time later he found himself in exactly the same position, resting on his crutch and looking at the empty sofa. Upstairs the bath was running, a guiltless gurgle. In his hand was a tumblerful of brandy. It seemed he had been trying to detect the flaw in the evening which would reveal it as a sham. But he concluded instead that everything else was the sham. His sudden awakening to the things around him produced an acute and embarrassing self-consciousness, as if he had been abruptly left alone on stage in front of a sceptical audience.

Lighting a cigarillo he deliberately dropped the spent match on the coffee-table top and watched the polish mist over and begin to blacken. At the same moment Sykes crept into the room again and gave him a wide berth.

'Watch out!' Dudley said to the dog. 'I'm a soldier of fortune.'

Sykes slunk into the kitchen and another smell gathered behind him.

'Tell me what you're doing here!' Dudley called after him. 'I want you to tell me what you've been doing, you little shit!'

It was much later when he ventured upstairs. When he knocked on the bathroom door Bethanay cried out in a nervous voice, 'Yes?' as if it could have been anyone, then, 'I won't be long.' Perched on the toilet seat a moment later, seeing her magnified in transparent bathwater, distractingly naked, he tried not to wish he had taken her hint. He had not realized what an exact scene-setter domestic crisis is, expunging those soft lines and unfocused comforts, and leaving only the strict essentials, the cold water tap dripping on to a big toe, the awkward angle of white knees, the sheen on flattened breasts.

'There was a woodlouse in the bath when I came up,' she said quietly. 'I thought you'd put some stuff down.'

He began to play with a spare toilet roll.

'How did you really injure your foot?'

'It's not important.'

'Tell me. Tell me the truth for once.'

'I didn't think you'd want to get to the truth so soon.'

Together they watched the lapping water dilate round her knees.

'It'll only end in tears,' she said and immediately began to cry. 'It can't go on,' she said between sobs.

He glanced up and back at the toilet tissue in his hand. Its skin was breakable, delicate and white. He stared at it intently. A tissue of lies is such a beautiful image, much more than a figure of speech, more a metaphor of something, of a certain kind of life. It meant failure and fragility.

'You bastard!' Bethanay said, choking. 'You bastard!'

51

'Do you mind?' he said. 'I'm the one who's meant to be angry.' She was almost drowning in the bath, but he was conscious of his right to choose a role and on the spur of the moment he chose disdain.

'I presume you're fucking him,' he said. Slowly he revolved the toilet roll in his hands.

She made a disgusted noise. Above the sucking of the bathwater, she sobbed, 'I can't live with you any more. I can't.'

He caressed the toilet roll with elaborate care, as if it were a living thing. 'Have you noticed that the obvious is always dull, even when unexpected? It seems to make no difference if it materializes out of nothing.'

'Yes, we were fucking, that's exactly what we were doing.'

A thumbprint appeared in the toilet roll which he immediately began to smooth away.

'There's fucking and there's fucking,' he said at last. A distance had opened up between his voice and his riven thoughts. He devoted himself to the damaged skin of the tissue. Lies were vulnerable and precious. He sighed. 'What are we going to do?' he said.

'I don't know.'

'Do you want me to leave?'

'I don't know.'

Fresh sobs convulsed her, tears ran down her cheeks and mingled with the bathwater. Unsure whether the part he was playing allowed him to pass her some of his toilet paper to blow her nose on, he frowned. Eventually he tore off a few sheets, folded them neatly, and passed them to her.

'Here.'

She blew and gagged.

'I'll leave,' he said. 'It doesn't have to be permanent. I'll leave for a bit. A short break. I don't know why I'm being so sensible. Don't ask me why, I don't know.'

'Where will you go?'

'I don't know. Abroad. I was thinking of going abroad anyway.'

'What for?'

'No reason.'

'How long?'

'A week.'

'What are you going for?'

'Doesn't matter.'

'You didn't tell me. On business?'

'Never mind why, it makes no difference if I'm going on business or going on holiday or going on a quest for fame and fortune. It's the same thing.'

'A quest? What do you mean, a quest?'

'Nothing, I meant nothing.'

'Did you say quest?'

'Yes, quest, that's what I said.'

'Meaning what?'

'It doesn't matter.'

'A quest for what?'

'It's not important what for.'

'Quests are always for something. Why did you suddenly mention a quest?'

Dudley moaned. 'Forget about the quest.'

'You make it sound like some old Charlton Heston film.'

'Forget it. Forget I ever said it.'

He went out stumping heavily on his crutch. 'I don't know why I'm being so bloody reasonable!' he shouted. 'I don't *want* to be reasonable!'

At the top of the stairs he looked back and saw that she had sunk down in the bath, submerged in the water. She was muttering to herself and peering forward as if looking at her reflection in the taps at the end of the bath: she would see her huge knees, tiny head, tinier face too small to possess any expression, as if her true emotions lagged behind her appearance, her thoughts racing ahead of it, out of control, like Dudley jolting down the stairs.

It was dark and the narrow strip of garden at the back of the house was chequered with shadows. Above him one window –

the bathroom window – still shone. In front of him the lawn, one yard wide, tunnelled for five yards between unkempt privet hedges and stopped dead at the side wall of a neighbour's house, a tall slab of black with chimneys. When he was depressed Dudley came to sit out here and stare at the simple geometry of drainpipes and shadows.

He breathed in the night air; it was cool and rank. Cars passed the house at regular intervals, all sounding the same: echoes of distant violence.

In the biography of himself which he carried in his head he tried to write the scene in which he left one life behind in Oxford and began another in New York. It was a great turning point. He had left behind a woman, it seemed; some said his wife. But it was his destiny. Alas. The night his life changed he sat in his little garden in little Oxford, very drunk, waiting for the dawn and dreaming of the future.

Groping under the seat he found the bottle of brandy and poured himself another glass. The garden increased his depression as it always did but, when he waved his hand to conjure it all away, the movement and the echo of the passing cars lulled him, as if suspending him – a constellation – between past and future.

There was a horrendous, wet, sucking noise suddenly, and, flinching, he looked up at the square of frosted light above him. A slight play of shadows performed across it like finger-puppetry. Inside, the bath was draining and Bethanay was finally drying herself. She had been lying there for hours, thinking her own thoughts and letting the water turn cold. Moments later the light blipped out, and the whole garden took a step backwards, intricate foliage coalescing into inky clumps, darker and denser than the dim sky overhead, that grey fuzz with its faint grit of stars like a screen waiting for an image.

It was true, dreams of the future preoccupied him.

Another hour passed and he drank steadily. Drunk and quiet, he heard a singing in his ears, the throb of his own blood beating like distant footsteps along an iron corridor. The garden seat was getting cold. It was very late. With a shiver he made to finish off his brandy and found that a slug had got into his glass. He thought of the ways in which a man might recognize moments of crisis in his life and ride them as a surfer rides dangerous waves. The muffled noise of a distant car sounded like surf, the stuff of nostalgia.

He staggered back up the garden, ducking with a cry as the washing line snagged on his ear and madly beating back a clinging shirt with his crutch. His shout set off a rondo of neighbours' dogs and their barks followed him into the house.

His biography had broken up in his head; only bits of it remained, disconnected like snapshots in an album. One showed him tottering into the dark lounge, his legs and crutch forming a crude tripod. In another he had stripped down to his boxer shorts, and was shuffling forward to locate the sofa with his arms held out in front of him like a child playing blind-man's-buff. In the last he lay on the sofa with the crutch resting at his feet like the dog on which entombed crusaders stand. Half-heartedly, one hand on his crotch, he tried to muster up a fantasy of a floor-show artiste named Jig-Jig, but he was too drunk and tired. All the images were disappearing. The last thing he heard as he fell asleep was Bethanay turning in the bed directly above him, and then the house was silent.

9

Although it was raining, Martin stood without a coat on one of the short approach roads to Gatwick's South Terminal and would not go inside. This was how it had always been, the same as standing by the labs first thing in the morning with the drizzle coming down and his blazer shoulders sodden like black blotting paper, watching his classmates through peepholes in the fogged windows, watching their games, watching their friendships, watching it all. His left arm was in a sling. He had told them he had fallen down the steps at the front of the school. There didn't seem to be a time when he wasn't carrying some injury; it was as if he was afraid of ever being completely whole and Proctor was merely his accomplice.

The beatings never did him any harm, they toughened him up, they made him alert to his real enemies, those who ignored him, those who were weak but safe, those who wore worsted jackets and wool trousers and carried in their briefcases the texts of Shakespeare's plays, the libretti of eighteenth-century German opera and an apple for teacher.

Rain dripped off the end of his nose.

Eventually he went through the electronic doors into the terminal, soaked, his hair dripping, limping through the crowds and looking anxiously round. Both his hands were dug deep in his pockets for he carried no luggage, not even a toothbrush. His only concession to travel was a lucky brass amulet round his wrist. The newspapers were full of record-breaking disasters, the whole aviation industry *in extremis*.

The plastic-floored building was long and low and ugly; it seemed to create a limbo which swallowed up the trivial sounds of trolleys, announcements and children, and gave the place the weird hush of a museum. Illuminated in supermarket brightness people looked separate and alone, even when queuing in mazes or riding the escalators together. Their faces were distinct and self-contained, and they were most themselves, not as they would be later in sun-drenched snapshots, blurred by fun.

Looking round, he saw Dudley appear from behind the Avis counter struggling with a loaded trolley, a halter of overstuffed handgrips hanging pendulously from his shoulders. Seeing Martin but making no gesture he veered slowly in his direction. At a distance of twenty yards Martin could see that something had happened to his hair.

He came to a halt and stood with a foot resting on his luggage like a gamehunter of old. Holding out a scalding hand he said with feeling, 'Blind, insensate lunatics are responsible for the design and manufacture of my baggage. Sadistic misanthropes built these trolleys. Megalomaniac perverts drew up the plans for this airport. I stand before you only by a miracle of endeavour. Every obstacle has been put in my way.'

'What's this?'

'My luggage?'

'Your hair.'

The oiled loops had been replaced by a mathematical side-parting and a fringe which seemed to rise and fall on the slightest waft of air. It was lighter in colour than before, and less natural.

'It's called a "Brideshead". Suitable for a young man from Oxford.'

'And what are these?' Martin pointed at the flaming-orange boots with built-up heels and winkle-picker toes.

'It's the cowboy in me. Butch Cassidy and the Sundance Kid and Wild Big Buffalo Hitchcock. Would you call me Butch if I wanted you to?'

'No, never.'

He smiled blandly and peered at Martin. 'Your voice sounds funny. You're soaking wet. You're wearing something odd round your wrist. Are you feeling all right? Don't say anything, I understand. Nervous of flying. There's no need to say a word. We go straight to the bar. Alcohol is what you need, alcohol and distraction.'

For the next hour or so Dudley explained how Martin could overcome his fear of flying. They were seated in the Gatwick Village Inn (*Purveyors of Fine Ales, Grog, Spirits and Wines*), an astounding transplant of bucolic England to the plastic setting of the airport. Through fake-weathered latticework was a view of a sweetshop, a newsagent, a coffee-shop, Her Majesty's Post Office, and an expanse of ugly carpet stretching to the duty-free area.

'All this', Dudley said, 'makes you realize how awful villages are.'

While they drank they watched departure information pulsate on a television screen. Beyond huge picture windows aeroplanes were being refuelled, impossibly heavy objects which lumbered across the asphalt, awkward as dinosaurs, fumes rippling round them like the shadows of water on aquarium glass.

'It's a miracle they get up in the air at all,' Dudley said. He glanced at Martin and added, 'A common miracle.' The banality of miracles in the age of technology became his theme. 'It's not my age,' he said in parenthesis. 'I belong to a more innocent era when people still believed in the pursuit of something more than common happiness.'

When their time came they rode a rubber velomat to their exit gate, Dudley standing slightly ahead of Martin, still talking.

'Do you know,' he said, 'I've just thought that if I like it in America I may decide to live there.'

'What for?'

'I don't know. Just if I like it.'

They came to the end of one velomat, walked a few paces, and joined another.

'What about your wife?'

Dudley looked vague. 'Did I not tell you? I've left her.'

'Left your wife? When?'

'Well, today actually. Now. As I speak. That's one of the reasons for changing my mind and coming with you.'

They rode in silence down the centre of the carpeted aisle like a very primitive form of animation.

'I see myself in American media, now that I think about it. Television. The key to it is contacts – the producers, the directors, the financial advisers. I see myself importuning, impressing, persuading, wheedling, begging. I think I'd be very determined. I'd be unshakeable.'

They arrived at their exit gate.

'But don't worry, I'm going to look after you too. Responsibility, I thrive on responsibility. I'm your minder, a sort of Jeeves or Sancho Panza. Think of me as totally dependable, think of me as indispensable.'

Minutes later, as the call for boarding was announced,

Martin suffered a panic attack and was comforted by Dudley into a state of pure funk. Dudley had never seen anyone so abruptly incapable.

'We have to go now,' he said helplessly. 'Off we go. Nothing to be afraid of.'

Martin shook head. His face was livid.

'Nonsense.' Dudley tried to think of something to say. 'You can only die once.'

Martin's eyes had sunk into his head.

Examining him, taking up his wrist and pinching it between thumb and finger, Dudley said, 'Are you telling me you need something stronger than persuasion?'

Martin lolled forward in his seat and his head butted Dudley's chest. People in the queue at the boarding gate had turned to look back at them, a small, packed audience holding their passports to their faces like fans.

'Wait a minute.' Dudley was rummaging in one of his bags, Velcro rending, as Martin knuckled shut his eyes against the overhead lighting, his breathing loud and erratic like the magnified echoes a deep-sea diver makes in his helmet.

'Here,' Dudley said. 'Take your pick.' Bottles, tubes, jars and packets spilled on to the carpet. 'Look. Diarrhoea tablets, Hedex, aspirin, sleeping pills, laxatives, Night Nurse, throat pastilles, TCP, calamine lotion, paracetamol, flatulence pills . . .'

Martin twitched and lifted an arm, an enormous, slow gesture reaching all the way from the playground, but Nurse Dudley fended him off.

'Take your pick, Martin. Any one you fancy, or a mixture of your favourites if you like.'

Martin's colour was changing from green to red. 'For fuck's sake,' he hissed.

'All completely bona fide medication. Lucky for you I'm a hypochondriac.'

'You jerk.'

'Thank you. And now for your choice.'

Martin breathed heavily through his nostrils and pointed.

'The sleeping pills? Sure you're not bad enough for the diarrhoea tablets?'

'Give me them, for fuck's sake.'

They were alone, everyone else had boarded the plane. Dudley (fraternal, compassionate, distracted by his bags) took Martin's arm and guided him (sick, resentful and compliant) on the last few steps out of the lounge into the plastic tunnel that led to the plane.

'Nearly there,' he said.

They went slowly together, followed by a single stewardess walking at a distance more slowly still with an indifferent air like a courtier or warder.

10

255. There is always another character, what of him? He has dark hair; he is long-faced, short, untalkative, aggressive in manner and he walks with a limp. There is pain in his eyes. He believes he knows me from a past life. Mon Semblable . . .
    My catalyst.
    The mysteries of human usage.

Flashing sunlight dazzled him as he squinted out at a frozen surf of cloud. In the distance a great cloud-mound squatted on the rest like a ruined sphinx, lit up orange and violet. With his hand shading his eyes he watched it pass. What questions did he have for it? What answers would it give him? Down the aisle a svelte hostess was bending over a bald patch.

For a long time he stared out of the window. Eventually the cloudscape's dilapidated majesty palled, he pocketed his pen, folded shut his notebook and shook open the copy of *The Village Voice* which he had bought earlier from one of the hostesses. Flicking through it, he considered how so often with British papers one searches in vain through turgid articles for an interesting advert, but with American papers it is exactly the reverse: turgid adverts and the odd interesting article. He read of a seventeen-year-old boy who made a pop record one day and the next was obliged to hire a team of bodyguards to protect him from his adoring fans. One of Dudley's ambitions was to employ bodyguards.

Half an hour passed in silence. Resting the paper in his lap, he woke Martin.

'I was asleep,' Martin said.

'There's a heatwave in New York.'

Martin let his head slide back on to Dudley's shoulder, and when it was at rest, Dudley nudged it again.

'I've been sampling the local newspapers. Ridiculously bad.'

'Wake me up when we land.'

'Incidentally,' Dudley said, 'regarding our quest for publicity, we shall be facing some stiff competition in New York. The place is a circus. Every day is packed with surreal events. Listen to this from *Downtown Diary*. "Fat Sam Wurtzkopf takes his one-man binge to show to Raphael's next Saturday." And this: "Jacques Brun's new collection is modelled by Bella LaRose at the Envy Club all next week. As before, Brun's costumes will necessitate a total body shave." Did you hear that? Total body shave. We seem to be talking poodles.' Martin grunted and Dudley lowered the paper to look him up and down. 'I suppose if all else fails we can always fall back on the body shave.'

The plane began to descend with an elevator-lurch, followed by the announcement that their descent was about to begin. Those sitting in the seats across the aisle from Dudley murmured as Manhattan revolved obligingly below them like an expensive toy. On the wrong side of the plane Dudley squashed his nose against the perspex of his porthole and saw nothing but a dingy stretch of water flecked with tugs, and the turning sky.

'By the way, Martin, here we are about to land and we haven't yet discussed your agenda.'

'Leave it to Slezinger.' Martin's voice was muffled by his

knees. His hands were clasped round the back of his head. Dudley questioned aloud the necessity of Slezinger at all, and was in the middle of this when the plane landed. It bounced twice, rubber yelping, and thumped home, tarmac rushing past the portholes like the end of a film flapping loose from the projector. Martin was whimpering, thumping the seat in front of him and surprising the man who sat there.

'I could tell you a thing or two about agents to make your blood run cold,' Dudley said cheerfully.

When the plane came to a standstill he was fine-tuning his fringe with his comb, humming. He seemed immensely pleased with their arrival and he nodded to his fellow passengers as they rose, cramped and fatigued, and reached above their heads for their luggage. People were already disembarking, awkwardly shunting their bags down the aisle and murmuring instructions to one another. Martin unwound and made an ambiguous noise.

'Not too bad, was it?' Dudley said.

Martin thrust his face up at him. 'You wouldn't fucking know,' he said. 'You have no idea, how can you know? You didn't spend three hours in the toilet, you weren't in pain the whole time. Flying doesn't scare you. Dying doesn't scare you. You don't know *anything*.' Tears made his eyes bulge and shine, he blinked and bit his lip, and Dudley stared at him, horrified.

'Martin,' he began.

'Fucking shut up.'

'It's over, you can relax. We're on the ground. We survived.'

'Get me off this fucking plane.'

Dudley's face was a mask of agonized apology. Busying himself with his bags from the overhead locker, he murmured reassurance. Elbowing people and excusing himself in a hasty undertone, he turned and turned like an animal in a hole, and in a few moments they moved into the aisle and began to edge towards the exit where the valedictorian hostesses were dispensing smiles. Awkwardly pressed together by the crush, they went as if chained to each other, out of the plane and into a plastic tunnel exactly like the one they had left behind at Gatwick.

11

American heat immured them in Immigration, a claustrophobic room with a low ceiling clad in bright pine like a sauna, containing five hundred sweating people in a concertina-shaped queue. Smartly dressed officials in white short-sleeved shirts sat impassively in their perspex booths, bathed in the glare of strip lighting. Brown-uniformed guards patrolled the queues, shouting to each other.

They had been there an hour, not speaking, each lost in his own thoughts. As the heat grew unbearable, people stripped off jackets and shirts and the air ripened. The hum of voices rose with the temperature.

'Hot,' Dudley commented to a guard, mopping his forehead with his cravat. His cricket sweater was tied schoolboy-style round his waist.

'You noticed?'

'I did, actually.'

'Major heatwave,' the guard said. He chewed once and looked away.

When they reached the front of the queue and went up, one at a time, to the immigration officers' booths, Dudley had forgotten all the smart remarks he wanted to make about his arrival. He was content to hand over the forms he had filled in and answer the man's questions, then to walk the last few steps into America with a sober, measured tread. Not once did the man look up at him. Watching the methodical hands, the bored eyes and disappointed mouth, Dudley thought that he must remember all this, it was exactly the sort of moment, typified by nothing, which should be recalled and given body but he was tired, there would be time later, when he wasn't so tired, to invent it all.

Men who communicated only in imperatives and interrogatives hustled them through Customs. 'Gimme your card. Got ya card? Short stay? Go through the main exit.' A poster on the wall said *The US Government Wants You to Think Twice*. A smell of detergent pervaded the corridors. Gone was the lifeless acrylic of England; here everything was busy and sharp. Ordinary details – the way people walked, their voices, the clothes they were wearing – imposed themselves on the general scene with unselfconscious urgency, like atoms milling in their natural chaos. Dudley strove to make sense of this movement by locating the background, to fix the setting, but there was no background to speak of, it was all foreground and everyone was centre-stage.

At the Arrivals Gate there was no one to meet them, no Ed Slezinger of Ed Slezinger Inc. Those waiting at the fence were all strangers. Dudley and Martin slowly passed down the line like unwanted baggage on a conveyer belt and emerged unclaimed into America.

Here where it was quieter and more spacious they were struck by the architecture of the airport. Its foreignness quietened them both, even Dudley. Everything was the colour of metal, the walls, the linoleum, the carousels in the baggage reclaim: all were interlocking parts in a drudging, efficient machine. There were no carpets, no upholstered seats or furry doormats to soothe and inhibit. Not even a common language redeemed the difference: signposts advertising NJ Transit Company and Greyhound were meaningless. Worst of all, everyone else was in the know; they passed without a glance, hurrying and relentless, while Dudley and Martin guarded their luggage, mildly panic-stricken, Dudley loping to and fro, craning his head in all directions, Martin standing still and stiff, as if balancing on tiptoe.

'What does this Slezinger look like?'

'How should I know? Never met him.'

'But you must have talked to him. What do you imagine he looks like?'

'I don't know. About fifty. Fit. Pushy. I don't know.'

Dudley looked around. 'I don't see him. He's late. He's forgotten us. Never trust an agent, Martin, I beg you. Let's have a drink on expenses.'

They bought martinis in plastic cups and sat on their bags next to a carousel. Nearby, two orthodox Jews were discussing something earnestly with their heads bowed together, beards touching, breaking off at intervals to dash to the Arrivals Board and back again. A group of Orientals went past at speed and returned almost immediately. At the fence, a few hopefuls were still waiting for those who would never turn up. Dudley looked them over – an elderly woman with whiskers; a thin man with a tattoo and greased hair; a young Negress in shorts and T-shirt; a fat Asian in a tight shirt. None of these was Slezinger, unless in disguise.

Martin had brought no record of Slezinger's address or telephone number. Dudley made the point that if they stirred from that spot, if they ventured into New York, they would irretrievably miss Slezinger, they would never be found, they would be lost men, dispossessed, invisible, anonymous. This was not the case, but he pretended it was, growing more eloquently nihilistic.

'You wanted to change identity,' Martin said, but Dudley began to explain how he had foreseen Slezinger's incompetence.

'I'd like to bet you three hundred thousand American dollars that we don't catch a glimpse of this Slezinger all week. That's the amount of money I'd like to bet. Not a cent less. A fortune says Slezinger is a fraud.' As he spoke – as if on cue – a wiry, grey-haired man in a double-breasted suit came hurrying towards them, his manner both fit and pushy. Martin snorted and Dudley, rising, murmured, 'No bet is valid until shaken on,' and then the man hurried past them and with smiles accosted the plump Asian who had been waiting at the fence.

'Slezinger?' Dudley crowed. 'A fraud, a cheat, a waster, a twister, a crook. Possibly a fiction. Have you thought of that? You've never met him, he might not exist. Someone has been impersonating him. Here we are at the airport, friendless, moneyless and hopeless, with nowhere to go. Don't think the scenario isn't a common one, it is the fate of all the dispossessed and disenfranchised, the millions who sink under the weight of chance circumstance and overnight are transformed into tramps and villains and the sexual slaves of New York's grossest. In a moment we will be approached by a character calling himself Jefferson Dwight the Third or The Kid who will offer us advice and a "shot" of something called Wild Snakestooth or Bright Lights Bourbon, and a place to stay the night, and by this time next month we will have sunk through every known level of human degradation and be working as prostitutes on Forty-Second Street, basement level. I see it all. In the interests of symmetry, we will be asked to service a client called Edward Long Prong Slezinger, a man known for the extent and vicious-ness of his appetites.'

'You're too ugly,' Martin said, 'to be a rent boy.'

Dudley talked wildly of Slezinger for some minutes, then stopped. A black girl in shorts and T-shirt stood over them.

'You're Prout, right?' she said to Martin. Her voice was hard and economical; she tapped her foot on the metal-coloured floor. They looked at her, and Dudley looked at Martin. 'Martin Prout. That's you, right?' Her chin jutted towards them.

'Your reputation goes before us,' Dudley said to Martin. 'I think she wants your autograph.'

'You lost a lot of weight, Martin Prout, what you been doing, trying to starve yourself to death?' She handed Martin a photograph of himself which was labelled *Edwin Slezinger Theatrical Agency*.

'Where did you get this?' Dudley asked.

'You hadn't lost so much weight I would've spotted you straightaway. Plus I was expecting you were travelling alone.' Her impatience showed itself in the flexing of a leg which

Dudley stared at. It was the leg of an athlete, strong and shapely, tapering to a thick white coil of sports sock and chunky basketball boot. Raising his eyes, he looked up at her baggy white T-shirt which disclosed, as she put her hands on her hips, the legend *Deep American Mouth* running crookedly from the brief embossment of one nipple to the other. He raised his head further. Her lipsticked mouth was working her gum, her jaw ticking round. Her skin was so dark it was almost maroon, tight and glossy over the trajectories of her forehead, cheekbones and chin, and her hair was braided into crisp knots, black and bright like links in a well-oiled bicycle chain. She was the most beautiful woman he had ever seen and she was looking at him with undisguised scorn.

'You're a friend of this Slezinger?' Dudley asked. 'He exists?' She blinked slowly, as if clearing her vision of a defect, and turned back to Martin.

'It's a business arrangement,' she said. 'Come on, Prout, the car's double-parked.'

She went ahead with a long stride, leading them out of the building, through loitering cars, cabs and buses. Engine noise, a guttural throbbing, seemed to make a voice for the simmering air which pressed against their faces and plastered their shirts against their chests. In a minute they were drenched. Roads the colour of glittering steel reflecting back the fierce sunlight led away from the airport into an enormous white sky, and in the distance was a solitary skyscraper, flat and grey, a neat and suggestive image, like a trailer for a forthcoming film or a vision of the future. Dudley's spirits revived.

'Look, Martin.' He pointed. 'Fantasia!' But Martin was looking in the opposite direction back at the airport.

When they reached her double-parked Mustang the girl turned and said to Martin, 'Is your friend wanting a ride somewhere or is this a long farewell?'

'He's coming with me.'

'Oh, really?'

'I'm Martin's UK manager. Pleased to meet you.' He put out a hand. 'Geoff Dudley, some people call me Butch.'

'I don't recall Ed mentioning any friend.'

'I'll tell him when we see him,' Martin said.

'You going to visit him in hospital?' The girl had stopped chewing and was looking at them.

Diesel fumes drifted round them, liquefying the hot air.

'Hospital?' Dudley asked.

'Ed's in the Blue River Hospital in Vermont. Broke his hip two days ago.'

'I'm very sorry to hear that,' Dudley said with a wild expression caused by his attempt to suppress a smile.

The girl went on, 'I'm running this thing for Ed, okay? You can tell me about your friend in the car. Let's go, we're way late.' She yanked open her car door. 'Well?'

Dudley had insinuated himself into her line of vision. 'I'm terribly sorry, I didn't catch your name.'

'Name's Bella LaRose.'

'Bella LaRose? Bella LaRose?'

'Will it do?'

He paused with his hand on the door, frowning.

'Well? Can we go?'

'I've heard that name before. Bella LaRose?'

'Must be some other Bella LaRose. Are you getting in the car or what?'

'I remember.' He looked at her with fresh interest. 'It's coming back to me: Jacques Brun, the Envy Club, Bella LaRose. Shouldn't you be bald?'

12

The imposing concrete façade of the airport, in style part industrial, part Islamic, receded as they drove into a wasteland of swamp and vacant lots, pylons, warehouses and oil sumps. Flyovers looped over rusted railway tracks, bending towards distant tollgates. Billboards hemmed in the roads. *Old English 800. Newport Lights Alive With Pleasure. NJ Lottery – Next Jackpot $4.5m.*

Dudley talked non-stop to establish presence, a technique he favoured. Of American landscape, travel, quest literature, myth. But Bella LaRose's eyes were hidden behind sun-glasses and Martin stared silently out of the window, biting his thumbnail. One of Dudley's theories was that travel had been cheapened by travel writing.

'They say that travel broadens the mind. I'd say it loosens the tongue.'

Martin snorted.

Monologues were his forte and his refuge. He spoke aloud of his career with a publishing house known for its scholarly editions of masterpieces of European pornography. Ediciones Sexual was the name of this house, a family business with offices in Berlin, London, Barcelona and Aix-en-Provence. It influenced the policies of national governments and made yearly donations to the monastic order of St Thomas the Doubter. 'For interest, can anything match the ambiguity of charity in our age?' Dudley asked. No one was listening to him. He asked Bella LaRose about her modelling career and she lit a cigarette and did not answer.

As they bumped down a flyover towards the Holland Tunnel, Manhattan came into view, indistinct in the haze, a postcard dawn Avalon. For a long time as they approached, its miniature silhouettes seemed to slide away from them like a mirage slowly receding from the slowly advancing delirious explorer. Fantasia. The City of Miracles. Dudley recognized the twin stilts of the World Trade Center, the Empire State Building and, eventually, the Chrysler with its hubcap and radiator spire. All this in the distance. Between lay wasteland: crumbling factories, outhouses and garbage dumps. An American flag hung from a pole in a field of wild grass. Hillocks of gravel and sand and spare parts appeared, choked with weeds. The heatwave lay over everything like a curfew.

69

At the Holland Tunnel they joined a queue behind a bus which said on the back *NJ Transit Easy Rider*. Twenty minutes later they had not moved.

'If we get to New York before nightfall,' Dudley said, 'I'd like to chew over some ideas I have for the coming week.' Ideas arose out of his monologue without premeditation: a media blitz, openings, happenings, political link-ins, a clothing allowance. Without speaking, Bella LaRose tossed a thick dossier headed *Itinerary Martin Prout* on to the back seat, and Dudley thanked her and was silent. The size of the dossier startled him into admiration. The sun was beating through the glass, waves of heat with the same lulling rhythm as the car's sloppy suspension, almost giving the impression that they were still moving, still undulating over bumps and holes, sailing in a dream. Dudley fell asleep, and while he slept they edged into the city. When he woke, parched and disorientated, they were stuck in another jam on Sixth Avenue, Manhattan's towers all around them, a fantastic eruption of architecture.

After so long looking forward to it, his first impression was not, oddly, of height and splendour, but of shrinkage and confinement. Towers cut off his view, their packed Piranesian bulk penned him in, forming a prison, a city of cells, like a honeycomb. When he pushed his doubtful face doglike between the front seats, he saw only the tunnel of Sixth Avenue stretching northwards, like the long corridor of a penitentiary. Shadows angled across it created a second city of shapes, of haphazard geometry, a double network of walls impossible to escape. His shocked face was no more than a microscopic detail in all this.

This was not the impression he wanted to retain and in later years remember with affection and humour, and he instantly tried to shake it off. He tried to flood it with other impressions, and as Bella LaRose turned the car down another street and accelerated sharply (to an abrupt medley of horns), he submitted himself to occasional details flashing past: Chemical Bank; syncopated bursts of police sirens; sunlight off glass; Burger Heaven; sooty brickwork; Must Vacate Entire Inventory

Reduced; blackened grilles; blackened windows; gold-glass skyscrapers glinting like krugerrands; a snatch of sky; Madison Avenue Muscle-Tanning Solarium; people streaming along the sidewalks; wooden planks patching the pitted roads; Terry's Gourmet; a truck with chrome fenders like moose antlers; Camel Smooth Character; a fountain in the shape of a dandelion-poll; a half-timbered Tudor cottage seventeen storeys high; a skyscraper shaped like a wave; a tree; Walk, Don't Walk; a bum with a bag; Vets International Armoured Car Inc.; Jockey, Minolta, Skimpy Yoghurt; a stretch limo; Fame Gourmet Gallery Cold Beer Salad Bar; Scuba Lessons; vertical marble, metal, glass; Frozen Gurt; deserted roadworks; sunlight off windscreens; chrome lettering; an awning; a footman; a hotel.

Bella LaRose stopped the car, gave the finger to a passing cab and got out, leaving the engine running. Dudley got out too, slightly shaken, and instinctively craned his head back to find the sky. He felt uncomfortably inconspicuous.

'There's one room booked,' Bella LaRose said. 'He wants a playmate, what do I care? But you make it on your own.' She turned her head, giving him the bonus of her profile, and glanced towards the footman who started obediently in their direction. Nervous admiration consumed Dudley, engulfed him. No response was left him but thoughtless wonder and the appreciation of these moments, these details of Bella LaRose's scrap-heap hair, her smooth, fierce face, her loose breasts in her T-shirt, the bunched muscles in her legs.

He told her how much he liked her city.

'Born in Chicago,' she said.

'I meant your country.'

She did not look at him, but at the hotel façade, the approaching footman, her dirty Mustang.

'He's going to stay in there all day?' she asked.

Martin was still sitting inside the car, slumped in the seat like a Guy Fawkes, staring at his thumbs.

Dudley felt the second tremor of worry. 'In England we've made rather a tradition of introspection.'

'And turning up unexpected.'

71

'Habit fostered by insecurity. We aim only to please.'

'You talk real weird. Get him out of the car.'

While the footman consulted with Bella LaRose, Dudley tapped on the car window and gestured for Martin to join him on the sidewalk. The window rolled down, and Martin's face appeared, pale and taut.

'Get back in the car,' he said to Dudley.

Dudley stared blankly at him. 'Wouldn't that be a rather retrograde step?'

'Get in the car. We're not stopping here.'

'But, Martin – '

'Get in the fucking car.' The window went up.

The footman had retreated a little way and was talking into a walkie-talkie; he had seen the extent of Dudley's luggage and needed assistance. Dudley attracted Bella LaRose's attention with a stage cough and explained the situation.

'He doesn't like the hotel? He has *seen* the hotel?'

'I'm afraid it's slightly more indefinable than that.'

A scene followed, played partly on the sidewalk and partly in the car, in which Bella LaRose was tight-lipped, impatient and sarcastic; Martin, hostile and uncommunicative; and Dudley compromising, distracting and futile. Finally they all got back into the car and drove away from the hotel and the footman, back through the honeycombed city.

'You see anything takes your fancy, just give the word. If that's the way you want it, that's the way we'll do it. I'm just the chauffeur.'

In a low voice Dudley remonstrated, pleaded with Martin, but Martin set his face to the window. In the distance, from several different directions they heard the warbling of police sirens.

'It didn't seem so bad to me,' Dudley was saying. 'At a distance.'

'Left,' Martin said abruptly. 'Down here.' They swung into a street where the buildings were lower and dirtier. A lone skyscraper stood empty at the far end, its windows advertising itself: F O R R E N T. In front of it part of the road was dug up;

there was a hole surrounded by orange cones and a skip filled half with rubble, half with shadow. Beyond, in a strip of sunlight which veered across the road as if it had an ulterior purpose, two men were loudly arguing.

'Here,' Martin said.

Central Hotel had a peeling door and a cracked window. A handwritten notice advertised second-hand beds. The brickwork had split and buckled, and the steps that led up to the door were piled with litter. It was not central. It did not look like a hotel. Bella LaRose lit a cigarette and glanced once towards the building.

'Big treat for you, Butch,' she said.

'Oh, I don't think we'll be stopping here,' Dudley said, nervous.

'Get out of the car,' said Martin.

They stood on the sidewalk and argued while Bella LaRose smoked in her Mustang.

'I hate this posturing,' Martin said. 'Why don't you hate it?'

'Posturing?'

'The pretence. I don't believe you're as stupid as you sound.'

'You're right, I'm craftier than you realize. It's part of my cunning plan to get you to go back to the other hotel.'

It took a long time for Dudley to understand that Martin wanted to stay at Central Hotel because he thought it was the kind of place which wouldn't patronize or cheapen him.

'Cheapen?' Dudley said. '*Cheapen*? Martin, look at it. They don't come any cheaper.'

They both looked at the hotel front. The Becks sign above the door which incorporated the hotel's name was a plastic box, split open, with the bulb gone.

Martin was expressionless. 'I like it. I like the look of it.'

Dudley mimed incredulity, his forehead wrinkled, his eyes bulging. 'I'm baffled, I'm bewildered, it's all deeply unintelligible.'

He watched Martin walk away, climb the litter-strewn steps and disappear through the door, all done with the kind of smooth, dreamlike movement which does not belong to the dream except as a puzzle, a wrong note in the harmony of the narrative. The door gave a helpless creak as it shut. He took four or five deep breaths as he tried to collect his thoughts and steady his nerves. The possibility that this hotel, this street, these ruins, would become his own particular corner of New York, the only New York he might be allotted, shortened his breath. The unexpected comes in many forms; the expected too has a variety of disguises. Dudley thought of the haphazard city of shadows laying confusingly aslant the real one. Confusion was the theme of his own experiences but perhaps, with a concentration of effort or with the passing of time, the picture would become clearer, focussed, and the experiences he had anticipated would appear.

Tapping on the car window, he gestured for Bella LaRose to wind it down. He stared at her a moment before he spoke.

'Looks like we'll stop here tonight. Martin is curious as to the low-life, about which we've heard so much. This curiosity is the source of his astonishing theatrical genius, of course.'

'Your friend.'

'Yes. Martin. We're very close.'

'Needs help.'

'You may be right.'

'Here.' She passed to Dudley the Martin Prout itinerary, and told him she was not wasting her time for nothing, that Martin's value to Ed Slezinger was negligible, that her own loyalties to Ed Slezinger were limited, that from now on she regarded Dudley as responsible for his screwy buddy. She was bowing out. She also gave to him an envelope containing one thousand dollars.

'I understand,' Dudley said, presenting through the car window a grave face.

'This much I'll do,' Bella LaRose said. 'Tomorrow. Lunch. We have to run through the agenda. After that he's on his own. Get him there. The restaurant's in the itinerary. No other restaurant will do, okay, no cruising the streets for low-rent kebab joints. Tell him that. One other thing.'

'Of course.'

74

'Butch isn't your name.'

'It's one of my names.'

'What are the others?'

'Geoffrey and Dudley. And, I'm afraid, Cyril.'

'I'll call you Dud.'

'Thank you.'

'One last thing, Dud.'

'Anything.'

'You don't need to be at the restaurant. Let's keep expenses to a minimum.'

'I was about to suggest it.'

The window went up, wiping a grease-smear across his reflection. Dudley bent forwards and tapped twice on the perspex, thoughtful.

'Drive carefully,' he said. His imagination tended to the carnal despite his solemn face. The engine revved, he stepped back, and the car slithered away, banging over a crater, bearing away all his luggage which he had forgotten to unload.

13

Cradling his chin in thought, sitting in his vest and Y-fronts at the windowsill, he experienced the compromised elation of arrival and sought the right words to capture it. On the one hand, in Slezinger's absence, he found himself unexpectedly influential in matters of Martin's publicity. On the other hand he was excruciatingly tired, it was 1 a.m., unbearably hot, and Martin, who had gone out before ten, still had not returned. Neither had Dudley's luggage. He was conscious of an alternative series of events in which he sat at a leather-topped desk in his suite at the Plaza, dressed in his quilted silk dressing-gown, confiding his thoughts to a moroccan-bound *cahier* bought specially for the purpose. He sighed, adjusted his vest and leaned forward.

261. So, if I write: we drove for miles and miles through barren stretches of swampland, warehouses and pylons, all dirty and dark with piles of rubbish everywhere as if it were a land fallen into dereliction, before crossing the river, a sticky, brown Styx far below, and nosing our way, traffic-bound, into the city – perhaps I also mean: the hero quested forth from the woodman's cottage where he had been reared as an orphan by a kindly hermit, and after many curious encounters fetched up at the sumptuous castle where, in a joust, he killed the king his father.

I am being metaphorical.

Dudley left off writing and looked at his watch. One thirty. He looked round the room. It was small, hot and dirty, with walls the colour of dishwater. Two narrow beds filled it. Besides the chair on which he sat there was no other furniture, only a partially dismantled television sitting on a shelf in an alcove which doubled as the wardrobe. A doorway hung with a bead curtain led to a squalid toilet which Dudley had no wish to see again. He wondered whether in New York lavatories were leased out by the hour, like certain rooms he had read about. There was a smell of trapped people, squashed bodies sweating in the night. Outside, there was a constant noise of talk, traffic and alarms. The City of Miracles never sleeps.

He wrote:

262. Martin Prout, Melancholy, that figure brooding, face sullen, back bunched, was waiting for me in this room when I arrived. He ignored my entrance, he was absorbed in the view from the window. I went over to him, eager to look over the city. The window gives out on to an expanse of brickwork three feet away. A similar view can be obtained by staring into a bucket.

When we arrived in this country I suggested that our fate was to be sold into slavery, and in a sense he has made it come true. He is a dangerous creature if he can take my fantasies and make them real. I can't.

76

He went out some time ago. To find a brothel, he said. Before he went he expressed a general sense of disappointment connected with his memory of our schoolboy friendship.

The door was suddenly thumped, giving Dudley a terrific fright and propelling him off his chair and into a copulative position on the bed. His notebook and pen leaped in different directions. Someone was rattling the handle of the door, trying to get in. Such incidents in dosshouses were well known to him from cheap fiction, he could imagine them; he twisted on the bed, alive to all dramatic possibilities. Appealing to his watch (3 a.m., surely not, had he nodded off, was he dreaming?), he called softly, 'Who is it?' and the scrabbling at the door handle intensified. 'Who is it, please?' Another thump. Thoughts racing, he anxiously judged the distance to the door. Had he locked it? He had not. Would he reach it before it was flung open by whatever brute was battering it? He would not. It took him only a second to live through the whole scenario about to unfold: the bursting-in of the drunken hammer-wielding navvy on the prowl for drugs and money and rough sex (his pocky face leering); the brief chase; the tragi-comic absurdity of Dudley trying to lock himself in a bathroom closed only by a bead curtain; the dragging of Dudley out of the bathroom (hot, vomity breath in his face); the blows to his head, ribs, kidneys (his squeals high-pitched and shamefully girlish); the stretching out of his genitals on the windowsill and the pounding flat of them with the hammer (hoots of mad navvy accompanying him into unconsciousness). In a small panicky movement which would always remain incomprehensible to him, he rolled off the bed, squatted by the wall, shut his eyes and waited.

When he reopened his eyes he found Martin swaying above him.

'Martin, it's you.'

Martin looked at him dazed. 'What are you doing?'

'Help me find my contact lens, will you?' Dudley said,

77

moving his hands over the stained carpet in slow, swimming movements.

They sat on their beds, Dudley talking, Martin watching. The heat, even in the hour before dawn, was uncomfortable, a grubby, airless pressure which left everything oily to the touch. The room seemed to bulge with it. There was no air-conditioning and the window wouldn't open.

Dudley sipped duty-free brandy, and talked. A vast monologue. Martin watched.

'I must get to bed,' Dudley said, filling his plastic beaker again. 'There are things to do, worlds to conquer.'

Martin listened to the words, their tone and resonance, and watched the gestures that accompanied them, the hand-waving and head-scratching and finger-wagging. They betrayed a new nervousness.

'What are you doing here?' he asked suddenly.

Dudley paused. 'You mean, here, in this room?'

'In New York. What are you doing here with me?'

Dudley looked furtive, as if he detected a trick question. 'Well, I'm looking after you. I'm your minder.'

'Don't tell me that, tell me why you're really here.'

Dudley rose and poured himself another drink. His furtive manner vanished.

'There *is* another reason.' He sipped. Martin was silent. 'I'm not sure how to put it. It's shamelessly personal. I'm going to change my life.'

Martin was still staring at him.

'You know, a fresh start, a new deal of the pack, a change of scene, a dying of the old self and the unimaginably resplendent rising of the new. Don't worry, I won't let it get in the way of my other responsibilities.'

Martin shook his head.

'Don't you believe in the changeability of character?'

'I don't believe in character.'

Dudley explained the procedure in medieval quest literature. 'There is a period of basic questing. The scenery rolls by. There are moments of self-denial and self-doubt. Things become confused. Finally it all ends in the miraculous. Our finales are always transcendental. It's quite simple.'

'Day-dreams,' Martin said.

'Harmless day-dreams.'

'Pure fantasy.'

'Fantasy? Fantasy is life. Everyone fantasizes.'

Martin got up and poured out the last of the brandy and drank it down. 'What's the difference between the day-dreamer and the madman?'

'No difference. That's my point.'

Martin went back to his bed, lay down and closed his eyes. Dudley looked at him with a pleased expression, then went to the window. Detail of the brickwork was visible in the dank, grey light.

'Dawn comes early with rosy fingers. We should get some sleep.'

Martin appeared to be asleep already; he lay like a waif on his side.

When the light was switched off, the room became grainy monochrome, the objects in it forming mute versions of themselves, flat and weightless – the charcoal diagram of the television, the dark nick of a sprinkler overhead, the black strip of the door, the hanging veil of the bead curtain.

'By the way, I've been reading the itinerary,' Dudley said. 'I have to admit that these Yanks are very thorough. I'm impressed, we're going to be busy. But tomorrow is a free day. Do some sightseeing.' He grunted as he tried to make himself comfortable. 'I'll be having lunch with a friend who happened to get in touch with me. Nice chap. Runs an import-export business.' He coughed. 'Writes poetry in his spare time.'

They were silent. A few minutes passed while each lay listening to the sounds from outside, the traffic, the alarms, the footfalls. Suddenly Martin said, 'You're happy unless you've a reason not to be. You think that the worst won't happen. You trust people before you doubt them. You think that character is something real.'

Dudley opened his eyes and watched the slow, filtered light diluting the dark alcove. 'Yes,' he said.

They were both silent for a while.

'I'm the opposite,' Martin said. His voice sounded far away, and before the alcove could get any lighter, and the door handle emerge out of the darkness of the door, and the television set change into itself, Dudley was asleep.

14

Up and down the steep ravine of Fifth Avenue the solid mid-air was a tremulous blaze of windows. Sunlight made New York wobble. Glass, steel and concrete seemed to be turning to steam and melted tar.

Unable to hold the city's gaze Dudley dropped his eyes to the sidewalk. Dark blotches appeared as drops of sweat fell from the end of his nose. He recalled the weather message on the television earlier: RIGHT NOW 85* TEMP 90* HUMID – just the right sort of hard-hitting, no-nonsense approach for a heatwave in New York. English heatwaves turned lawns yellow; in America they melted the shirt off your back. For the last hour he had been hobbling along the sidewalk, his head craned back, dizzied and entranced and dripping with sweat.

He had not anticipated heatwaves; they had not been part of his plan. Worse, having been parted from his suitcases, he was forced to wear what he had arrived in: cricket jumper, corduroy trousers, cowboy boots. The boots, he had discovered, were too small.

He hobbled on, wiping his face with the cravat, seeking new sights.

The rush hour was long over, but the sidewalks were solid

with people; they came past, their eyes fixed on the middle distance, their expressions set against the heat, against the diesel fumes and stink of garbage and clamour of car horns, against the city itself. Dudley stared at them as much as he stared at the buildings. Caucasians, Negroes, Arabs, Orientals, Asians, Caribbeans, Latins. Where were the Americans? he thought.

Hobbling on, he found a diner and went in.

Seated in the window with a lumberjack breakfast of eggs easy-over, sausages and pancakes, he spent an hour watching everything that happened at the junction of Fifth Avenue and Thirty-Seventh Street. He had time to kill before meeting Bella LaRose for lunch. Martin was conveniently occupied in buying himself some smart new clothes.

Immense trucks crawled by, bull-nosed monsters with aluminium smokestacks and dinosaurian fenders. They were called *United City Interior Demolition* or *Duffy Disposal Co. Inc.* or *Radio Despatch Zonker Towing* and in each of their squat cabs was a gum-chewing sixteen-year-old with a baseball cap and skinny arms, his hand pressed to the horn. Smaller trucks went by too, towing clapped-out Chevrolets and Lincolns. Truckiness was the main characteristic of nearly every vehicle on the road: even an old people's coach looked like a truck, with a prognathous cab and armour plating. American cars were not neat and stylish like European cars, they were frank and powerful and ugly. Many were beaten up as if to say that life is for the living, you're bound to take a few knocks.

Dudley wondered if, on the highway of life, he were a truck. In his notebook marked *Pensées* he wrote:

278. *Eggs easy-over slightly disappointing, They don't live up to the implication, given by their name, of relaxed sex.*

Real trucks, the original trucks, were everywhere, busy dismantling the city, clearing the way for new excess: bigger office blocks, taller skyscrapers, more massive stores. Excess was obvious, both urban and egoistical. He thought about the buildings he had seen: the Chrysler Building, the Rockefeller Center, the Woolworth Building, Trump Tower – all those towering egos. Like him, those people equated New York with one thing: making it big. Gratefully he aspired to their dimension. They had made their dreams come true in brick, concrete, glass and steel: lucid, ludicrous buildings hundreds of feet high.

The diner filled with people, men in business suits between meetings, men in overalls and women in cheap stretchpants or chic jewellery. The proprietors were Greeks, they yelled at each other in their own language, and addressed their customers in brisk, casual English: 'Hello, what is it you want? What coffee, please? To go? Yes, hello …' A sign above the cappuccino machines said *May Peace Prevail On Earth*. A woman with a nasal voice sitting alone was reading aloud atrocities from the morning's paper and the radio was playing 'Those Were The Days My Friend'. Dudley wanted to write it all down, to become a part of it, to live out the lives the city offered.

He reflected, and wrote:

279. City of games. People come to it to win or lose. It even looks like a city of games: a huge chess-board, a maze, a funhouse. The whole thing is a new toy, with shiny building-blocks, early-learning-puzzle skyline and ten-foot-high spelling mistakes in neon ('Eezy-fit', 'Fone Fun', 'R Snax R Max'). Children built it for themselves out of wishes and dreams. Wishes and dreams – not real estate or pork bellies or futures – are its true business.

Outside, having finished his breakfast, he stood under an official road sign which said *No Parking No Standing No Stopping No Kidding* and consulted his Hagstrom. Then, by several chess moves across Manhattan's enormous board, he hobbled towards Macy's.

On his way he admired the beautiful buses that passed him, all chrome and rivets with massive snub noses like dogfish.

They revved and whooshed and glided by. The people on the sidewalks were just as numerous and insensible as before. A bald man with a head wound came by shouting, 'Fuck God! Fuck God! Fuck God!' apparently to the surprise of no one.

He was prepared to find Macy's impressive, even overwhelmingly so, but he was disappointed. The dowdy wooden escalators were familiar, so too the racks of safe clothes and the lethargy of the sales assistants. It was an English experience, only magnified. But he was short of time: he was already late for lunch, and first he had to buy some suitable clothes. He could go no further in his cowboy boots.

In ten minutes he had bought (out of the expenses Bella LaRose had given him) a T-shirt with a yellow smiling face on it, a pair of blue-striped, knee-length shorts, basketball boots, a pair of Ray Bans and a New York Yankees baseball cap.

His old shirt, cravat, jumper, corduroys and cowboy boots he left in the end cubicle of the Gentlemen's cloakroom on the seventh floor (self-abandonment begins with an irrevocable gesture) and went down the creaking wooden escalators to emerge into Broadway a new man.

He was late for lunch, but checking his reflection in Macy's windows his eye was caught by the display of merchandise behind the glass, and he stopped for a moment to stare. Several nude manikins, each wearing at least a hundred watches up their arms and round their legs, many in uncomfortable positions, were posed in front of a curtain spray-painted with the words Thirst, Emotion, Love, Drive, Ambition, Trust, Sadness, Lust, Hunger – graffiti which seemed to represent the range of possibilities from which watch-wearers might select their guiding passions.

He read through the list again, slowly. Drive appealed to him. Ambition too. Lust as well. Glancing at his own watch, then back at his reflection, he murmured, 'This is it.' He turned, he almost span on his heels, an overweight Fred Astaire, and entered the crowd, and as he did, the smile still on his face, a girl went past wearing a scarlet skirt, her hair bobbed and dark. It was such a small thing, a detail in a million, but it swung him back suddenly to Bethanay crying and Sykes slouching into the kitchen and all the dear and unbearable details of his life before he was a man on the make.

Someone jostled Dudley as he went by shouting, 'Come on, Lucifer! Come on, Devil!' and he remembered his lunch appointment.

He set off, bouncing in his basketball boots.

'Drive,' he said thoughtfully.

He lolloped along.

'Ambition,' he said, more loudly.

Bounce, bounce, bounce in his new boots.

'Lust,' he whispered. 'Lust, lust, lust.'

15

He was very late, it was his nature to be very late, and Bella LaRose who had purposely turned up late herself had been waiting for half an hour when he arrived. Mopping his brow with the loose sleeve of his T-shirt and shivering, he edged his way through the freezing, leafy interior of Casa Fina. Bella was sitting at the back. Smoking a Marlboro Light and holding a frosted glass against her cheek, she looked past Dudley to where the leaded window, framed with cool foliage, gave out on to blazing East Thirty-Fourth. Muted chatter filled the restaurant. Waiters in dress shirts swanned diligently between tables.

He didn't recognize her at first, her hair had utterly changed. The previous night it had been a high mound of crisp, oily coils and now it was a punkish whirl of tufts sloppily tied with scarlet ribbons. Gone was the hieratic jade mask, and in its place was the face of a tomboy – pouting mouth, stubborn chin, lazy eyes. Only her air of self-possession was unchanged.

'Bellissima,' he said, from close range, unexpectedly.

She started, Dudley's first triumph, her eyes swivelling on to him. They held his for a moment, dropped to his sneakers and rose to his baseball cap slung on backwards. With a twirl Dudley removed his Ray Bans.

'Jesus,' she said.

'All over American,' Dudley said. 'You didn't recognize me.'

'I wasn't even expecting you.'

He pulled out a chair.

'Hey.'

'I thought I might sit down.'

'Stay on your feet. Move that way. Over there. People will think you're with me.'

Dudley backed out of her line of vision, and while she pretended he wasn't there, he observed her with renewed awe and lust. A scarlet leather bustier contained some but by no means all of her torso, a bizarre E-cup version of the fifties lift-and-separate brassière, its two padded and ribbed cups spiralling from her chest, conical in shape like miniature warheads. For the rest, she appeared to be naked.

'I was thinking,' Dudley said, momentarily not thinking at all. He paused. 'I was thinking, as I say, thinking that you might in fact be bald by now. I'm relieved, I confess, to be lunching with someone with normal amounts of hair.'

Without taking her eyes from the front of the restaurant, she said, 'First thing. I'm looking, but I don't see.'

'Martin? He's indisposed, actually.'

'Second thing. You're here.'

'I am. Complicated, isn't it?'

'Tell me.'

'May I sit?'

Bella stubbed out her cigarette. 'All right, you get to sit.'

He removed his baseball cap, slicked back his damp fringe with a damp palm and grinned. He nodded towards Bella's glass.

'What are you drinking? I think I'll have the same.'

'Don't think it. Think of seven good reasons why you're here and your insane friend isn't.' Her voice contrasted nicely with his, a precision motor after the distant rumour of an aeroplane.

'It's going to take some time.'

Bella made a slight movement with her shoulders. 'Let me give you an incentive. In one minute I'm through that door, away, gone, never to be seen again, and you and your crazy friend are nowhere. Is that an incentive?' She spoke casually, but with an expectancy which suggested total control. Her eyelids were seductive but Dudley had no doubt that at the slightest slackening of his performance she would leave.

He began to talk, carefully, smoothly, slyly and rapidly. He told her about Martin's 'bashfulness'. He pointed out that Martin was brilliant, charismatic, irresistible, lovable if you knew him – but shy. He described how Martin, desperately wanting to please, found the responsibilities of pleasure bafflingly onerous. Several anecdotes supported this claim. In conclusion Martin was the hottest property in British theatre, film and television but must be handled with extraordinary sensitivity, in other words: by Dudley.

There was a long pause. Bella leaned forward.

'Do you *believe* any of this?'

Dudley looked at her, then shook his head. 'No.'

'Why tell me?'

'I wanted to create a good impression.'

'What's the truth?'

'The truth? Martin is moody, anti-social, immature, semi-skilled, inanimate, uncivilized, hostile and odd. That's why I'm here.'

Shaking a cigarette out of her carton, she lit up, keeping her eyes on him, brilliant whites under heavy lids, incorruptible and mocking. Blue smoke plumed like a veil across her face. Her lips were glossier, perter, more *liplike* than any lips he had seen before. He smiled, his eyes fixed on her mouth as she spoke.

'So. This friend of yours.'

'Yes. Martin.'

'Is an asshole.'

'I certainly wouldn't expect you to like him straightaway.'

'He's vicious.'

86

'He has a sort of righteous anger. A short person's view of the world.'

'He hates the world.'

Dudley nodded. 'Possibly it's more extreme than that.'

Bella nodded with him. 'And you? You're not an asshole?'

'I hope not. Not exclusively.'

'You're friendly and intelligent and all the rest of it.'

'One hates to make claims.'

'And your relations with the world? I'm assuming you belong to this world, despite appearances.'

'The world and I get on. Our relations are cordial. I wouldn't say they were close.'

Bella was nodding slowly, wreathed in smoke.

'Now tell me what you're really doing here.'

Dudley winced, raised his hands in a gesture of surrender and sighed. 'You've got to help me,' he said. 'I need help. That's why I'm here. You're the only who can help me.'

He began to talk again. Two stories evolved, linked but distinct, one concerning Martin Prout and his savagery; and the other – by way of contrast – introducing a character whose charm and willingness to please and not inconsiderable abilities had been neither satisfied nor snuffed out by his native country, and who had therefore decamped to the land of opportunity, arriving socially hampered and relatively friendless but unmistakably likely, in need only of a helping hand. He would have said more, but Bella cut him off him with a groan.

'You know. Another guy would have walked clean out of here half an hour ago. Half of what you say you just made up. The other half is crazy. What am I doing here?'

'I think they're still serving.' Dudley looked round to catch a waiter's eye.

'You're a dork.'

'Thank you. Dork?'

Bella was shaking her head. 'If I'm not going to get rid of you, let's get through lunch as quick as we can.'

The waiter was poised scrupulously at Dudley's shoulder.

'Hi, I'm Brad. Can I get you something?'

87

Dudley threw his arm across the back of his chair. 'Dry Martini. One olive.' Brad went.

Dudley fingered the menu, glancing at Bella who gazed back, lips parted to blow smoke, mocking. 'Is it always this hot in New York?' he asked, his face wily and wide-open. 'Quite amazing.'

'Been here before?'

'Only in my dreams.'

'Listen to me for one minute. I'm giving you my time.' Talking evenly, as if ridding herself of a small burden of memory, she told Dudley what to do over the coming days. A copy of the itinerary appeared. Listed in it were both major interviews and the interviews that could be skipped, the names of interviewers who must be deferred to, and those who could be put in their place, the things to say and the things to leave unsaid, the biographical details which were compelling and character-enhancing, and those which were tedious and forbidden.

He flipped pages, smiling. 'Is there radio?'

'There's radio. Plenty of radio.'

'Television?'

'One slot.'

'Is that enough?'

'More than he deserves.'

'What kind of slot?'

'Arty trendy. Everyone hates it. You'll love it. Now some words of general advice.'

She told him to take cabs and give the drivers a hard time; never to use the subway. Never to walk when there's an elevator. Never to talk to a cop except to complain. Never to catch anyone's eye in a crowd. Never to go to a hooker, always to get her to come to you. To get a change of clothes immediately. To speak politely when mugged. Dudley's martini arrived, huge, in a small vase, a swizzler-stick the size of a pop-gun casting a shadow across the surface of the liquid.

'Ask me why I'm telling you all this.'

'Why are you telling me all this?'

'Because now I don't have to care what happens to you, you're not on my conscience, you're history.'

'Thank you.'

He was history. He was lunching at the famous Casa Fina, East Thirty-Fourth. He was delighted. Clearing his throat, he pushed his elbows forward, businesslike, and began to talk about his innovative work in the UK television industry. 'The point is,' he said, 'I can foresee a time when I might move across to the American side of things. You probably deal with a lot of people in television here.'

'You don't need contacts, Dud. You need protection.'

Brad presented a small pad and stump of pencil, beaming. 'How are we doing here?'

'We'll order,' Bella said. 'I'll have the sole. Mixed salad, no tomatoes. French. Dud?'

'We have some real good specials today,' Brad said as Dudley nosed through the menu. 'Lobster and apple salad in a piquant sauce; Chinese-sautéed baby chicken wings with wild thyme mayonnaise; chilled curried sea fruits and hot corn bread with fresh herbs; forest mushroom crêpes with sugared garlic croutons and a hot Stilton sauce.'

'Thank you,' Dudley said.

'Spinach and coconut pasta bake with hot bacon doughballs and a gratin dip; crab, avocado and sour cream pie with . . .'

Dudley held up his hand. 'I believe in simplicity in all things. I'll have the mushroom crêpe, but can you render the exotic bits optional by bringing them on separate plates?'

'Sure. And to drink? You want to see the wine list?'

'A bottle of Puligny-Montrachet for the lady, very cold, and for me a bottle of Pouilly-Fuissé. I think you'll enjoy that,' he said to Bella.

Brad flashed a smile and was gone, leaving Dudley to talk about his hopes of New York.

'Le Corbusier called New York a magnificent catastrophe. Did you know that?'

'I just live here, Dud.'

89

He talked on. Every few minutes Bella LaRose shook a cigarette from her pack and put it in her mouth. Lips, slightly apart, showed their moist purplish inner surfaces. She never stopped chewing gum, even when she smoked. She never laughed at his jokes, she never responded to his gambits but listened to him with lazy, faintly mocking eyes. Dudley's nostrils twitched as he smelled – or imagined he smelled – a scent off her, of perfume, tobacco, synthetic watermelon and perspiration.

'I've talked enough,' Dudley said. 'Tell me about your city.'

'New York? You really want to know about New York?' She exhaled blue smoke. 'You can die in New York. A guy like you who knows nothing and thinks he knows everything, you can get killed within minutes of arrival. You can get pushed under a truck, whacked in a bar-room brawl, knifed by a stranger who just doesn't like your style. You can get bashed on the head by an eleven-year-old in Central Park. You can get shot by a junkie for the resale value of your sneakers. You can get accidentally beaten to death by the New York Police Department. Downtown, the bums will get you. Midtown, it's the wandering psychos. Uptown, it's the gangs, the Ricos and the Yardies. It can happen anywhere. In a restaurant like this you can eat a pork chop and be set on fire by a whole range of people from fundamentalist Muslims to militant vegans. Guy like you, you're a walking target, there's a big sign in flashing neon over your head which says, "Kill Me. Go Ahead, Kill Me, I'm Yours." Guy like you has no chance. Zero survival rating. I'm having lunch with a dead man.'

Dudley was no longer smiling. He shifted on his seat. 'I'm just here to get rich,' he said.

'Get rich? In New York?' She reminded him of the empty shops he had seen, the closing-down sales, the patched-up roads, the piles of garbage on the sidewalks, the deserted skyscrapers.

'You mean you think the object of my quest may be illusory?'

Her lighter flared blue, her eyelids flicked and he shivered. After the swelter outside, the restaurant's air-conditioning had turned his T-shirt to a sheet of melting ice. Mysteriously he continued to sweat. He was bewitched by the climate, the buildings, the women and their talk of death.

He rose clutching his napkin.

'Excuse me a moment. Nature calls.'

'Nerves,' she said, exhaling smoke.

Alone in the spacious, steaming-hot Rest Room (but surrounded by twelve different reflections of himself), he urinated. 'Hombres' was a marvel in glazed terracotta, its cubicles and urinals so sensitively designed as to be almost invisible; its wash-basins, by contrast, strong and vulgar, large, smooth scoops out of mock turquoise-veined marble overhung with gilt taps in an exaggerated double droop.

He, however, was in an uncomfortable state of arousal, his whole body sweating, his heart palpitating and his eyes itching. Vertigo, or something similar, afflicted him. Turning, buttoning, to the wash-basins, he decided to wash his armpits.

Glimpses of someone in difficulty doubled in two mirrors: arms trussed in coils of damp T-shirt, neck throttled, face flushed, hair doggy, a yellow moon-face smiling through crumpled anguish. Dudley wrenched himself free and stood naked to the waist, considering his reflection over the wash-basin. His heart was pounding but for a few minutes he was motionless.

'Interesting,' he said through a slitted mouth. 'If you didn't talk, if you didn't smile or frown or squint or leer, if you did your best to breathe as little as possible, you'd be passably handsome. Don't you think?' The reflection leered, squinted, frowned, shuddered and turned aside.

'All is vanity, Geoffrey. Geoff. Butch. Vanity, mirth and folly.'

With quick clumsy movements he lathered his armpits, his face distorting at the absurd discomfort of it. Just when he needed to be at his brilliant best he felt unsettled and lacking conviction. And his body seemed to be disintegrating, leaking

91

away; soon nothing would be left of him but a pile of damp clothing. He felt himself to be on the verge of a tremendous illness; he scratched his scalp violently and checked his finger-nails. Both his dandruff and his hypochondria had flared up nastily. Bending, he felt carefully at his throat, neck and groin for buboes.

'Check, check, check. Plague-free. What is wrong? What can it be?'

From the pocket of his shorts he took *Pensées* and wrote:

280. Questing disorder: psychotic behaviour deriving from retarded and obsessive desire for approval. In extreme cases sufferer develops complementary disorders such as dandruff and athlete's foot.

He had been away rather longer than expected; the food was already on the table. The ashtray was full.

'Sorry for the delay. I got cornered in the Gents by a man who claimed he knew me from somewhere.' Dudley described this man, a disagreeable executive from Johannesburg with a drink problem and a badly fitting wig. As he examined his Deep-Breton-style wild mushroom crêpe, he murmured, 'But I haven't been to Johannesburg for years.'

'Dud.'

'I'm sorry, I couldn't shake him off, he kept on about his mining interests in the Transvaal.'

'Dud, for the sake of brevity, can we talk about something neutral like art or automobiles or something? I can't cope with your television moguls and South African diamond magnates.'

He chewed a sugared garlic crouton, then removed the plate of them to the furthest extremity of the table. 'How much do you know of medieval quest literature?' he asked. Without waiting for an answer he began a one-sided conversation about the meaning of the grail and its place in European culture, in the course of which, as he became animated, he knocked over first his glass, then hers and finally most of his wild mushroom crêpe.

'You're the clumsiest guy I ever met,' Bella said.

'Things,' Dudley said. 'I have problems with things. Handbags, crockery, *objets d'art*, glassware – the expensive end of the market. Things like that rush into collision with me, they hate me, they want to be revenged on me. But people, people are quite different, people find me irresistible.' He smiled at her in a peculiar way. He had drunk most of his bottle of Pouilly-Fuissé.

Bella LaRose looked as cool as ever. Flushed, he mechanically forked crêpe into his mouth, chewed, swallowed and burped. He was heavy-headed and short of breath and for the first time the thought of missed opportunities occurred to him. Before he knew it, the lunch was almost over and despite his strenuous efforts he lacked the skill to keep Bella's interest.

'One thing,' he said, and paused to wonder what this was.

'Yes?'

'Yes, one thing. I'm having difficulty imagining you hairless.'

'You have problems with your imagination? This I can't believe.'

'It's the thought of your modelling, it's very provoking.'

'Provoking?'

'The blur between image and reality. You know. Images realized, reality depicted. An ancient tradition. One thinks of icons, the lesser saints and martyrs. The grail even, one even thinks of the grail.'

'I don't do religious stuff.'

'It would be lovely to know what it is you do do.'

'What would you like me to model, Dud?'

'Don't ask.'

'Garden furniture? Kitchen gadgets? Pet food?'

'You appal me.'

'Lingerie? Rubberwear? Sex aids?'

'This conversation.' He put an unsteady hand up to his eyes.

93

'Ex-conversation. Let me get the check.'
'That martini.'

They were standing in the sudden white heat of Fifth Avenue waiting for a cab, Dudley slipping on his sun-glasses to look at her surreptitiously, groping vaguely for the traffic lights to lean against. To his surprise she was wearing a red leather mini-skirt which had not been noticeable when she was seated at the restaurant table. Tanned animal skin packed with the meat of her haunches.

'Don't stare, Dud, it's impolite.'

He realized that he did not know, could not guess, her age; she could have been sixteen or thirty, there was no trace of age on her impassive features.

'I expect we'll be seeing quite a bit of you over the next few days,' he said. His voice was hopeful.

'Hardly a thing. I'm leaving Psycho to you.'

People pushed past them, commuters leaving work, their ties loosened, eyes glazed, faces pinched. They marched up the sidewalks six abreast.

'I may need your advice from time to time.' His voice verged on the desperate.

'I'm at the Plaza. You can phone. I just don't want to see you there.'

'I understand.'

The traffic stood churning in the heat as if it had been there for thousands of years, a flood of metal, an ancient mass. Mirrored skyscrapers disappeared into glare with a flash as if the air were caving in. The alcohol he had drunk played havoc with perspectives.

'Bella, don't you think that Martin should be *seen*? Wherever the gossip columnists hang out, wherever the paparazzi and the photographers go.'

'Sure. Buy yourself a grand's worth. That's what it's for. There's a list of venues in the itinerary.'

'And perhaps we'll see you there.'

'Who knows, you may get lucky. But, as I said, in my opinion I doubt you've got long to live.'

He watched her settle into a cab which took her still profile twenty yards into the jam. With great effort he restrained himself from running after. He had nothing to say, he just wanted to follow her. He wished he were properly in disguise, he wished he could get into her cab and share a ride to the Plaza where he would be staying while he told her about his mining interests in the Transvaal and his early days in television. He wished he were alone with her not with Martin Prout who would be waiting for him in their dosshouse. As if he saw himself through Bella's eyes he despairingly considered his T-shirt and shorts and baseball cap. Images of more suitable outfits appeared to him, zoot suits, spats, kid-leather gloves and fedoras. He still had a lot to learn.

16

In the long, greasy mirror above the bar Dudley saw his face, a cigarette smouldering in its centre. Something was wrong. After a moment or two he remembered that he did not usually smoke cigarettes.

He was not happy. His hair looked tired. The alternative events of his life now included gatherings at the classier Manhattan clubs where, amidst a swirl of celebrities, Bella LaRose and he plotted his rise; where, against a background as lurid as the end of empire, they conversed tête-à-tête about the secrets of the heart. Bella's image stood out vividly in his mind like a promotional poster but his own image was less forceful, it blurred into other images which hardly seemed to belong to him: a tired face and tired hair, an inexplicable cigarette and a greasy mirror. He had been drunk since lunch and was getting drunker, and he could not stop thinking of Bella LaRose.

'The man said he *couldn't* recommend this bar,' he said, turning to Martin.

'That's what I like about it.'

At eleven o'clock they had descended to the hotel lobby, and asked the porter if there were any bars nearby that he could recommend. 'There's one a block that way, and there's one a block that way, but I can't recommend them.' His teeth were shiny white when he laughed, like a stage Negro's.

The bar was called *Bar Beer Spirits*. Its door was a mobile poster-montage on a loose spring bearing no name and all names – Budweiser, King of Beers; Miller, Champagne of Beers; Wild Turkey Bourbon; Camels Clean Taste; Marlboro Lights. Inside, the room was long and narrow with a faded red linoleum floor and black formica bar-top. Down one wall was a frieze of baseball pennants, some car numberplates and a collection of framed 1950s photographs showing aspects of the Manhattan skyline. Behind the bar was a sign saying *Onion Rings Buffalo Wings Chicken Nuggets Delight Platter*. The women wore tight dresses, the men large belt buckles. For a moment all eyes were on them. There was a smell of grease, dope and smoke, and the noise of conversations composed entirely of laughter and whoops.

'A man who knows bars, he's an expert on bars, and he can't recommend it. *I* can't recommend it.'

'I like it.'

'When I said you should be seen, I was referring to the more exclusive end of the nightclub scene, I was referring to Larry Tee's Love Machine, to Frank Roccio's Lift Up Your Skirts And Fly, to Maurice Brahm's Red Zone.'

Martin ordered beers and, after a pause, whiskey chasers.

'What I mean is, what kind of exposure are you getting in a place like this?'

'Exposure?'

'Air time, column inches, full-page spreads.'

'Fuck the inches and spreads.'

'My idea is this: you are surrounded by celebrities, I'm introducing you to them, there are flashbulbs popping and a low, questioning murmur. "Liza, this is Martin Prout," I say. "The hottest property in British film at the moment. Martin, meet Ms Minelli. Martin, Liza, Liza, Martin. You met the other day, I think, at Zabaglioni's Erogenous Zone."'

'Don't you ever stop?'

'A man in alligator-skin shoes and a toupee comes over and says, "Are you that handsome son of a gun Prout, I want to make you an offer." And I say, "No, but this is Martin over here. Martin, meet Zeff Barcadi. Zeff, Martin, Martin, Zeff. Zeff wants you in his next motion picture, Martin."'

'Listen.'

'Do you get the idea?'

Martin turned sideways to see him. 'Don't you realize?'

'Realize what?'

'I don't even want to be here.'

'Well, I didn't want to be here in the first place, finish your drink and we'll go.'

'In this city, doing these things.'

'But we've only just arrived.'

'I'd rather be somewhere else.'

'This is the place to be, this is the capital of the known world.'

'We could drive across the country. Mississippi, Texas, Arizona. Travel. See the Pacific. I'm serious. Get out while there's still time. Why not?'

He ordered more beer and bourbons, and Dudley enquired as to the wisdom of this. Along the bar two thin women stood talking to a fat man whose bulk was supported on a slender stool. The man was inexpressive, the women shrill; every few minutes one of them shrieked, 'That's the *funniest* thing I *ever* heard!' and backed into a crouch, wheezing with stage laughter. She was one of the tormented, a classical archetype in a tight purple dress. Dudley had to shout to make himself heard above her anguish.

'I'm your promotional adviser, I have to think of these things.'

She crouched low, wheezing. 'That is the funniest, the

absolute, the frigging, absolute, *funniest* thing I *ever* . . .' She hauled herself upright on the bar-top and looked through slitted eyes at Dudley, who had turned to stare at her.

As he developed his theme of abstinence they both got drunk. It was one of those bars into which hardly anyone comes and from which no one leaves. At one o'clock nothing had changed, no one was ever going to go home. Dudley caught sight of his reflection again, put on his baseball cap, took it off, put it on again.

'What is wrong', he said, 'with my *hair*?' As if conjuring up a vision to replace his own he instantly began to talk about Bella LaRose, her hair, her looks, her manner of conversation, her athletic way of walking, her laconic sense of humour and – finally – her contacts: the media people, entertainments personalities, fix-its, spin-doctors and fellow celebrities.

Martin was looking at him.

'When are you going to have lunch with her again?'

Dudley blinked. 'What do you mean?'

'You know what I mean.'

'What do you mean, "again"?'

'You had lunch with her today.'

Dudley choked. 'What do you mean, lunch?'

'East Thirty-Fourth Street. Looking like a wanker.'

Dudley's eyes slid all round the bar and found no refuge.

'Lunch,' he said at last. 'East Thirty-Fourth Street. It rings a bell. I'm guessing but I think it would have been a business lunch. We talked about you, about your itinerary. I had a job persuading her that you were serious. I had to stick up for you.' His manner was frivolous but his voice was frightened. Martin was still staring at him. 'Martin, you terrify me. What did you do, follow me?'

'Yes.'

'You terrify me.'

'You know nothing about me.'

Laughter clotted behind them where the hysterical thin

woman crouched and wheezed in torment. The other thin woman was trying to get her to go home, but her efforts were being treated as a joke. '*Funny*? Every goddamn time you open your mouth I'm going to pee my pants!'

Dudley was preparing to leave, he got off his stool unsteadily and jammed his cap on to his head. 'I'm glad we talked, Martin, but it's late. It's two o'clock. Bedtime.'

But Martin was calling to the barmaid for more drinks. Dudley rolled his eyes. 'Come on, Martin. Look, it's late, I'm not making it up, it really is, it's gone two o'clock. Look at my watch, look where the hands are.' After a minute or two he sat down again and fidgeted. Reluctantly he accepted another beer, and Martin said:

'Do you remember the lavatories at Shammings, the ones near the library?'

Now Dudley stared. Martin spoke so quietly that he had to lean towards him to hear him.

'Big room, wide, always wet on the floor. Old urinals with long brass pipes. A double row of wash-basins. Naked plumbing. Every basin clogged with paper towels, footprints in the wet, cubical doors covered with graffiti. *Headcase*, BTFC, *Shit Here*. There was a sort of wet light coming through a pebbled window high up in the wall, it wasn't really wet but it looked like it was. And it wasn't quite silent, even when you were there alone, there was always a noise, a gurgle or gushing, but it was *like* silence. And there was that smell, chemical strawberry. Do you remember?'

'No,' Dudley said. 'I'm glad to have forgotten.'

'It's where I used to go when I didn't go to lessons. I'd be in there, and everything would be almost silent, and wet, and I'd walk up and down, just walk, slowly, opening the doors and looking inside. Just to see. I'd open a door, and I'd see a ripped-off seat and bare porcelain. Or a flooded floor. Or paper towels stuck to the wall with shit. Do you remember?'

'I wasn't there, Martin, how could I remember?'

'So I walked along and I pushed the door and there was a blocked bowl. And I looked at it for a while, then I walked to the next and opened the door and there was a soaked exercise book on the floor with geometry exercises melted all over it. I'm remembering this. Then I went on to the next one, and in that there were dog ends floating in the water. And then to the last. The one at the end, the one I'd left till the end. And I opened the door and Proctor was standing there, just standing, not pissing or anything, just standing there.'

'A figure of nightmare. Typical of Proctor. But why are you telling me this?'

'And he put out his fists and he opened them, and in one was his lighter, in the other a compass, and he·said, "Take off your shoes."'

Dudley looked at him and said nothing. Suddenly he thought of Martin's limp and he swallowed and put down his beer. Martin was saying something else but there was a rumpus down the bar, a tussle and laughter, and he couldn't hear what it was, he only saw the mouth moving, the cupid's-bow lips parting and closing. The hysterical woman in the purple dress would not get up off the floor. Dudley brayed over the top of her laughter about how late it was. He felt nauseous with fatigue and fear.

'In hospital for a month,' Martin said.

Dudley desperately tried to finish his beer.

'Dominic Proctor,' Martin said. 'He was expelled. There were three or four others as well. A gang of them.'

'I know,' Dudley said. 'Expelled for bestiality. I'm proud to say I had something to do with it. Proctor was the worst but they were all monsters, monsters, depravity incarnate.' He was shaking his head and squinting sideways at Martin.

'I was one of them, I was one of them expelled.'

The flux of the bar roared. A small crowd had gathered round the woman in the purple dress who crouched at the foot of the Cherry Master video machine, screaming.

Dudley shouted. 'I don't understand. You weren't a friend of Proctor's.'

'You told him, expel these bastards.'

'Proctor. And one or two of his accomplices.'

'There was a mistake. My name was mentioned. No one believed me.'

'But how?'

'It had been mentioned before, when I went into hospital. People believe what they want to believe. Proctor was in your house, you were asked about it and you said, "Expel them all."'

'I don't remember one of them being you.'

Martin put down his beer. 'Who were they then?'

'All right. All right, I'll tell you. I can remember them all.'

'You remember nothing.'

'In this case I make an exception.'

He chewed his knuckles. He was hunched over on his stool and Martin stared at him. They lacked only the spotlight to make a scene of conventional interrogation. He sensed dimly the confusion into which this accusation was leading him.

'You don't remember.'

'Wait a minute.'

'You don't remember anything.'

'Wait, wait. It's on the tip of my tongue.'

'Whole areas of your life gone, of my life, as if they never existed.'

Dudley's face unwound itself. 'Henderson,' he said. He sighed deeply. 'He was one.'

Martin's face was inflexible. 'Who else?'

Dudley scowled again. 'Someone else. I'd know if it you said it. If you gave me a list of names I'd pick it out.' He drummed on the bar-top with his fingers. 'Proctor and Henderson and someone else.'

Martin said nothing. Dudley was sweating.

'Begins with G, sounds like Gold, Golder. Gobbler. No, not Gobbler.' He reared up as if his strings had been jerked. 'Godley! Somebody Godley, Paul or Mark or James or something. I remember! That's the three, that's all three of them, Proctor, Henderson and Godley!'

Martin said, 'There were four.'

He was lost in the wash of voices and juke-box noise and ringing in his ears.

Martin was saying, 'You talked to me about character. What's character? What do you know, what do you remember? Hardly anything. How can you talk to me about your character?'

It was three o'clock and people were wandering slowly round the bar in pursuit of the woman in the purple dress who was loudly sobbing. They would never catch her and she would never find relief. All the unhappiness in the world seemed concentrated in that place, and they left it together unsteadily, and stood outside in the street. Moonlight divided it into diagonals, dark and pale shades like remnants of buildings draped from perfect, solid verticals above. They could see nothing of Manhattan but the street they walked down; nothing of it existed except a faint glow crowning the skyline. Forwards and backwards were frail links of lights, the occasional neon sign, parked cars, a fleeting cab drained of colour passing across their street, entering and exiting, a one-line actor, a messenger from the battlefield.

Dudley stopped. He would say nothing to upset Martin.

'Probably you'll never forgive me,' he said. Martin didn't look at him.

'Forgiving isn't the point,' he said.

'You're right. There's never a point.'

'The point is, do I trust you?'

Dudley nodded. They walked on.

All night he tossed in fitful sleep, disturbed by dreams involving taxicabs. Several times he rose to get a drink of water from the bathroom and Martin's bed was always empty. He had gone. Vaguely he remembered him going, a silent gliding, like a dog returning to the night. An expulsion. A myth of expulsion which has no sense but its own resonance.

A thrum of electricity in the street outside was indistinguishable from a reverberation in his own head. Somehow it made him thirsty. In the distance police sirens were breaking the peace, and his dreams were full of yellow cabs, their horns blaring.

<h1 style="text-align:center">17</h1>

Cooper Square was a region of intense heat intensified by the industrial grind and fumes of locked traffic. The old buildings surrounding it, their crumbling arches and pilasters, were dull in the strong light as if they had soaked up dirt out of the hot air. Avoiding the rollerbladers and cyclists who weaved between the cars, Dudley and Martin crossed into the sudden shadow of a modest six-storey former warehouse in sooty sandstone. The heatwave continued. Violent crimes were up twenty per cent on the same period last year, the radio said.

Dudley had reverted to a Van Heusen and lightweight slacks, but still wore his Ray Bans which gave him the appearance of an officious clerk. Under his arm he had the itinerary of Martin's appointments, as thick as the average typescript of a novel. Martin, trailing behind, wore new jeans and a singlet which Dudley had bought for him. Around them was the noise of the traffic, horns and revving engines and, from several directions, the whooping of car alarms. Dudley was talking about the initiatives and responsibilities of international fame. He paused and said, 'Ask not for whom the car alarm whoops, it whoops for thee.' Holding up a hand to indicate the noises, he made it clear he had made a point. Then they entered the building and the noises faded.

Cramped in the same wedge of space they revolved with the door and Martin saw in the glass their double reflection, heads joined but facing in different directions, a Janus in a pointless whirl.

From the corner of the lobby where the brass elevator doors

were flanked by small trees of basil in polished tubs, a black concierge came towards them.

'Which floor for the magazine *Go For It*?'

'Top.'

As the elevator doors shut them in, Dudley said, 'This is it, Martin. The first of many. One small chat for a ridiculous magazine and the opening lines in a dialogue with the whole world.'

Martin stared at the floor while Dudley chattered above the whining vacuum of their levitation.

'How do you feel this morning, by the way? I feel dreadful, I can't remember feeling worse.' He would not mention more.

'I hate all this,' Martin said.

'We should perhaps have talked about the kind of image we want you to present, but if there are any difficulties I'll be on hand to help you out.'

The receptionist talked to someone called Chas on her telephone and told them that Mr Allen would be along in a moment. Soon a loose-limbed young man in beige chinos and baggy lemon shirt came towards them.

'Mr Prout?' he said, his eyes flicking over Dudley, onto Martin, and back to Dudley. Dudley pointed. 'Chas Allen, good to meet you, glad you could make it. We got all the details from Slezinger's, and some good glossies. I've been really looking forward to meeting you.' Squinting at Martin, he added in a naïve tone, 'Didn't recognize you straight off. You look . . . younger. But you can't count on recognizing anyone from their publicity shots these days. Must be new techniques they're using or something.' His gaze drifted sideways as the elevator doors opened and a smart young woman stepped out. 'Bella taking good care of you?' he asked.

'Who?'

'Bella LaRose. Is she something.'

Martin stared at him.

'She's having her head shaved next week,' Dudley said.

104

Ignoring him, Chas Allen ushered Martin to a pair of swing doors, then turned to face Dudley who was closely following.

'Excuse me?'

'That's all right,' Dudley said. 'I'm with Martin here. Liaising with Bella. It's a pity about Ed, isn't it?'

'This is Dudley,' Martin said.

'Call me Geoff. Or Butch.'

'We don't usually.'

'I go everywhere with Martin. Wherever it happens to be, Tokyo, Rome, Jo'burg. Mainly to do with the legal side of things. You won't notice I'm here.'

They zigzagged together across an open-plan office marked out with baffle-boards in long dog-legs. Everywhere they saw fleeting impressions of work, glimpses of luminous screens, keyboards, fax machines, micro telephones, bent heads and talking faces. Syncopated urgent monologues blended into a general buzz. Lifestyles were made here.

Chas Allen led them to a quietish corner with a low, round table and four easy chairs upholstered in olive-green leather. Tacked to the back of a baffle-board was a poster of a dolphin emerging from brilliant blue wavelets with a grin. Beneath was a rubber plant in a brass pot.

'Our Relaxation Zone,' Chas Allen said. 'Sounds terrifying. Make yourselves comfortable. Can I get you coffee?' Martin shook his head.

'Espresso,' Dudley said. 'Very kind.'

'It's just from the machine. Estelle, would you get two coffees?' A girl with a back-combed mound of flame-red hair disappeared into the maze of boards.

Chas Allen's smooth, assured face, short blond hair and thin-wristed gestures gave him the air of a minor, eager to please, deferential and easily distracted.

'Okay. You happy? Got everything you want? Okay. Here's the game plan.' Briefly he outlined the nature and purpose of his questionnaire, the specifics of a- and b-type questions.

Martin bit his thumbnail. 'A-type?' he said. 'B-type?'

'Okay. Maybe I should explain exactly what our magazine's

about, I mean its philosophy and marketing strategy. *Go For It* is aimed pretty well at the Young Aspirant, age group eleven to fourteen, family background affluent, ethnic group WASP. The way it works is, we target both the teen dreamer and the prematurely career-conscious, so basically we have really quite serious features, interviews, reports, but also a whole bunch of colour pix. Result is, the Young Aspirants love it.'

'In England we strangle such children at birth,' Dudley said.

'Take an interview like this, okay. To the Young Aspirant you're a successful careerist but you're a pin-up also, so basically the questions are a mix of stuff about your general lifestyle, your financial expectations, career strategy, all sorts of angles.'

Chas Allen lowered his voice and bent towards Martin, veering away from Dudley who simultaneously bent forward as well.

'You have to remember basically they're kids. Some of these questions, well, you'll see. It's sort of fun, think of it like that. We haven't got long.' He looked at his watch. 'I'll do what I can. Look at it this way. It's all publicity.'

Estelle put coffees in front of him.

'I love you, Estelle. Let me get my pad. I'll be right back.'

As soon as he was out of sight Martin got to his feet. 'Fuck this,' he said.

'The man is mildly deranged,' Dudley said, 'that's all. With a little fortitude we will prevail.'

'Fuck it all.' But he had delayed too long, Chas Allen came back into view.

'You want the bathroom. Sure? Okay. Let's get straight down to the stage ones.'

He wanted to know Martin's birth date, place of birth, occupations of his parents, his education, qualifications and early theatrical work. When he asked a question he made a neat gesture with his pen, a rounded shape circumscribing his words. Listening to Martin's answers, he hummed encourage-ment through closed lips, and appeared occasionally to drift off, distracted by fluff on his chinos or the progress of Estelle's profile and flame hair above the top of a baffle-board.

Martin uttered monosyllables. Dudley watched him struggle with the easiest enquiries as if they were advanced mathematical problems. His memories seemed freighted with ambiguous meanings; he would say one thing and then change his mind and insist that Chas Allen revise his notes accordingly, and then change his mind again. He varied the history of his childhood four times before he was satisfied. It was almost as if he were putting together a fictional person. But gradually he became firmer and his autobiography developed, solidifying out of obscurity, the details clustering together like filings round a magnet.

'I was expelled from my school and went to Borstal,' he said.

'Excuse me? Borstal?'

'Borstal?' Dudley said. '*Borstal*!'

'Not called Borstal now. Detention Centre, Youth Custody Centre. For juvenile delinquents.'

'Like, you mean prison?' A flicker of interest crossed Chas Allen's face.

'Of course, our juvenile delinquents are probably not much different from your Young Aspirants,' Dudley said hurriedly. He looked at Martin, panicking.

'Prison's good, it's a good story. Off the record, what did you do?'

'I want it on the record,' Martin said. 'I want it all on. I did nothing. I was accused of sodomizing a pupil at my school.'

Chas Allen whistled. Dudley moaned.

'You were framed?' Chas Allen asked. 'You were attacked by your enemies and betrayed by your friends, that sort of thing?'

'I had no friends.'

'Few,' Dudley said. 'Few friends.'

'You were a loner?'

'I was alone. In Borstal I went to drama classes. People like me acting out their nightmares, stupid enough to think we'd find out why.'

107

'You learned enough to go professional.'

'In Borstal's everything's professional, even privacy.'

'You know, Mr Prout, this is a very American story. Triumph over adversity.'

'One slight problem is that he's not actually American,' Dudley said.

Martin smiled, frightening Dudley who had never seen this before. 'My story is Everyman's,' he said.

Chas Allen brightened. He asked Martin about his career, his achievements, his ambitions. He asked him about his work in British theatre, film and television. He asked him where he lived, and why. Martin pieced himself together, choosing hard, impersonal facts, seldom revealing anything of an inner life. Occasionally Dudley fielded questions which didn't directly involve him.

'What's the scene in Oxford?'

Martin looked at Dudley, and Dudley said, 'Primarily Gothic, with some superb infusions of the English Baroque.' His voice was still shaky and he gave Martin perplexed looks.

After more coffee Chas Allen moved on to the b-type questions, and the situation worsened.

'Okay, this is the real stuff, Mr Prout. We've nailed your biog, now we lay bare your soul. It'll help when you answer these questions if you keep the Young Aspirants in mind. Don't worry, like I said, they're basically kids, they want to know the *strangest* things. Fun-things too. Think publicity. Okay.'

'I've given you the facts.'

'Here we go. The Young Aspirant wants to know what inspires you.'

There was a pause.

'Perhaps you could move on to the next question,' Dudley said after a few minutes.

'Let's put it another way. The Young Aspirant wants to know what makes you tick, what makes you get up in the morning and say Shoot, today I'm going to go for it?'

'I have problems getting up in the mornings.'

'Problems?'

'And in the afternoons.'

Chas Allen thought about this. 'It's okay. I'll put down Inner Drive.'

Dudley objected. 'You know Freud's thing? "The only motive is honour, power, wealth, fame and the love of women." How about that? We could select from it if you think it pleonastic. It seems to me admirably concise.'

Martin was hunched forward, brooding.

Chas Allen said, 'Next question. The Young Aspirant wants to know what you think of love.'

'Love?'

'Do you see yourself as a romantic?'

'What do you mean?'

'Flowers, chocolates, gifts of underwear, that sort of thing.'

'Are you serious?'

'Be serious, be humorous, the Young Aspirant is interested in all your moods.'

They sat in silence for a minute.

'No problem, we'll skip it. Next question. What is the thing you most hate about yourself?'

'Wait. I've told you the facts. I live in a bedsit, I think about Borstal, I've nothing I can call mine. What can I say about love?'

'It's okay, I understand. Let's move on. What's the thing you like best about yourself?'

'Wait. Love's an obsession. Like all obsessions it betrays you. There's nothing else to say.'

'Don't worry about love, Mr Prout. Next question. The Young Aspirant wants to know who you admire most.'

Martin shook his head. 'Love destroys. First it destroys the thing you love. Then it destroys you. I don't want to talk about love.'

Amused, worried, Chas Allen smiled, stopped smiling and glanced towards Estelle. 'The Young Aspirant wants to know what annoys you most. You know, like shaving, or the phone ringing when you're making love, or the smell of tar. Whatever.'

'Shit,' Martin said contemptuously.

'You mean excrement?'

The Young Aspirant wanted to know Martin's favourite colour, time of day, movie, item of clothing. He wanted to know his favourite cartoon character ('they're only kids'), flavour aftershave, baseball team ('I usually put other nationals down for the Yankees'), drink ('non-alcoholic, say a milk shake') and popular phrase or saying.

Martin had been silent for a long time; he got to his feet white-faced and said, 'Fuck it.'

'Suppose we put "Darn it"?'

'I've had enough, this is pathetic.'

'Isn't it? And I have to do it for a living. But let me ask you one last question, Mr Prout. From what you've said, despite being non-American you personify what we call the High Achievers Phenomenon. All our featured celebrities do in fact. Do you have a view on that?'

Martin was moving away.

'He has no view on that,' Dudley said promptly. 'No view whatsoever. An utter absence of view. Now we must leave you, I'm afraid. We're on a very tight schedule, as you can imagine. In fact we're due at the Plaza, there's a reception for us.'

'One last thing. There's a rumour going round about a movie for Columbia, some kind of romance.'

Dudley gave a huge smile. 'We never confirm rumours of that nature. You must wait until they ripen into facts.'

For the first time in his life Stuff was following him, he could hear him breathing heavily as he negotiated the path that ran between the baffle-boards. There was a noise which he himself was making, an obscenity moaned loud enough to silence the telephonic chatter in office pods around him. Faces appeared, then people to go with them, watching. Stuff was up with him.

'I'd like to think that this could work to our advantage. But don't ask me how.'

Then he was going downstairs very fast, jerking on and off

110

his bad foot, no longer shouting. Stuff had fallen behind. The Young Aspirant wanted to know about facts. Facts coalesced into truth. Facts were solid but fragmentary. Facts were discriminate. Facts had no obligations or meaning. Facts conjured you up, made you appear, over and over, exactly the same, like a single image on a roll of film flickering on and on and on. The Young Aspirant wanted to know what he was going to do next.

18

Through the lobby with its dangerous cargo of waiting fifteen-year-olds, beyond the porter in his reinforced glass booth, beyond the out-of-order elevator, in a recess on the far side of the pile of building materials kept permanently for unknown purposes and incidentally marking the entrance to the staircase (*Fire Door Keep Closed*), was a payphone. It was ten o'clock; the night was young. Heat lingered in pockets, bulged and would not shift. At the bottom of the stairs Martin, sweating, carrying a brown paper bag which contained one triple pastrami on rye, one cherry soda and one bottle of brandy, heard a familiar voice and paused.

'Yes, LaRose, as in the well-known *Romaunt de*. If you would.'

He slipped inside the fire door and waited.

'Perhaps you could keep trying, she might be in the bath, she often has a bath about this time. Well, how about a message? Message, not massage. I left a message yesterday too. Three messages in fact. All right. Tell her: consultation an urgent necessity. Tell her: the balloon has gone up. Ask her: how many PR disasters can big Ed handle? Ask her – yes, I'm being as brief as I can – ask her: where can I get my head shaved should I become a top model? Yes, shaved. Shaved. S-H-A-V-E-D. Thank you, you've been as helpful as you could be. Goodbye.'

Martin moved away. When he reached his floor he heard the fire door below swing open and the sound of Dudley humming operatically. Themes of lust and betrayal. He went through their room into the bathroom where he stood on the balls of his feet in front of the mirror, staring at himself. His forehead and eyes were visible but no expression of any kind could be read in them. One of Dudley's cravats was in his hand and he put it loosely round his neck and said to the mirror, 'The balloon has gone up. Yes. Up. U-P.' The voice was not his own. Under the basin he found Dudley's washbag. It was a large bag made of a cheap plastic treated to give the impression of leather, and someone had handwritten GCD in gold lettering on the side in imitation of a monogram. Among the tubs and tubes of creams, ointments, gels, oils and powders he found another object, long and hard with a shiny surface like certain sea shells: an old-fashioned razor with a Bakelite handle. Outside the sound of hummed opera grew and the door was opened. Putting the razor into his pocket with the cravat, he replaced the bag under the wash-basin and went out.

It was eleven o'clock. The heat in the room was still unbearable. Dudley swished aside the bead curtain and stepped from the squalid bathroom, wearing his silk dressing-gown and maroon leather slippers. His face was pink, his hair slicked. Such an entrance effected nothing.

'I wouldn't go in there for a while if I were you,' he said.

Martin had made no move to go anywhere.

'By the way, you haven't seen my razor, have you? The one with the pearl handle.'

'No.'

'A family heirloom.'

'Haven't seen it.'

'I had to shave with my second-best razor. If I do that too often I'll develop a complex.'

Martin lay on his bed and put on his Walkman. It was too early and too hot to go out. The hiss of the tape in his ears was like the rush of air from a puncture inside him – suddenly plugged by the tremendous noise of song.

Dudley was still talking, his mouth working noiselessly, his cheeks quivering. Martin turned the other way and Dudley tapped him on the shoulder, found the Walkman and cut the music.

'What now?'

'Are we going to sit here all night? Tonight's the night we go clubbing.'

'Go if you want.'

'You need to be seen. Bella and I are agreed. Visibility, that's the thing. It's your duty, Martin. Clubland expects.'

'Miss Black America'll take you. You don't want me. She's more your style.'

Aggrieved, Dudley began to brag. 'Did I tell you she's going to introduce me to some television people here? Preliminary talks. I'm expecting a call at any moment.' He coughed modestly. 'I think she rather took a shine to me.' The expression on his face betrayed the nature of his thoughts about Bella LaRose: they were luminous and rapid, a series of quick movements involving her lips, eyes, hair and leather bustier. 'Of course, she doesn't like you much, I had to defend you against some pretty severe criticisms.'

'Just another American, all mouth. Do this, do that.'

'You've started off on the wrong foot with her, that's all.'

Martin switched on his Walkman and Dudley reached over and turned it off again.

'It's you I want to go clubbing with, Martin. It's important. Listen, I see a city ablaze with rumour, I hear your name on everybody's lips; they're discussing your forthcoming triumph in the Awards ceremony, they're swapping comments about your face, your build, your style. The manufacture of your clothes is a topic of furious discussion. Speculation about your sexual orientation is rife.'

'You're sick, you're so sick you're virtually an American.' He pressed Play, and the room was silent except for the muted hiss of the tape.

Dudley sighed through his nostrils. It was astonishing how long Martin could remain inactive. Hour after hour he lay on his bed, eyes glued to the ceiling, doing nothing, perhaps not even aware of time passing. This inactivity filled Dudley with panic. He picked up his pen and wrote:

317. Character is based on memory which is a form of fantasy, therefore character is illusory. Examine.

Standing at the window now, smoking and thinking – his view of that smallish area of dirty brickwork and fretted, unloved corner of fire-escape about three feet away – he could see neither the sky nor the ground, he was looking into a well of shadow, dark the way some lives are dark: uninterestingly dark.

'This view is disappointing,' he said out loud. He wanted to see the whole city spread out sparkling below him, all the famous landmarks stark and foreign, the sky-burst of towers, the Mondrian grid lit with neon, the gleaming sweep of the Hudson rounding it off like a circumscribing gesture. He wanted to balance above it like a high diver on a springboard ready to take a header down into it all.

He went into the bathroom to dispose of his cigar stump.

'Give it a few minutes' grace,' he said when he came out. 'It's still rather ripe in there.'

Martin was staring at the ceiling, smoking, a plastic glass of brandy balanced on his chest. The Walkman clicked off and began to rewind.

'By the way,' Dudley said. 'We must remember to lock the door tonight. I feel slightly anxious about security.'

Martin looked across. 'You've been anxious since we got here. This city makes you anxious.'

Dudley pooh-poohed the idea. 'A passing mood.'

'You're scared.'

'I wouldn't say *scared*.'

'And you'll go on being scared.'

'What do you mean?'

'Fear has its own momentum, doesn't it?' Martin's face was blank, his voice unsympathetic.

'Let's not exaggerate.'

'So what are you scared of? What scares you?'

Midnight. He was back at the window, looking out at nothing, a plump, lonely man with pale skin and crumpled chin standing in thought, his arms loose at his sides, his shoulders slumped as if his whole body had been slackened by a sudden change in atmospheric pressure. It was impossible not to smile. Impossible not to see the lanky, lonely boy in ill-fitting school uniform bouncing on his toes across the playground, shiny briefcase in one hand, slim volume of a lesser Romantic poet in the other, trailed by a crowd of jeering fourth-formers who ape his loping stride and conceited, anxious manner. Across the playground, into the future, bouncing on his toes. Lust and betrayal will be his life but he cannot outrun revenge for ever.

Dudley stood at the window looking out on nothing. Always a window, a view or absence of view.

'Things are not going well,' he said suddenly. 'Today didn't go well. "Well" is not the word I'd use. I'll have to call Bella, talk things through, develop a strategy, we can't go on like this. Bella and I understand each other, we've developed an understanding. "Intuition" is the word I'd use.' He turned and spoke directly to Martin. 'Today was not a PR success,' he said. 'Allow me to state the obvious.'

From *Go For It* they had gone to *The Cutting Edge*, magazine of the film industry. Together they filled in a questionnaire. From *The Cutting Edge* they went to *Look Now*, an independent guide to television viewing. From there to *Vox* where Martin was rude to the design director. Earlier than expected they arrived at *The New York City Guide to Everything* and sat drinking Diet Pepsi in a packing room for an hour, conscious only of the heat and the day's deterioration. Logistic confusion and the afternoon traffic prevented them from getting to *The Advertizer* at all. The cab did a U-turn and took them uptown towards radio station WA57. An accident delayed them. The cab did another U-turn and took them downtown to radio station WA99. And so it went on. In interview, Martin was monosyllabic and edgy. But he continued to astound Dudley with anecdotes of Borstal, documentary-style stories richer and fuller with each airing. He never mentioned Dudley who stood outside, nose to the window, straining to hear his name. Everything Martin said made his heart race. It made no difference if he didn't believe Martin's stories about Borstal, the time to deny Martin was passed, he had missed his opportunity; now he had to collude in his myths. Myths of expulsion, myths of exile. Dudley's nose squashed against glass, his heart racing.

It was twelve thirty, hot and cramped.

'It's not too late to go clubbing.'

Martin was lying on the bed, transfixed by the ceiling, his ears plugged by his Walkman.

'It's not too late, the man downstairs said it's never too late. He's a funny man.'

From his position, even if he had been *compos mentis*, Martin could not have seen Dudley's mouth move. He lay on the bed, his doll's body outstretched, the soles of his feet pointing up like a dead man's.

'I'm talking to myself, aren't I?' Dudley said wearily. He sighed, turned to the window and talked anyway. 'Why do I bother? It's not only the refusal to promote himself, to be frank it's the reluctance to play the slightest part in ordinary social intercourse. He's cut himself off from the world, the world goes on without him.' The window showed Dudley the reflection of the television, and vice versa, a nightmarish series of infinite regression. He raised his voice. 'I could give him the names of two dozen top clubs, the hottest venues – he's not interested,

116

he's deeply uninterested, he's virtually catatonic, I could make a bigger sensation in New York with a below-average chimp.'

'I know a strip joint,' Martin said, making Dudley jump and spin round. 'We could go there.'

Dudley eyed him as he might an unpredictable piece of machinery. 'A *strip joint*? Martin, I want you to be seen with Liza Minelli not some knicker-kicking tart.'

'Live entertainment. Girls, Girls, Girls. Non-stop Music. Rubber novelties.'

'I would like to make a serious point.'

'Called the Purple Palace.'

'We're going in different directions. Completely different. I'm changing my life for the better, you're staying the same to your own great detriment. I'm being cautionary, that's why I'm being unusually honest. It's my duty to caution you.'

'What makes you think your life is changing?'

'These things develop a momentum of their own. You said it.'

Martin said, 'You're out of control.'

'Martin, think. We could be in the Plaza instead of this sixth circle of hell.'

'Go to the Plaza. I'm going to the Purple Palace.'

He got off the bed and put on his shoes and walked to the door. That stiff walk. Dudley watched, fascinated despite himself, frowning almost with pleasure, almost smiling. He could not quite believe in Martin, even if he had to collude in his lies.

'You're not going really.'

'What a naughty boy I am.'

'I don't believe you're going to go.'

'What are you going to do, report me, have me expelled?'

His going took something from the room Dudley could not explain, more than a physical presence, more like an aspect of its heat. The groove in Martin's bed was the scar where the heat had been sucked out. Forgetting that the window had no view he went to it to watch Martin emerge on to the street, and the dirty bricks confronted him, black with shadow. His legs were trembling. He wanted another city from a different window, a razzle of neon, but instead what he imagined was a night sky like pale, hot ash, a city like an enormous demolition site. Was it too late to ring the Plaza again? It was never too late, the funny man had said, never too late to change your mind or your life. First he took his *Pensées* from the side of his bed and began to write.

19

318. *We met at a spot convenient for clubland and apparently notorious for pick-ups. Informing me of this, she gave me a playful look. I picture her now stepping from the cab, twenty minutes late, wearing a sleeveless aluminium (a-loo-minum) top and leopardskin-patterned ski-pants, yellow stilettos and elbow-length gloves. Her hair, still intact, is massed bouffant, sort of savage, powerful and deepest black. It muscles against the top of the cab as she ducks out and, seeing me, she lets out a vulgar yell.*

I had undergone a transformation. It would have been interesting to see myself at that moment as she did, pale-armed in black leather sleeveless vest, sturdy in black leather trousers and motor-cycle boots, mean in Young Marlon Brando crew-cut and raw ears. Yes, gone was my 'Brideshead', mourn it no more.

'Dud,' she said. 'You are one goofball.'

'Thank you,' I said. 'Goofball?'

319. *The European feels out of time in America. I feel ancient and irrelevant, like a Victorian lady traveller fallen among the natives of some primitive tribe. They approach without refinement to show off a chant or song, but remain nervous of me, apparently in awe of the manner of my conversation*

and my many skirts. I am, of course, completely in their
power, these adults in children's clothing.

320. We visited a great many clubs: the Underground, Red
Zone, Lift Up Your Skirts And Fly, MARS, Space Machine,
the Factory, Zee Zee Casanova, Electric Storm, CBGBs, One
Jet, the Mudd Club, Funk Lounge, Hole in the Wall, Love
Top, Riporama, the Flying Aquarium, Flim Flam and the
Rub. We made a night of it.

At the Rub I was introduced to a number of her friends.
Conversation was impeded by the intensity of the light show
and the chaos of the noise (they play no music at these clubs,
not what you would call music), but with a little sign
language we got the gist of what we were trying to say.

'This is Nick Crest,' Bella said. 'Crest.' (Miming a wave
with her hand.) 'He plays nano-moog with The Angel Dust.'

'Dangerous?' I said. 'Dangerous what?' (Baring my teeth,
scratching the air with my fingers, shrugging my shoulders.)

'Angel Dust.' (Flapping her arms, closing them in prayer,
sprinkling the air with her fingers.)

'Excellent,' I said. 'An excellent band.'

Nick Crest nodded. He signed to me that a large quad-
ruped with horns was coming to take him away. I am not
sure I quite understood him.

Later I was introduced to the disc jockey, the man who
made the noise. After we had gestured at each other for a
while he asked me if I would like to 'spin a few discs'. At
least I think he did. I mounted the podium anyway (he
hustled close behind) and said a few words to the quopping
masses on the floor and put on one of the records he had
lined up for me. I told people that I was a psychologist and
that they should behave exactly as normal. My voice was
taken from me and turned into one of the many discordant
strands in the record I played, and the noises it made mingled
with the stroboscopic lights, and it seemed to me that a basic
law of physics was being transgressed and we were all
crossing a boundary to a new world.

119

321. *Travel is not merely geographical, but also temporal and mental. Travel to America is particularly deranging, for America is both the past and the future, the past because it is the worlds of our childhoods, and the future because its gadgets, fashions, business techniques, health-fads and perversions will not be seen in the Old World for months, possibly years to come. In America you spin forwards and backwards at once.*

322. *Bella and I danced, frequently photographed for the gossip columns. I exist in white glare, my arms above my head, a nub of black hair showing where my biceps meet the straps of my vest. (Shouldn't my arms have more definition?) The lower half of the photograph is confused, it is not clear if my legs are below the level of my waist.*

After dancing we retired to a quieter corner of the city and she talked to me. Her manner was confiding and intimate; she offered to take me up the Empire State, she invited me to her shaving ceremony. Dawn was breaking. My hearing was still impaired. We shared a last cocktail and she told me of her relationship with Ed Slezinger, the heartbreak when she heard of the amatory escapades in Vermont which have done for his hip. He is a powerful, inventive man but she can no longer love him.

'Dud, tell me what to do. I want to kill him, I want a list of all the possible ways he could die.'

It was a tender scene. Neither love nor murder were problems, I said, they never were, but she must get some rest. She put her head on my shoulder and fell asleep.

323. *The penis is a tropical fish and likes to swim in warm waters.*

324. *There is an obvious dividing line between fantasy and reality, but this line shifts. The purpose of there being a line at all is that it should shift.*

20

Ingenuous in sleep as he never was in waking life, Dudley lay on his bed in dressing-gown and slippers, his *Pensées* face-down across his chest, his hair matted, his mouth open, laying bare his soul to the empty room. Contradictory, naïve, verbose, comic – Dudley, Dud or Stuff. But his sleeping expression revealed something usually hidden: a slyness and rigour – as if a Disneyland character had unexpectedly removed its huge foam head to expose the overworked manipulative actor within.

It was late in the morning, traffic roared in the street, the temperature was ninety and climbing, and Dudley's sinuses were blocked.

There was a bang on the door and his mouth snapped shut.

'Hey, in there! Telephone call!'

His head swung through a hundred and eighty degrees and an eye opened. He grunted, amazed at himself, at his dressing-gown, his slippers, his aching neck and gummed eyes. He cleared his throat hesitantly. He did not know where he was; he seemed to hear from a great distance the peals of a telephone, not the familiar English half-impatient, half-timorous ahem, but a long, confident drawl.

Half-asleep, he listened vaguely. A minute passed. Then both eyes came unstuck and he sat up.

'Hello,' he called to nobody. 'Hello. I don't suppose you would take a message?'

On the landing he bumped into the porter who said, 'Run like hell. Probably rung off by now.'

'Are you sure it was for me?'

'Plaza Hotel calling Mr Dud.'

He ran.

*

'Hello? Hello? Hello? Hello? Anybody there?'

There was silence. Not even the sound of breathing.

'Hello? Here I am. Is that you, Bella? Hello? It's me now. Can you hear me?'

'Hey. Dud.'

'Bella. Bellissima. Can you hear me properly? This line's very bad. Bella, how kind of you to phone.'

Panting, he peeked round the alcove into the lobby where loitering teenagers stood staring at him. They had witnessed his explosive entry through the fire door, a mange-haired fat man in a flapping dressing-gown, and had assumed the rococo design stitched on to the back of it to be a boxing thing. This did not excuse him in their eyes but it intrigued them. Dudley forced himself deeper into the recess and secured the belt of his gown.

'Bella,' he said breathlessly.

'Just wanted to chat, Dud. If you're about to die, don't worry, some other time.'

'No, this is fine, it's a very good time, an excellent time, I can't think of a better.'

'I wondered how you were. You know your welfare's dear to me.'

Dudley felt the blood rush to his head, he actually felt it, a prickling sensation as if he were about to sneeze. 'And vice versa,' he said. 'Very vice versa.' He smiled as if trying to create an impression on the telephone receiver.

'First thing I thought about when I woke up was you, Dud. Don't know how, but I've got to admit you're working on me.'

'Really?' Dudley's voice was incredulous, his mouth dry.

'Just rolled on to my side and picked up the phone, Dud, I swear. Still not dressed.'

'Not dressed? Really?' The receiver squirmed in Dudley's moist palm.

'Not what you'd call dressed, I've bits on, a few items of a lingerie nature, you know the kind of thing, I don't need to describe them to a guy like you.'

'Actually,' Dudley began, hopefully.

'So give me an update. Talk some business.'

'Business?' Dudley said with a dying fall.

'We don't want to waste time, Dud. You remember business. You're in charge of a dangerous, talentless lunatic. Isn't that how you'd describe him?'

'An understatement in fact, I'm revising my opinion all the time.'

'Your friend.'

'Martin.'

'Belongs in a cage.'

'You may have a point.'

'Tell me.'

'To coin a phrase, he is nasty, brutish and short.'

There was a pause.

'You knew this already. You're his big pal.'

'Actually I know nothing about him. And the longer I know him the less I know. He seems to be one of those people who are always strangers. I can't imagine anyone *wanting* to get to know him.'

Another pause.

'Hello? Bella? Are you still there?'

'What?'

'You sound very funny. Is it this line?' Dudley shook the phone and scowled threateningly at it.

'Keep talking.'

'Now that we've got the business out of the way, I was wondering, when are you free to meet? I think it would be a good idea. Obviously you will need time to get dressed, but . . .'

'Talk, Dud.'

'Perhaps we could have dinner, take in a few of the clubs. Martin needn't know, it's probably best if he didn't, he might start killing people, he's very sensitive.'

'Are you asking me out on a date?'

'Sort of.'

'A *hot* date?'

Dudley's mouth was dry again.

'Hottish.'

A pause.

'Hello? Bella?'

'You make me sick.'

'Bella?'

'I didn't realize how fucking sick you were.'

'I'm sorry?'

'You cunt.'

'Who is this? Bella, is that you?'

'This is the man in the cage. This is the creature without a name.'

'Martin?' Dudley's voice cracked and broke. 'Martin? Am I speaking to Martin?'

'Call me Martin. That'll do. That's who I am.'

'What are you doing on the phone? Is Bella with you?'

'You cretin.'

'Where's Bella gone?'

'You cretin. That was me.'

Dudley stood aghast, staring at the receiver as if it had metamorphosed into a turd. In one disorientating moment he was lost in the funhouse, humpbacked and craving-faced in the distorting mirrors, walls buckling, trap-doors flying open; he was hurtling through space.

Martin was laughing, a sound like a cry of pain.

'Martin, what are you doing?'

The cries stopped. 'It's called mimicry, it's what I did for a job, remember?'

'Christ, Martin.'

'You stupid prick.'

Through the silence Dudley heard faint voices as other telephone lines nudged their own: a ghostly audience. As if to drown them out, he began to speak quickly.

'Martin, forgive me. A little brio, a bit of frivolity, no harm intended.'

'Do you know what I want to say to you?'

'I don't.'

'It's later than you think, that's what I want to say.'

'Is it? What time is it? Goodness, it's nearly ten. We have interviews to go to.'

124

'Late for you, that's what I mean.'

'Late for me?' Dudley's mouth was so dry now his voice cracked as he spoke.

'You think it's going to be okay?'

'We've no time to talk now. Jump in a cab, we have to be at something called *Sports Line*. They cover the social calendar, I can't think why. Three eighty, Sixth Avenue, eleventh floor.'

'See ya, Dud.'

'Martin, please, not that voice.'

But Martin had gone.

He replaced the receiver and knuckled his eyes with his fists. For a long time he remained like that, it was only the sound of voices from the lobby which eventually brought him to himself. Finding some loose change in his dressing-gown pocket, he lifted the receiver again, and dialled with a trembling finger.

He breathed out heavily and ran his hands through his hair.

'Hello. Plaza Hotel? Yes, would you put me through to one of your guests, Miss Bella LaRose? Yes, it's urgent. Of course it's urgent. Do I sound like someone who wouldn't be urgent?'

21

Eighth Avenue lay in front of him and behind him, stinking in the heat, and as he walked the last few blocks to the corner of W14th to meet Martin at NYFM studios, sweat ran into his eyes. He wiped his forehead with his finger ends and winced. All the money he had advanced himself out of Martin's expenses had been spent; he couldn't afford to take a cab any more. He had walked from 42nd Street, through the ruins of the red light district, past magazine shops and photo booths with their sooty signs, *Sex Shoppe*, *Peep Land*, *Nude Review*, *Table Dancing*, *Sex Explosion*, *I'm Not Feeling Myself Tonite*; past unmarked doorways and glimpses of stairwells; past stores on the fringe selling marital aids and cutlery. *Don't blame us if you overpaid elsewhere*, they announced. The pornographic cinemas advertised family fun, boasted 'crystal vision' screens and 'zoom action' projectors, and all the models in the faded photographs had seventies hairstyles.

Sweat poured down his face. He wrinkled his nose at the stink of the street.

Eighth Avenue smelled even worse than 42nd Street, a hash of booze and piss deepening at the junction where the Port Authority Bus terminal sat rusting like a giant shopping basket under the blue, corrosive sky. Manhattan's famous energy evaporated here: derelicts lay on the sidewalks; the young middle-aged drifted from news-stand to kerb and back again; they all passed round the bottle, Wild Irish Rose Wine, Elderflower Brandy, liquids pink or mauve or blue. The shops were too hopeless to do much to advertise their cheap clothing, their second-hand electrical goods, old magazines, last year's videos and cassettes, tools, toys, buttons; they depended on handwritten signs and bargain bins on the street. The road had fallen apart a long time before, it was a fossil, like an ancient riverbed humped with the accumulation of ages.

A man moaned at Dudley from where he sprawled in the gutter, but he wanted nothing except perhaps momentary acknowledgement, he was busy trying to erase a tattoo from his forearm with a shard of bottle glass. Blood covered his hands. Street traders stepped round him, pushing trolleys and hauling boxes. Everybody was slow. Everything was cheap.

Meteorological reports declared that the heatwave was here to stay, this part of the world was getting hotter. Suicides were double what they were the same time last year. A man had killed his wife because their refrigerator stopped working.

Dudley liked to think that New York bore his imprint. All morning he and Martin had zigzagged across town from interview to interview, imposing their circuitry on the grid. Progress by cab was erratic: one minute they were lurching forward on a tide of other cabs, the next they sat motionless at traffic lights with the din of horns around them. Sunlight beat through the dusty windows, scorching the metal trim, but he and Martin said nothing to each other about the weather or anything else; in silence they looked at the buildings, vast glass towers reflecting each other, silver, blue and black. Dudley did not mention the telephone call in which Martin had impersonated Bella LaRose. He wound down his window and stared up the curve of number nine West Fifty-Seventh for so long that in the glare of the heat it seemed to ripple like a great black wave about to fall and engulf him. This is the way miracles work, making the inanimate live, and freezing the quick. Martin and he had reached a new level of understanding, an equilibrium based on mistrust.

The interviews had been relatively untroubled: Martin's performances were more assured now. Extra definition was given to his autobiography in new vignettes, scenes from the life and joking anecdotes. In these stories, told with a deadpan rigour, mentions of himself were always made with an air of surprise and assertion, as if through the processes of memory he claimed himself. He was always in character, but it was a different character from the one he showed Dudley when they were alone: more thoughtful, more controlled, almost aloof. Dudley didn't like it. Nor did the people who interviewed him; they were disappointed that he spent so long on mundane details like the place and date of his birth, his education and prison sentence, when what they wanted were his inflammatory views on sex, women, money and fame. Dudley suffered immense frustration; he would have been pleased to provide any such details, but he was never asked.

At lunchtime they had parted for a couple of hours. Mainly Dudley was relieved to have kept Martin out of trouble, but there were high points too: Martin had mentioned him by name in a couple of interviews, once to acknowledge his custody and once to commemorate their schoolboy friendship. Two, perhaps three people glanced at him. He nodded back, yes it was him, friend to the famous. You have to start somewhere.

He remembered all this as he crossed W15th Street towards the NYFM studios, plotting, smiling and sweating.

*

The former warehouse was a joyless building with flaky-brick walls and a rusting fire-escape. Going past the garbage and graffiti he entered the lobby and found the receptionist facing him through plate glass, headphones stopping her ears and a microphone guarding her mouth. He looked at her, then around the room. Signed photographs of people he did not recognize covered the walls.

'Geoffrey Dudley,' he said into the small grille. 'To meet Martin Prout.' She made no response. '*The* Martin Prout,' he added.

She appeared to be trying to make him disappear by telepathy.

'I'm his agent. Can you hear me all right with those things on?'

Without taking her eyes off him, she said into her microphone, 'Gentlemen for Mr Poop.'

'Prout, actually. I expect he's waiting for me, I'm a tad late.'

'Name?'

'Tell him Dudley.'

'Called Dudley,' she said into the microphone. 'Somebody Dudley.'

'Geoffrey in fact. Or Butch, if you prefer. Usually it's Butch. I handle the UK side of things for Slezinger. Ed Slezinger? Martin Prout's my responsibility. You might say property. Did you hear about Ed by the way? Hospitalized. Terrible business. Assaulted in Santa Monica by a maniac. Pelvis smashed to smithereens. Sometimes I feel like letting off steam myself. Perhaps I could talk to Martin if he's there.'

'Take a seat, Mr Budley.'

The magazines featured good-looking, wealthy, famous men and women whose lives were lists. Entranced, he read about their early-morning filming sessions, penthouse *pieds-à-terre*, gala openings, country residences, exciting divorces, million-dollar contracts, exquisite heartaches (caused by loss of custody of beautiful sons and daughters), drug scandals, health farm visits, photo-opportunities, red setters called Senator or Biff, Vegas comebacks, tributes from the feeble-minded and, late in life, undeserved joy.

The seat hurt his back.

After a while a man with a moustache and a clipboard came up to him.

'Are you Mr Prout's friend?'

'His agent actually.'

'I don't suppose you have any medical skills? We have a slight problem.'

The ante-room culminated in a long strip of window which disclosed the interiors of two tiny recording studios, cramped cubby holes piled up with equipment.

Near the window of one of them Martin was sitting alone, eyes fixed on his feet.

'Sorry I'm late,' Dudley said.

Martin looked up, removed his Walkman and focused slowly. 'The bastards got you as well,' he said at last.

'They told me you were drunk. You don't seem that drunk to me.'

Martin lifted an arm, swept it in front of him and fell out of his chair.

For some minutes Dudley talked anxiously about what they should do, but the details would not come clear. 'Christ,' he kept saying. 'Christ, Martin, why are you doing this to me?' He chewed his fingernails and frowned at everything in the room. Martin said, with an air of perverse satisfaction, that he was going to be sick. A hurried conference took place in which Dudley gave two NYFM people every possible kind of assurance as to Martin's reliability. (English hilarity, he reminded them, was essentially a product of the public house.) He mentioned that Martin had a slight speech impediment which should not be mistaken for a slur. Finally he implored them not to write them off at the beginning of their careers, so young, so talented, so impressionable and led astray.

129

A young woman in jeans and T-shirt came up to him and introduced herself as Stacy Sheldon.

'I'm Geoffrey Dudley. I'm here to look after Martin.'

'You're doing a lousy job.'

'He's fine actually. Someone told me he was drunk, but they were mistaken. He's mellow.'

'He was drunk as a skunk half an hour ago.'

'Slight nerves. You've no idea how much your show means to him.'

She had dry hair cut in a fringe and long red-knuckled hands which were never still. Together they walked over to where Martin sat, head in hands.

'Is he going to take his Walkman off or what?'

Dudley waved a hand in front of Martin's face.

'Can we get on, are you going to make it?'

'He'll make it.'

'Can he speak?'

'He can speak.'

'Say something.'

'Go ahead, Martin.'

'Where's that fucking sick bag I asked for?'

Dudley and Stacy Sheldon stood aside and talked some more. In one of the studios someone put on a record to buy them time, and pop drifted over their argument like music remembered from disastrous parties.

'I should tell you both to take a flying jump. If we weren't short on back-up I would.'

Puckish suddenly now that it was clear that disaster could no longer be averted, Dudley suggested that she interview Martin and him together. 'I'm his oldest friend,' he said. 'There are lots of anecdotes about his early life which I could relate.'

She glanced at her watch. 'I must be crazy,' she said.

'Martin will be very grateful.'

She sat on one side of the desk wearing headphones, Martin sat on the other side and Dudley perched at his shoulder on a

130

tall stool he had found in the corner. Like a kindly warden, he smiled frequently at the other two. But he was not calm. The excitement of talking to the world on radio was compromised by the impossibility of guessing what Martin might do next.

A final refrain of pop was playing.

'You,' Stacy Sheldon said to Dudley. 'When he's talking, *if* he's talking, you don't make a sound.'

'I have an unusual capacity for silence,' Dudley said. 'Incidentally, how long will we be on the air?'

'The slot is the half-hour. Outstandingly interesting, he goes all the way. Moderately interesting, he might make twenty minutes. Dull and I'll cut it at ten. By the look of him I'd give him five.'

They watched her as she adjusted instruments with her long hands, music fading about them. 'I forgot one thing. He does anything crazy I pull the plug right there.' With fingers bitten at the nail she pushed levers down a monitor board and in a vastly different, speeded-up voice said to the microphone:

'Okay, boys and girls, that was Carlo Vanderbilt's Funk Factory, and this is Stacy Sheldon, and with me is Martin Prout, the boyish British star of acclaimed commercials who's about to become a sensation over here, hi, Martin.'

Martin nodded.

'He's right here, but he's a little shy, we're going to have to get him to open up, tell us how your trip's going, Martin, this is your first time in the USA, having fun?'

Sounding like those victims of air disasters who are seized by television crews and interviewed within seconds on being spilt from the wreckage of the plane and the jumble of bodies, Martin began to relate a few details of his life. Dudley gazed round. The room reminded him of the bedsits of teenage electronics freaks; it was full of cardboard boxes packed with spare cables, terminals and circuit boards. A typewriter on a table contained a dusty curl of paper. But from this unlikely place their voices were going out to New York, like spirits descending on that vast city. He scratched his ears and winked

131

at Stacy Sheldon. Martin's voice was a brief monotone punctuating her bubbling torrent.

'We've been talking about your childhood, Martin, sometimes it was a little tough, you've had your share of sadness, but is there anything you remember with affection, any events stand out, moments, friends, tell us about the happy side of Martin Prout.'

There was a silence.

'Nothing at all?'

Silence.

'How about a friend?' Her tone was sharp.

Martin considered this. He nodded.

Stacy Sheldon clenched her teeth and hissed, 'Tell us who, Martin, don't be shy.'

There was a pause.

'Him,' Martin said.

Cocking his head on one side as if he hadn't heard properly, Dudley raised an eyebrow and an enormous smile possessed him. He edged his stool forward and automatically slicked back his hair. Stacy Sheldon was gesturing at them both furiously.

'Maybe a word of explanation here, okay? "Him" is Geoffrey Dudley, who joins us now, Geoffrey is Martin's agent and childhood friend, hi, Geoffrey, nice to have you along.'

'Very nice to be here.'

Martin looked over his shoulder to see Dudley's big, hopeful face homing in on the microphone.

'We were at school together,' he said, unprompted for the first time.

'Formative years,' Dudley said, nodding and smiling. 'Formative years.'

'We went around together.'

'We even acted together.'

'We talked, we discussed things.'

'I have to say, we've been more or less constant companions.' A lump came into Dudley's throat. Making up a shared past was an intimate thing, memories of events that had never

132

happened sprang to mind, and in them he and Martin lived. 'I was his head boy at school actually,' he added truthfully.

'Borstal,' Martin said. 'We were in prison together.'

Dudley flinched. Too late he realized his mistake.

Stacy Sheldon said, 'We heard this story already, you served time too, Geoffrey?'

His mind was suddenly as jumbled as the room around him, his mouth moved as if he were trying to formulate a complicated sentence.

'Um,' he said.

'Constant companions,' Martin said. 'Adjoining cells.'

'Let me get this straight: you were both young offenders?'

There was a pause in which it seemed his life might go in several different directions. He winced. 'In a manner of speaking,' he said at last, reluctantly.

'Bad boys made good?'

'Well,' Dudley said. He hummed and hawed. 'I suppose we were quite a handful.' He attempted a mellow chuckle. 'All behind us now. Our later careers are rather more interesting.'

'You don't strike me as hardened criminals.'

'Oh, hardish, we were hardish. But I wouldn't want to exaggerate.' Dudley began to talk quickly about ethics in an individualistic society. 'Crime is so much a matter of interpretation, don't you think? In England there is quite a tradition of the gentleman thief. But as you suggest, it's all behind us now. Isn't that right, Martin?'

'Dare I ask what put you inside?'

'Sodomy,' Martin said. 'Rape. Assault. Torture of small boys.'

They stood sweating together on the sidewalk waiting for a cab. The roar of homebound traffic filled the air. Dudley still could not bring himself to look at Martin; he glanced away at the cars and buses, the lurch of metal.

'She *said* she would pull the plug. You knew that.'

Martin shrugged.

'You knew it, but it didn't stop you. One of our most important interviews. Why?'

'Why not?'

'But think, Martin. Think of it. Think of me.'

'You've got the jitters.'

'This is a low spot, one of the low spots of my life. I can go no lower. The people of New York believe me a rapist, a sodomite and a child-torturer. How will I get them to love me again?'

'You're running scared.' He smiled, a brief, formal display of teeth. Crowds walked past them. They were the only stationary people on the sidewalk.

'When I came here,' Dudley said, 'I thought splendid things were within my grasp. Now I'm having trouble just remaining human.'

Martin grunted.

'These jokes,' Dudley went on. 'These jokes about being with you in prison.'

Martin said nothing.

'Listen. I want to stop living in the past. That's all I want. It's not much, is it?'

Martin stirred. 'You thought it was simple. You thought I was a small part of your life, just enough to be useful, just enough to get rid off easily. But it's better than that. You're a part of my life now.'

Traffic filled the road, a single creature. One minute it banged past, the next it was frozen at the lights. Windscreens, mirrors, hoods, all caught the sunlight. A Negro in a slashed grey suit was fishing in a subway ventilation shaft with a magnet on a string. Dudley looked away and up, and thought that from the top of a skyscraper he and Martin would appear – if they appeared at all – as an infinitesimal part of one slow movement, a shifting layer that meant nothing to the city, not even disturbing its pattern. He was lost, he was not himself any more.

A cab stopped and they got in. Wiping his forehead he noticed that his hands were still trembling.

134

'It can only get better,' he said as calmly as he could. 'I believe that, I almost believe it. When this is all over you can forget Borstal. No one will ask you about Borstal, they'll want to know about New York, the First Visit. You can say "New York? Dudley was with me in New York."'

22

The elevator rose with hurtling, imperceptible speed.

'It is conventional in European quest literature for the knight errant to occasionally ascend towers to rescue maidens in distress, but in the USA naturally things are the other way round. I'm ascending the tower, and *I* am in distress, and you are the only person who can help me.'

'Can anyone help you?'

Dudley raised a hand and brushed the rim of his new fedora. The hat was light grey with a darker grey band round it, and a smooth crease in its crown softly reflected the elevator's harsh light. It was a present from Martin, although Martin didn't know it: Dudley had advanced himself some more money from his expenses fund.

'Let's be clear about this. When I say I need help I don't mean I could do with some help, I mean help is indispensable, I mean that without help I am utterly lost, doomed, destitute, a wanderer in the lower shades of hell. That's what I mean.'

'Am I meant to take it you worry about Psycho?'

He glanced at her.

'Look at me. I'm falling apart with worry. Look. My hair's disappearing, my teeth hurt. I go to sleep drunk at three in the morning and wake to find I've lost all sense of smell. I feel nauseous. I feel dizzy. I itch all over.'

'This isn't normal?'

'I need your help. I really, really, really need your help. Really.'

There was a distant clunk, and as they rocked slightly on their heels, the doors buzzed open. Trooping out of the elevator with the others, they went past the kiosks selling Empire State accessories to the edge of the wire cage that held them in nine hundred feet above Manhattan, and found the sunset all around them. A hot breeze gusted Dudley's hat almost off his head.

His first sight was of the sky, an artist's palette smeared with yellows, greens, rusts and golds. Then he looked down and saw the technology, the big chips stuck in the circuit, a crystalline design intricate with tiny faint lights: the city. Between the two, belonging to neither, he stood and stared. ·

'Over here,' he said at last and he led her to a shadowy corner of the compound. 'I'm not so unself-aware that I can't detect in myself the beginnings of a paranoia about being followed.' He glanced round and pulled down the brim of his hat in conventional fashion. 'I think we're safe here.'

Taking no notice of him, she stood with her hands in the pockets of her long, white coat, looking westward into the landmass. The coat, zippered at her throat and hanging to her feet in a smooth column, gave her the look of a Giacometti, the essence of a figure with nothing added, nothing interpretative or contextual. Her hair was in stiff little ringlets. Longingly Dudley looked at her remote face and inflexible profile.

'If I had to choose a single word to describe all this,' he said, gesturing to the view, 'it would be phallocentric.' He looked at her hopefully, and, without indicating that she had heard him, she moved away.

They walked round the perimeter of the cage, and while he talked despairingly of Martin, she pointed out to him the main landmarks – the buildings, the monuments and the parks, the empty homes of billionaires, the scenes of riots, presidential cavalcades and Thanksgiving Day Parades. Every so often, when his own story became too much for him, he put his head through the big waffles of the cage and gazed down, tracing the line of the building to the sidewalk, a line so sheer it seemed to bend like the curve of the world, picking up speed as it fell, an accelerating trajectory. He felt that he had been given the means to understand why the cage was there: the sense of the vertical was so beautiful it could make people want to throw themselves into its slipstream and become part of the dizzying descent, to rush like a blip of pure energy into the transistorized heart of Manhattan, their own heroes for a moment. Speed, flight, destiny: he liked to think that these were his themes. The worst thing would be for the angels to bear him up now.

'There's something else too,' he said. 'Another reason for wanting to see you. Apart from the awfulness of Martin, apart from the delirious joy of our reunion. Do you want to know what it is?'

'Do I have a choice?'

'I want you to introduce me to some television people. Would you do that?'

They were both looking down at the river, a solid shape brown as furniture.

Bella said, 'What for?'

'For interest. I'd be interested.'

She said, 'You've got the wrong person, Dud. Contacts is my business. I don't work for free.'

'It's difficult for me to know who you are and what you do. I know nothing whatever about you.'

He watched her considering him, her face motionless as if her undisclosed thoughts required absolute stillness as they ranged over endless possibilities, a sense of wide, rapid movement.

'First you want my advice. Then you want information. Now you want my life story.' She seemed amused. 'Is this a good backdrop to a life?'

'Almost perfect.' He waved a hand at the sky behind her. 'Sunset. The vastness of America. Casper David Friedrich. Hints of apocalypse and revelation. I have so much to learn.'

'What do you want to know? Let me guess. The magazine facts. What clothes I buy, where I eat, how I work out, what car I drive, which clubs I go to, where I get my money from, my zip code, my pants size.'

He reluctantly denied it.

137

'These facts belong to everyone, they're not mine. That's an important distinction. I was sixteen when I discovered this, and I left home and moved into a hotel, and I've lived in hotels ever since. No one knows where I come from, I come from nowhere, it's what makes me believable. That's the way to start a life, by getting rid of the facts. Never give the whole picture. People don't want to *just* believe, they want to make that leap of faith, they want to be consumed by you. So get rid of facts. You could make a career out of it.'

'I was going to ask about your career.'

'Last year retail. This year, media. Next year, who knows, maybe politics.'

'But what do you do?'

'I let people do what they want. Some people call it consultancy.'

'The Slezinger thing is just consultancy?'

'Check the compay records, you won't find my name. I could give Slezinger the finger today, he knows that – and maybe I will. Or maybe I want to shave my head, because I'm in control and why not? In this city, you think you stand out because you've got a shaved head? You blend in. You drop out of circulation for a while, do time on the streets, see what's happening.'

'That must be very interesting.'

'Bums coming out of the early morning mist off the Hudson, men weeping into their whiskey, the bodies of tourists in the streets.'

She looked out over the river to where the lights failed, and the distance seemed to flicker.

'It's madness, of course.'

'What do you mean, madness?'

'Pay attention, Dud, I'm giving you my time.'

'But what madness?'

'You. Me. Our madness. What else have we got?'

*

138

They walked together round the perimeter once more, Dudley seeing her lit from the blazing observatory against the deep, blank, blue sky, a sky the colour of wet ink.

Bella asked, 'Is it my turn to ask about you? Is that the game?' Her voice was mocking.

Dudley shook his head.

'If you choose the game, Dud, you have to play it. The seduction game. Don't tell me you don't know it. You tell me your life and I'll tell you mine, and it all ends with the big movie clinch.'

Dudley equivocated, his hat in his hands and on his head at the same time. Everything in his face showed that he knew he was ridiculous.

Bella said, 'Let me start on the questions, Mr Dudley.'

'If you must.' He braced himself, like a vast tangled bird, against the wire.

'What is your favourite colour?'

'Favourite *colour*?' He looked surprised. 'I don't know, it changes from day to day. Today it's . . .' He turned his head and looked through the wire mesh into space, into the blue, the trailing rags of purple and green. 'The colour of the sky. Always a hopeful colour, I think. I'm not religious however. Ask me about my view of religion.'

'Favourite drink?'

He stared at her. 'Martini, actually. Ice, no olive.'

'Item of clothing?'

He was confused. 'Hang on.' He raised his hand. 'Aren't you rather neglecting the major issues? What about my ambitions and fears and dreams and longings?'

'Favourite automobile?'

'I don't know anything about cars. Look, I want to be asked about my formative experiences, my earliest encounters with the opposite sex, my intimations of death and the afterlife.'

'Aftershave?'

'I refuse to answer. I want to be asked interesting questions.'

'*Interesting* questions?'

139

'That's right.'

'Okay. Tell me what you like best about yourself.'

He raised an eyebrow. His mouth opened, and closed. Frowning, he turned, raised his arms above his head and looked down into Manhattan. The pinnacle on which he balanced was only a few feet wide, a frail shaft of masonry that hung over the city, somehow resisting the velocity of gravity which plunged past him. If the wire had not been there he would have gratefully dropped over the edge. He had no answer.

Then, as he swung back round – lifting his head to her – the wind took his new hat and flung it against the wire mesh. He grabbed at it, missed, and it went through a hole and vanished. Putting his head out as far as he could, he looked for it in the sky but there was nothing, not even the conventional drifting speck; it had written him out of its existence.

He turned back to Bella LaRose, moaning and gesturing helplessly.

She made no reaction. 'The question,' she said.

'Christ,' he said and stood there embarrassed. 'I don't know,' he said at last. 'I don't know the answer to that. It's a trick question, isn't it?'

In the elevator he reverted to his worried theme of Martin.

'You spoke of madness. Madness is the word that springs to mind. I'd like to be funny about it, but I can't any more. I don't know what he's going to do next. He could do anything. I think he might be the suicidal type. I don't want to wake up one morning with the bed next to me full of blood.'

'How's the hotel, by the way?'

'Awful. Screams in the night. I feel like screaming myself. I need your advice.'

'Now you want advice about your accommodation?'

'About Martin. About everything.'

'I just told you everything I know, and you're still asking me for advice? Think, Dud.'

They emerged into the great movement of the street, a sensation of shrinkage and struggle.

He squinted round into the razzle of neon and fluorescence. 'You know, I still have this feeling I'm being followed.'

Vendors had set up stalls on the sidewalks, men in Hawaiian shirts performing tricks with three cups and a coin on folding card-tables, their hands moving with brilliant speed. They shouted to passers-by and there was always someone to stop and argue with them. Four lanes of traffic began to move at the change of lights, sliding forward out of a cloud of smog.

'Will I see you again?' he said.

She shrugged.

'There's a big party tomorrow night, I remember it from the itinerary, at the something something gymnasium.'

'Gold Coast Muscle Club.'

'Will you be there?'

'I may drop in.'

She raised an arm for a cab.

'So what are my plans?' Dudley asked suddenly, rhetorically and desperately. 'What am I taking away from our little meeting?'

She waved goodbye. He watched her get into the cab, and as it pulled away he was still thinking about her question, still failing to answer it.

Indecisive, worried, randy, he stood next to the street conjurers attempting to flag down a cab, flapping his arms in a parody of theirs.

23

It was eleven o'clock and the room was suffocatingly hot. Martin sat on his bed scrutinizing the bedspread as if to read a sign in it. Dudley was sitting by the window in his dressing-

141

gown and slippers, eating a triple pastrami on rye, and trying to read *Itinerary Martin Prout*.

A light sweat covered Martin's face. There was no space, no margin of relief, between the surface of his body and the slick heat. It lay against him and he breathed it in; he felt utterly absorbed in it as if it were a disgusting aspect of himself. Noises outside took on a quality of this heat: sirens in the distance and alarms in the street below sounded febrile and insistent like the mewling of birds. Closer and equally suggestive were the faint sounds of Dudley chewing pastrami.

Martin stared at Dudley. His ostentatious dressing-gown was open to the waist, exposing one white leg, flesh of a shocking bloodless colour, paler than his face even which was the colour of veal. A very unexciting face, a non-face, with non-features and non-hair.

'I suppose I'll be taking the trip to clubland alone this evening,' Dudley said. Nonchalance was the effect he aimed at, but his tone was too loud; after he had spoken the room felt hotter and grimier.

Martin shrugged.

'Fine by me,' Dudley said. 'I have people to see, television producers and so on. I mean, I have to think of myself sometimes.'

'I've just remembered why you were called Stuff,' Martin said.

Dudley frowned and picked a scrap of pastrami out of his dressing-gown's florid front pocket. He began to hum.

'It was short for stuffing. You had the stuffing knocked out of you by Proctor.'

'I don't think that can be true.'

'He beat you up so you got him expelled.'

'Completely made up. I was called Stuff a long time before Shammings. Never knew why, in fact. I don't know why you're so interested. I think, in fact, I'm fed up of Shammings.' He took a cigar from a tube and began to smoke, looking out of the window at the brick wall.

'I'll be off shortly,' he said after a short while. 'Must get ready.' He stayed where he was. 'Probably I'll pick Bella up on the way,' he added.

Martin watched him. Creases in the back of his dressing-gown bunched the hem, exposing the back of one white calf. The skin was inflamed in the hinge of the knee showing the friction marks of a pair of tight Levis, another costume already abandoned.

'I hate Americans,' Martin said. 'Especially her.'

'Yes, I know.'

'I fucking hate them. They think we love them.'

'Do they?'

'You love them.'

'I don't dislike them as much as you do.'

'You love them, and you envy them. That's good, love and envy. The only two emotions they understand.'

Dudley sucked evasively on his cigar, removed it from his mouth and looked at its deft, glowing tip. How irresistible its cool, burning impersonality.

'They excite a certain anthropological interest,' he said.

Pale and fat and fancy in his creased silk gown, he was like a sacrificial victim, dolled up to be led dazed and bloated one early morning from dark cell to bright courtyard. When he spoke, his words, the lengthy sequences of sounds, gave off an anxious crackle, a bleat of static like the creak of chewing. Words for him were almost physical things, bits of gristle in the mouth, mucus at the back of his throat to be coughed up and extruded.

'You love them and you envy them and you'd like to fuck some of them.'

Dudley was quiet, fussing with his cigar. Martin stared at him for a while then sank back on his bed.

'One thing, talking of Americans,' Dudley said at last. 'Your impersonation of them. I mean, of Bella. Not bad. I didn't know you were a mimic.'

'It's just a knack.'

'Mimicry's not the highest form of dramatic expression or the most interesting, but it always gets a laugh. Can you turn it on at will?'

'Yes.'

'Could you do it now?'

'If I wanted. But I don't.'

Martin lay back on the bed and looked up at the ceiling. One corner of it had not been painted. Always some detail to show him his life was lacking. He took out a cigarette and blinked slowly.

When he turned on his side Dudley was still looking at him expectantly.

Martin pointed to the windowsill. 'Matches,' he said.

'You're not doing it. That wasn't it, that sounded just like you.'

'Throw the fucking matches.'

'I suppose sometimes you have the knack and sometimes you don't. Like most things.'

Without taking his eyes off him Martin said, 'Dud, you are pure goofball, I mean pure. When the shooting starts you're exactly the kind of guy who forgets to run. Deadmeat, that's what you are, Dud. Will you throw the frigging matches or what?'

Dudley was amazed and terrified all over again.

'Not bad,' he said in a shaky voice. 'I mean, really quite like her.'

'What is it you want from me, Dud, my life story? Don't you think that's a little obvious?'

Speechless, Dudley stared at him, suddenly realizing, slow as ever.

Martin continued: 'What is it you want, man of mystery? Want advice about accommodation? Where is it you're staying, the sixth circle of hell? No problems. A little fear never did anyone any harm, what are a few beatings between friends? Now some questions about your life. What makes you think you exist? Hey, goofball, don't you know it's dangerous to

144

walk out on a conversation in New York, you could get wasted, I mean like totalled, zeroed, wiped.'

He was in the bathroom clutching the wash-basin, like a criminal or a saint seeking sanctuary, staring in the mirror, his breath hoarse in that hot cell, the bead curtain clacking behind him, fading gradually into low noises of police sirens outside, car alarms and the beat of running footsteps. There was nowhere he could go without being followed, there would always be that small figure like Dürer's Melancholy sitting in the shadows or at the next table or on the bed, staring down at the unreadable bedspread, staring up at the ceiling with its unpainted corner, Melancholy the shabby symbol and the soul in torment.

It was eleven thirty, hotter than ever, and the room felt like an overinflated balloon.

The beads clacked and Dudley appeared. He murmured inaudibly and Martin said, 'What?'

'I wouldn't go in there for a while if I were you.'

Martin turned his head.

'I mean, no one craps *eau de cologne*.' His voice was too quiet now for nonchalance though he attempted it anyway. He went quickly to the window and looked out at nothing, the dead cigar in his hand again, his dressing-gown bunched again, his white legs slightly splayed again, his head hurting, all these things repeated in exact, exhausting detail in the manner of an afterlife. If he turned he would see Martin sitting hunched and remote on his bed. Taking up *Pensées* he scribbled furtively:

387. Melancholy. Myths of expulsion and exile. I think this: the briefest of moments can jar the world out of kilter, and on the margins of that world there are two figures, one in furious pursuit, the other sitting in exile.

'I'm going out in a minute,' he said after a while. 'It's not too late. I've some people to see.'

He stood staring at the window. It was eleven forty-five and the room seemed to pulse with the heat.

'Better get ready,' he said. He stayed where he was.

By midnight he had recovered some composure. With a few sighs and quizzical asides he began to change into his party-wear. Anticipating the moment of his entry into clubland he had borrowed a little more of Martin's money and bought another disguise. Button-down linen shirt, pleated white trousers, dotted silk tie, psychedelic waistcoat, perforated cream leather shoes. He was drenched in colours. For a while he looked for his new fedora hat before remembering that it had blown away from the top of the Empire State. Another sudden disappearance. An event too brief to include the custom-ary moment in which to recognize his life.

Turning to Martin he said, 'How do I look?'

'Scared.'

'I'm off. Off to clubland. I'm presuming you're not coming. It's okay, I'll be fine, no need to worry on my account, no need to wait up late.'

'I'll come.'

'Oh.'

Martin got off the bed, limped over to the door and pulled on his old black T-shirt.

'You're coming?' He was incredulous.

'Yes.'

'Well. I'm delighted, of course. But you can't go dressed like that.'

'Come on.'

'Are you sure?'

Reluctantly he followed Martin out of the room and down the stairs, their shadows chasing and struggling in the well.

'Which club are we going to?' Martin asked.

'I don't know,' Dudley said. 'I hadn't decided which to start with.'

'I know a club,' Martin said. 'We'll go there.'

'Fine.'

They came in silence to the bottom of the stairs and went through the fire door.

By the piles of building materials Dudley suddenly paused. 'It's not that strip club, is it, Martin?'

'Do you think I'd take you to a strip club? Trust me.'

The porter nodded to them as they left the lobby and pushed their way past the litter piled on the front steps, down on to the street, Dudley adjusting the hang of his psychedelic waistcoat, Martin staring at his shoes.

'Not a strip club at all?'

'That's right.'

'Good, I'm very pleased.' He looked up at the skyscrapers and began to hum.

24

'Martin, this is a strip club. Look, there are girls stripping. Strip club is the only reasonable definition of this place.'

Martin shrugged.

'There's a maximum of one dozen people here, three of whom are stripping. The words exclusive, stylish, chic, expensive are in no way applicable. You lied to me.'

'Don't talk to me about lies.'

Outside on Eighth Avenue, where they had hesitated only a moment, the signs in the display case said *Live Girls*, *Non-stop Shows*, *Erotic Entertainment*. There were photographs of girls grouped on stage, all smiles, curls, G-strings and star-bursts. These girls are live, they are in no way deceased. By the time Dudley had absorbed this Martin was already past the bouncer, and he was following, bleating into his waistcoat. Where were his ideals, where the objects of all his quests? Where else but in the Purple Palace?

With their tiny tots of outrageously expensive substandard

bourbon, they sat on low stools in a dark alcove at the back, commanding a partial view of the dim gallery, evil bar and brightly lit stage. Backed by floor-to-ceiling mirrors the stage stood immediately behind the bar, so that men watching the acts from their bar-stools were no more than a yard away, their faces on a level with the girls' ankles. It was important they were able to reach up with their dollar bills and tuck them into the girls' G-strings.

The three girls shuffling up and down to the cataclysmic rock music had nearly finished stripping. Only their G-strings and high heels remained. One was a tiny Korean who chewed gum; she had large breasts which she rubbed and powerful buttocks which she pressed against the mirror behind her, and whenever a man gave her money she giggled and covered her mouth with her hand like a schoolgirl. Dollar bills bristled from her G-string. The second girl was older, the image of American bar life with a washed-out face and large hips and dyed blonde hair; she worked hard for her tips. The third was an elderly Filipino with a small, cleft scar like a seamstress's tuck in the flesh of her hip; she moved very slowly and sometimes not at all, tired, or bored, or both.

'Look at these people,' Martin said. 'Real people. That's what they think.'

Half a dozen men sat at the bar, most of them staring into their drinks. From time to time, sometimes without even lifting their heads, one would reach up and give a girl a bill, a harsh but supplicatory gesture.

'Look at them,' Martin said again.

'Drink up, Martin, we ought to be moving on.'

'Anything could happen to these people.'

'It wouldn't surprise me.'

'It's like a film. People drinking at a bar. Somebody dives into them. There's a big fight, like a fight in a saloon in a western.'

'Perhaps when you've made your reputation as an actor you could direct.'

'People here with criminal records just fighting, getting up and starting a fight.'

'Why?'

'I don't know.' He swallowed his whiskey. 'Because of the women.'

Dudley said he felt queasy. Martin was rocking slowly to and fro on his stool, his face bobbing in and out of shadow, the shifting light and shade giving him a theatrical appearance, an insubstantiality as if he were a figure in a nightmare whose identity continuously shifts, bringing on feelings of panic, speeding up the plot, the chase, the children's game which must end in disaster.

'I feel queasy,' Dudley said again. He bent down and wiped a smut off his cream leather shoes.

Suddenly a man came round the corner of their booth and sat down with a bump at their table. The table was small and his head hung heavily towards theirs, so close they could feel his breath on their faces as he peered at them.

'Good evening,' Dudley said after a moment. He was an old man with a fat, grey face and creased eyes. There was a stain on the lapel of his light brown jacket. He did not speak but continued to breathe on them, looking in an abstract unsighted way first at Dudley, then at Martin, finding nothing worth his attention. His face began to show signs of confusion; he dashed a hand to his eyes, got up and went away.

'That sort of thing tends to put me on edge,' Dudley said.

'This is the right place for us. A good backdrop to a life story. Don't you think? Hints of fuck all and worse.'

'Martin, please.'

'When I first went to prison I didn't think I'd ever come out.'

'I don't think I want to hear about prison again.'

Martin stared at him. 'When I first went to prison I didn't think I'd ever come out,' he said again. 'Everyone feels that. And in a way it's true – you can never leave because you carry it around in your head for the rest of your life, everything, your cubicle, your pisspot, the corridors, the screws, the other cons, everything. Most of all the cons. It's the stories they tell. You can't escape their stories, those stories droning on and on. That's what prison is, stories, all different, changing all the time. Some bloke would start to tell you he was a five stretch for armed robbery and by the time he'd finished it was rape, almost like he'd have to begin again with a new version, each version different, again and again and again. Or you'd say to some other bloke, I'm in for rape, and he'd say, It's exactly the same with me, and then he'd tell you how he's in for murder. Real people, that's what they thought, but they hardly existed.'

'Oh God,' Dudley said.

'You don't exist either, you're just stories like them. You're a fool. Nothing will ever happen to you because you're not interesting enough. What did you think? You thought you'd come here and use me and you'd get what you wanted. Just stories. In prison you talked about two things, what you'd done to get put inside, and what you were going to do when you got out, and they were never the same, they changed all the time. The only thing you knew – that you were inside – you never talked about. That's what your life's like too.'

Dudley finished his bourbon and looked away. The girls were shuffling to and fro on the stage, collecting dollar bills.

'Actually I don't believe you went to Borstal,' he said quietly.

'Didn't go to Borstal?' Martin shouted. 'What am I doing here then? I went to Borstal, you cunt, I can give you the details, the dates, the hours of every day.'

Alarmed, Dudley shook his head. 'I think it's a lie.'

'Don't talk to me about lies! You say that you're an idealist, but what are your ideals? All that crap about the changeability of character. You don't even have a fucking character. Listen. When I was in prison we didn't have to sew mailbags or anything like that, we did exams – just like outside – and what do you think they wanted to study, all these fucking criminals who were in prison for murder and rape and GBH and extortion? They wanted to do psychology, drama, poetry, dance. It was pathetic. Like animals trying to stand on their hind legs and sing. Whenever you talk to me I think of them. You're the liar, the cheat, the twister, the Judas.'

Trembling slightly, Dudley lifted and looked into his inscrutable empty tumbler. 'Shall we go?' he said at last.

'All right, let's go.'

He rose and followed Martin out of their booth, then stopped. Martin was heading not for the door but for the bar, limping briskly towards the row of men whose heads were so oddly set against the backdrop of waving ankles. He hesitated, then edged forward. 'Martin!' he whispered. 'Martin!' Up here the music was louder and the girls' skin, close up, was damp; it glistened under the bright lights, streaks of sweat visible over their ribs and down their faces. Their bodies were solid, heavy-fleshed, and they banged the boards of the stage with their heels as they moved, the flesh of their legs bunching and quivering.

'Martin, what are you doing?' Dudley asked, catching up with him.

'This is a good place. It's the best. I've said what I wanted to say. Give me the money.'

'What money?'

'The money she gave you for me.'

'I don't have much on me.'

'Give me what you have.'

Martin took the envelope and removed one of the hundred-dollar bills, then another.

'I hate to say this, Martin.'

'Don't then.'

'I beg you to think.'

'I am thinking. I'm thinking of all of this.'

Dudley's eyes rolled. 'Did I say I could go no lower? "The worst is not as long as we can say *This is the worst*."'

'Shut up, you fake,' Martin said. He held up the bills, reaching forward until they were within an inch of the Korean girl's breasts. She giggled, half-nervously, arching her back and pushing forward her hips to sudden laughter along the bar.

151

Someone lazily whooped, and then she took the bills in her fingers and stuck them into the pad of her G-string. Then she was retreating, juggling with her breasts, and looking at Martin through half-closed eyes. Dudley, wincing, not knowing where to look, became aware of his reflection in the mirror at the back of the stage, head only, as if on a platter, resting between the Korean's feet. Her high heels were stamping on either side of his ears. His cheeks were flushed, his hair dead. What was left of his hair.

'No blacks,' Martin said. 'I bet you were hoping for blacks.'

'Oh, God,' Dudley said. 'I've got to go.' He couldn't take his eyes off his reflection. The worst thing, by a long way, was the state of his hair. Sadly he took another drink from Martin; it appeared in front of his reflection, and his face jerked out of the picture, and the drink was finished.

'Let's get out of here, Martin,' he said.

'We could get a couple of these girls for ourselves. We've got enough.'

Dudley turned back to his reflection. 'I think my whoring days are over.'

'No blacks. One American, two Orientals. Two of these girls or two others, it makes no difference.'

Along the bar a new noise rose and intensified. The blonde was slipping out of her G-string. Suddenly animated, the drinkers were baying as they fished into their wallets, half a dozen arms rising as if they all had the answer to the same question. Please sir.

'You want to run away, don't you?'

Dudley nodded.

'One girl for me. One for you. Scared?'

Dudley nodded again.

'Got a stiff one?'

Again the cry from down the bar, a vague, incomplete noise, a rumbling in the throat that never rose as far as the mouth – then suddenly high-pitched whoops, all air. The Korean stood centre stage on bunched legs, her thumbs inside the string, working outwards. Shy and serious: the mound of her belly,

152

the pinched roll of puppy-fat, the blackest pubic patch, and Dudley's face under it all, enduring.

'Going to run? Look at these girls. You want to run away from them.'

He said nothing, he couldn't speak.

'Two girls, one fat, one thin. You choose.'

There was another flicker of interest, but muted and partly charitable, as the Filipino limped to the front of the stage and eased out of her G-string to display her grizzled pubic hair. Dudley looked at his own hair, tortured in the bright lights, and turned to leave.

Martin caught hold of him. 'You can't bear it any more, you can't stomach it. This place is real, real as prison, real as you, real as me.'

At that moment the music ended, the girls stopped dancing and put their leotards and mini-skirts back on. Clothed, they were bulkier and sexier. Trooping off the stage they were met by a large blonde woman, middle-aged and butcher-faced, who began to introduce them to selected members of the audience.

'Desperate,' Martin began again, his voice cracking. He had talked more than ever before, too much. 'You're getting desperate,' he said. 'Here they come.' Clinging to Dudley, he wheeled round, keeping his distance from the madame and her short, powerful girls, and Dudley, looking down at him in amazement, realized that Martin was far more frightened than he was.

'You can't take it,' Martin was saying. 'All right, we'll go, let's go, don't fucking worry, panic over.' He was like a small boy hanging on to his elder brother. 'All right,' he said shrilly, but he had left it too late, the madame stopped him with a hand and spoke in an undertone, the Korean waiting obediently at her shoulder.

'Don't touch me,' Martin shouted, and at that moment the Korean came forward, a delicate, eager movement, her buttocks shoving together under the thin material of her mini-skirt, and put her hand on Martin's arm. Both arms flew up into the air, and the madame grabbed at Martin's wrist, and two men appeared from along the bar, spoiling for a fight. The music started up again, heralding three new girls who walked unconcerned on to the stage while the two men manoeuvred Martin to the floor, and along the floor towards the door.

'Hey,' Dudley yelled as he hustled after, and someone's elbow struck him in the face. He struggled to get to Martin but was held back, he got only one glimpse of Martin writhing on the wooden floorboards, his face briefly presented to him, his eyes seeking his, and then he was gone. It was a moment as brief as a vision or a blow to the head but in it Dudley felt a sudden and violent protectiveness. The woman with the butcher's face was coming towards him, calling over her shoulder to the two men just returning, and he edged sideways.

'Look here,' he said.

They came right up to him, their heads together, staring at his psychedelic waistcoat and pleated white trousers and perforated cream leather shoes.

'There's no need for violence,' he said. 'More violence than is necessary,' he added, and then they caught hold of him and he was hauled off.

Distraught, he reeled on the sidewalk, searching for a point of reference. Only the irreducible things of the world remained, traffic boiling along three intersecting streets, tail-lights blurring as they bounced into the distance, and opposite a single pizzeria lit up green and red between dark stores. Everything he knew had disappeared, evaporated into the hot air. Night seemed to have fallen abruptly that minute, the blank sky suffocating the street, the city darkening and hardening like lava.

Martin was nowhere to be seen. There was no point of reference. His face hurt and he did not know where he was. He barely knew who he was. But nothing that had happened was so frightening as that moment of tenderness when he had seen Martin dragged along the floor.

154

He began to walk along the sidewalk looking round him, and calling every few minutes.

'Martin? Martin?'

25

Once he had pursued ideals, followed his goals, but it was only now, he realized, that his proper quest began: the anxious plod, the footsore duty, the weary search for the misplaced, ordinary thing.

He made his way across Columbus Circle through knots of waiting tourists and joggers and vendors selling pretzels and donuts, then went eastward among leafless trees and scavenging pigeons and squirrels, looking around him all the time, until he came to Wollman Memorial Rink. There he consulted his map, lifting his head occasionally to watch the rollerbladers. Deep in the rink they were dancing to unheard music in their head-phones, a silent, surging crowd like a pantomimic chorus of mourners attendant on some unknown tragedy. But he could not stay to see how their drama unfolded, he had to push on. First he walked to the Bird Sanctuary, then to the Pond, then to the Zoo and the Arsenal. After that he slowly doubled back to the Mall, a shadow-filled avenue beneath overgrown elms lined with statues of the famous which he ignored, going past them to search the Sheep Meadow where a thousand obscure citizens were picnicking, lying immobile on the singed green like litter. With the watchfulness and toiling step of an ice-cream seller he went among them, peering down. Back to the Bandshell, he skirted Cherry Hill, went in a wide sweep over to Pilgrim Hill, and eventually reached the Lake at Bow Bridge. He was very tired.

Quests necessarily involve travel, often of an arduous nature. They take the hero in two directions: one a devious route towards an objective goal, a Chapel Perilous; and the other a more devious way still towards a state of grace or understanding. Dudley was still thinking about quests as he rested on the bridge, the soles of his feet tingling, sweat prickling his forehead. Four hours had passed since he entered Central Park, the sun was at its zenith, and he was exhausted. He went over to an ice-cream stall and bought a cornet. Next to the stall was a man selling toys and Dudley spent his last few dollars on a zebra-striped baseball cap with spring-loaded antennae and a sign which flashed on and off saying *Moon Loon*, a demeaning article of clothing and symbolic of his desperation.

The previous night, after leaving the Purple Palace, he had spent two hours looking for Martin in Eighth Avenue and the conjoining streets – a depressing neighbourbood of run-down tenements, shuttered stores and deserted kiosks – before returning defeated to the Central Hotel at 3 a.m. At seven he was woken by pounding on the door and a voice telling him he was wanted on the phone. He scuttled down the stairs into the booth.

'Martin,' he said. 'Thank God. Thank God. Are you all right?'

'You're off-beam, Dud. This is Bella.'

He stared, then laughed. 'Amazing how well you do it, the twang, the authority. Really, it's as if I can actually see her talking to me.'

'Doubt your eyes would let you down so bad.'

'And what are you dressed in today, may I ask? Not dressed at all, I bet, I see you in the scantiest, the most dispensable of filigree lace camisoles, a sort of wispy pattern on the lovely dark skin. But enough of this provocation. Where are you? Where have you been?'

There was a silence.

'Hello?' he said.

'Dud, do you remember what I told you? About giving Slezinger the finger?'

He looked in terror at the receiver.

'It's done with. I'll see you at the ceremony, but apart from that you're on your own. Enjoy.'

He bit his knuckles.

'Just a reminder to make the Channel 155 interview tonight.'

'Thank you,' Dudley said humbly.

'Filigree lace?'

'Bella, is that really you?'

'Wow. It's the speed of your thought impresses me.'

Dudley winced and whimpered. But there was no time to explain, no time even for him to be abject; he mentioned that Martin had disappeared, that he had no idea where he might be, and that he was afraid Martin would kill himself before he located him. Wearily and ambiguously Bella wished him luck.

'But where do I start?'

'Who knows. But you could do worse than start with the Park, it has a gravitational pull this time of year. Also, when night falls, it's the place to go if you want to die.'

After he hung up, he dragged himself upstairs, took a cold shower, and by eight o'clock was approaching Columbus Circle, a forlorn figure carrying a map, an overweight tourist among the joggers and rollerbladers, a man without hope or humour, with only a sense of involvement and, whenever he thought of Martin, stabs of that fierce tenderness, a feeling as ambivalent as the discovery of a capacity for self-destruction.

Sunlight glinted off the aluminium boats that sat on the Lake; the Lake itself did not reflect the light, the water was the colour of phlegm, a thick, dull green. The art deco towers of Central Park West loomed over the trees, a Camelot sinister in its bulk and extent, a Gothic asylum for the lost and lonely.

He took out his *Pensées* and wrote:

401. *Imagining our own death is in some ways more bearable than imagining other people's. Who can remain sane – who*

157

can remain alive – with the guilt of having caused someone else's death?

He finished his ice-cream, gave the stagnant scene one last look, and turned away. Limping as slowly as the loony bounce of the ping-pong moon-eyes on his cap, he went over Bow Bridge into the Ramble and east towards Cedar Hill.

For the next four hours he was only intermittently aware of his whereabouts. Occasionally landmarks presented themselves – Great Lawn, Summit Rock, Belvedere Lake, Shakespeare Lake – but most of the time he wandered uncertainly across stretches of brownish pasture and along twisting asphalt paths through sparse woodland, always emerging at basketball courts or baseball diamonds to the strenuous sounds of victory and defeat. In the late afternoon, as the unnatural shadows of urban trees lengthened and the day bowed to the ground, he reached the Reservoir.

His map carried a warning which read: *It is inadvisable to venture into the unfrequented northern area of the park, even during the day, except in groups.* According to the publishers of the map this area had been left in its uncultivated state; brief descriptions of its features suggested virgin forest and malarial swamp. Names filling these empty spaces were bleak or romantic – Harlem Meer, Nutter's Battery – and north of everything, like the *terra incognita* of ancient charts, Harlem was indicated in ominous red letters. Pausing only to remove his cap and wipe his forehead, he pushed on.

There were fewer landmarks to the north, and the landscape became general and interchangeable – East Meadow shading into North Meadow, the Pool running into the Loch – but he found the area to be devoid of danger. Picnickers, joggers and baseball players crowded on the pasture and scrub, and in the woodland friends and lovers strolled in twos and threes. Nothing disturbed the torpor of the hot afternoon unless it was Dudley's laboured breathing. For another two miles or so he walked without stopping, a cloud of insects accompanying him – apparently attracted by the movement of his cap's spring-loaded stalks – and he thought continuously of Martin and himself. Little by little, as the day wore on and his feet blistered and his face peeled, he convinced himself beyond any doubt that he would not see Martin alive again. His anguish was so great that he cried out, surprising himself and others. But there was no relief for his regret. Now that he tried to imagine what it was like to be Martin Prout, his imagination failed him.

On his blistered feet he went northward towards Harlem. Late sunlight caught the treetops ahead in a corona of orange light like the glare of a conflagration he was walking into. By now his anxiety had become so comprehensive, and his tread so regular and automatic, that he found it impossible to imagine what was going to happen next. He could only see himself walking for ever in exactly the same aimless and laborious manner beyond the Park into those forbidden suburbs, beyond them even, across North America, drifting like a somnambulist with nothing to think about but the past, memories of people and cities. Nothing about this image was familiar, but in its strangeness he recognized himself. Memories changed into dreams. He remembered sitting with Martin in a graveyard in Oxford, asking him, 'Do you think of death much?', and Martin shaking his head; and slowly it dawned on him, with an appalled sense of irony, that he himself was Death, and the shadow on the grass in front of him – a figure made shapeless by its expansive gestures and questioning manner – was the shadow of death.

His thoughts had become so unreal he did not realize how deserted the Park had become. The scrub he crossed now was bare, even the shadows of trees sliding off it. The woods which he entered were empty.

Silently, without reason, he climbed the narrow path that wound up the hill, stepping over the debris of fallen branches and encrusted leaves which seemed to have lain there for years. Overhead, dense foliage blocked out the sky and total shadow descended. Nothing moved in the wood, and no sounds reached him from outside. It was no cooler among these trees, it was hotter, and he removed his cap and carried it in his hand, the moon-eyes nagging his wrist. In time he came to some crumbling steps and mounted them slowly into greater shadow and heat and a profounder silence, the steps drawing him on, as steps will, with a purpose both obvious and undisclosed. They were steep and he couldn't see where they were leading until he arrived, suddenly, on a high, leafstrewn platform fronted with a classical balustrade and carved urns at either end. It was Nutter's Battery, or its ruin.

Perhaps once this platform had overlooked a view, but now the packed trees pressed round it, obliterating any such meaning. On every side there was nothing but this spillage of wood and leaf; it was as redundant as an Angkor temple in a jungle. He held his breath and listened to the silence. Not even a bird made a noise. There was only his heartbeat, and what he saw in front of him, the cracked balustrade, the lop-sided trees, the dark thatch of leaves overhead, the crumbling steps leading away and the neglected purpose of it all. He was alone with himself. His breathing quickened; he glanced over his shoulder and spun back, disorientated. Out of the silence, out of the surrounding trees, a moment of confrontation seemed to form and demand recognition. Something horrified him: himself. For a moment he stood absolutely still, barely breathing, and then he fled. Panic filled him, and he stumbled down the steps, sweeping past the trees, vaulting fallen branches and roots, down the bouncing path towards glimmers of daylight. Out of the emptiness he ran and fell and ran again away from what he could never define towards what he would never know.

At eight thirty, the sun was sinking into the western reaches of the Park, twilight about to fall, and he limped the last stretch home from Sheep Meadow to Columbus Circle. Gently the Park was transforming itself into the violent arena of the next day's newspaper headlines. Martin's body would probably feature. Obsessed by this thought he did not feel the blisters on his feet nor the cramps in his legs nor the last rays of sunlight

160

on his scorched face. His feeling was all in his memories, a naked exposure to them.

Heckscher Playground was nearly deserted. Once he had thought New York was a child's puzzle, something to be dismantled and rebuilt over and over, its big, funny shapes bigger and funnier, but he knew now that there were no fresh starts in New York, only, as elsewhere, the rigid cycles of luck, good and bad.

Exhausted, he leaned on the railings gazing at the slides, the roundabouts, climbing frames, sandpits and swings. Everyone had left the playground except one boy sitting alone on a swing. Dudley looked round for his parents, but there was no one in sight. How typical of New York to manage small tragedies as well as the big ones, lost children as well as gang rape. Over the playground the light seemed to flicker, and when he turned he saw the sun had gone down behind Central Park West, leaving its faceless, turreted masonry dark, waiting for the next dawn. The boy on the swing was sitting very still as if he was never going to go home. His head was down, a black wedge of hair canted up. Dudley sighed and turned again to go. Then he stopped and looked back.

'No,' he said.

For no reason he checked his watch and pockets. Looked again.

Then he was running towards the swings, shouting; and Martin, looking up from his shoes, saw the alarming sight of that fat, tall man lurching towards him all legs like a galloping cow, his red face distorted, his cap peeling off and sailing into the air.

They swung together awkwardly, Dudley over-large on the tiny plastic seat, not knowing what to say, Martin stiff and self-contained. Their eyes met. Martin nodded and looked down at his shoes again. There was a bruise on his forehead and a gash below his left eye. Twigs and grass were in his hair.

161

'I was just passing,' Dudley said at last.

Martin grunted.

They swung in silence.

'I thought I'd pop over and say it's okay.'

Martin said nothing.

'Television wants you. Did you know that?' He looked at his watch. They had a quarter of an hour to reach the studio.

Martin looked away and back. He said to the ground, 'Sometimes I want to smash your fucking face.'

'I've been looking for you everywhere,' Dudley said. 'I was worried.'

'Break your fucking nose.'

Dudley tried to explain.

'Knock your fucking head off,' Martin said. 'I want to get you in the toilets and carve my initials into your arm with my compass. I want to hit you so hard I puncture your lung. I want to make you drink your own piss.'

Dudley fell silent. The Park was quiet, sirens bleating faintly in the distance. Trees around the playground were solid with shadow, clenched like fists under the colourless sky. Martin swung softly, his shoes scraping the asphalt. Despite everything, Dudley could hardly stop himself from reaching out and touching Martin's shoulder, stroking his arm, his face. Instead he got off his swing and limped over to where his fallen cap lay on the ground, its antennae splayed and still. Dusting it down, he took it back to the swings, and when Martin didn't look up, he put it on Martin's head and pulled the peak over his eyes.

'Fuck. I don't want that.'

'It's a present. A magic hat.'

'Will you fuck off.'

'It helped me find you. It confers on its wearer special powers of optimism and forgiveness.'

'I don't want to be cheerful. I don't want to forgive you.'

'You won't be able to help yourself.'

'I don't want anything.'

'We can walk to the studio. It's not far. But we need to leave now. It's the truth.'

162

Martin was still and silent. 'I'll tell you one thing,' he said eventually. 'I'd like to walk. Out of this park, out of this city, right away from it, out there.' He looked over his shoulder. 'Just walk, into all that, never stop. In all that space there must be something better.'

'It's funny, I was thinking the same just a while ago.'

For the first time he looked directly at Dudley. 'Come with me.'

'Nothing would please me more.' Dudley glanced at his watch. 'But we have only ten minutes.'

Martin took off the moon cap and examined it.

'The cap's yours, Martin, keep it.'

Martin looked at the cap.

'It's ridiculous,' he said.

'I know,' Dudley said. 'But it's real. We need such rubbish because not everything can be said.'

It was night. They were hunched silhouettes among the mechanical silhouettes of the playground, their voices almost as soft as the circumambient noise of traffic. Rising like spectres in the grey light they walked away together, fading towards the distant noise of sirens, the only other noise the sound of Dudley beginning to hum as they went.

26

Through a dust-blurred, light-filled window he looked out on a grey collection of towers rising out of discount stores and diners. To the north, office blocks obscured his view of Central Park; southward, office blocks hid the theatre district. He was caught in that sweep of Broadway which crosses Eighth Avenue just south of the Park, an apparent blind alley of masonry, as difficult and unsympathetic as moments in human lives when the past and future seem separated by a void. He checked his watch. Nine fifty-five. He wanted to abandon himself to the

163

excitement of television, the drama of light and voices about to unfold, but he was tired from having walked round Central Park all day. And already there were difficulties of an unforeseen nature.

The voice at his ear.

'It's you I can't believe. You say you're his manager.'

'His friend too.'

'You say you're his manager *and* his friend, and you don't know where he is all day, you're spending all day searching for him? In my line of work they call this Fuck-Up Syndrome. I said Fuck-Up.'

'It's kind of you to mention it.'

Dudley turned and looked at the producer. His squashed features reminded him of a mammal which for the moment he couldn't name: it was Australasian, cousin to the duck-billed platypus, and made its home in areas of great desolation. He decided not to mention this. The man's hands never stopped worrying his beard or plucking his ears. His filmy eyes protruded, suggestive of anxiety or outrage.

'It's some kind of record. There's a record here. Central Park to seven hundred seventy Broadway in twelve hours? You could've flown from London quicker.' His purple-shimmer tracksuit was three sizes too big for him; bracelets and rings chinked as his fingers worked his cheeks and chin. 'What I'm saying is. You're a lucky man. Your pal, the con, he's a lucky man. We don't do this for everyone. We need that slot tonight.'

'Valuable footage,' Dudley said. 'Classic archive material. People are going to be very interested in your slot.'

'You ask anyone round here, they'll tell you I don't have patience. Patience, it's not me. You know what they call me? Blood Pressure, that's what they call me.'

'Oh God,' Dudley said under his breath.

The producer put a finger into his ear, withdrew it and stared at it in horror. He pointed it at Dudley.

'I've lived with stress for thirty years. Thirty, three zero, thirty. Emphysema, cardiogenic shock, coronary thrombosis, arrhythmia, mucous colitis, gastric ulcer. I had a seizure once.

But I'm still here, I'm not going to roll over, no matter what this country does to itself. What's wrong with your pal anyhow, he looks like someone shrunk him in the wash. What is he, some kind of midget?'

'Small but perfect,' Dudley said.

'I'm going to the studio now but I'll be right back. Understand? I don't want you to move from here. Your type make me nervous.'

The room was deserted, hot. There was one chair, a magazine face down on it, and an ashtray on an aluminium stalk. In a side room Martin was being made-up. If Martin were dead, as Dudley had imagined – his body mashed and divided, the scattered pieces decomposing on East Meadow – then he would be in that room suffering himself to be made beautiful. He could not stop himself thinking this. Because the show must go on, because Dudley is available and adamant, because this chair, this magazine, this ashtray on its silver stalk exist as solidly in an alternative world, he must take Martin's place on creaky-leather studio furniture to recompense the management of Channel 155 and the studio audience and the world at large. He will have a few words to say. 'He is dead, but his advert is immortal . . .' Elegy conferring its sensuous asceticism.

Distressed, he sighed and scratched his scalp. The lobby was deserted, hot and dull. Bored, he pushed through a door and trotted down a short corridor until he came to another door marked *Studio*. This was more exciting. Through a small chamber he went into a high-ceilinged, ill-lit bunker containing a steep, semicircular bank of seats, a black spray-painted dais and two stools. Idle cameras stood in a ring like silent devotees of the scene. Enormous black drapes covered the walls, disappearing into the dim, articulated ceiling, scaffolding of vacant lights, girders and cables. He looked round in awe. The ordinary dead do not merit such mausoleums. Then the producer was hustling towards him, and he cultivated nonchalance.

'You,' the producer said, coming up close. 'You don't listen, you're not a good listener. I frustrate easy when people don't listen. How can I make you listen?'

Dudley began to talk about the heat and dullness of the lobby, but while he was speaking the producer rolled up his tracksuit leg and turned a lumpy, discoloured calf towards him. 'Thrombophlebitis,' he said. '1988. Minor surgery.' He pulled up his tracksuit top and showed a whitish scar below his navel. 'Duodenal ulcer. 1989. Major surgery.' He pulled down the elastic waistband of his sweat pants, giving a glimpse of black jockeys and a small cleft scar in his hip. 'Hip replacement. 1990. Seven weeks on crutches. Constant pain, agony. Don't talk to me about heat, don't talk to me about boredom. Talk to me about life and death. Talk to me about your friend the con, the midget. Do you understand what I'm saying?'

Dudley was quiet.

'I frustrate very, very easy,' he went on. 'Also I have this other problem. I enrage easy. Rage is bad for the heart. Worse than frustration. The worst. Do you understand?'

'I take your point,' Dudley said. He looked past the producer to the dais. 'By the way, I notice that there are only two chairs laid out, I assume for Martin and the interviewer. They should certainly have priority. But is there any chance of putting out an extra one for me?'

The producer was holding his own wrist, apparently taking his pulse. 'You, you're coming with me. I don't want you on the set, you're a dangerous man, you could cause me lasting damage.'

'Will I have a chance to talk to Martin before you start shooting?'

'There are no consolations in this life. Ask me about consolations. There aren't any.'

They left together, and as they went a single spot suddenly lit up the dais, the stuff of showtime.

The observation room was a girdered eyrie clamped to the underside of the roof, a window running along its length from which the dais could be viewed directly below. Dudley stood with his back to this window, looking inward at the technology:

nine television screens set into a wall; a bank of dials; a long table-top of buttons and monitors. On three screens, like components of an abstract montage, were facets of the studio: a stool, the other stool, a corner of dais; and on another, a clock face with no numbers, a single hand gliding slowly round, encountering nothing. His reaction to all this was unexpected. He was startled by its purity. Television seemed to bear no relation to the world except in random fragments, and its style was cold and aloof. As he watched, Martin's face appeared on four of the screens, his hair swept back from his forehead and bound in a ponytail. The bruises and gashes had been erased by cosmetics, and his face was emptied of any expression. This too was an aspect of television's purity, the iconographic, empty face – but Dudley felt no jealousy, only a slight possessiveness in seeing Martin turn into an image for mass consumption. Going to the window, he tapped on the glass and waved, waiting for Martin to look up.

'You notice something?' the producer said behind him. 'Everyday more and more sickos. You notice that?'

His colleagues, busy with instruments, ignored him. Below, a technician was bending over Martin with a fistful of wires, delving in his clothes, fitting him with an earpiece. The spotlight shivered, faded, brightened, narrowed.

'They're all transsexuals, they're having all these operations, and getting all this therapy. And that's just the cameramen.' He put a cigarette in his mouth and crumpled the pack.

Dudley pressed his nose to the glass and waved. He was looking down on silent desolation, two survivors sitting bathed in light and shadowy figures on the margins hunched over cameras like gunners. He had not expected such loneliness. He tapped on the glass and waved again.

'Tell me you want to jump,' the producer said. 'We'll open the window. People live too long in this country.'

The countdown began.

'Know one thing?' the producer said. 'I waited all day for this. All day, that's how long I waited. For this homosexual shit. It's watched by no one, it's presented by some freak with

167

too much state education, and the only reason I'm here is because no one in this network can stand my guts.'

'Ten seconds,' his assistant said.

'Is it a wonder I don't relax? Once I did Carson, I did Letterman. Now I wait all day for five minutes of excrement. That's my day.'

'Five seconds,' his assistant said.

'It's what I do, it's who I am. I don't want your sympathy. Sympathy? It's not me, you can keep your sympathy for the sickos and weirdos.'

'Cue camera one.'

On four screens four identical faces gave a severe but playful look of self-importance. The faces were talking with one voice about the art of advertisements, citing McLuhan and Postman. The voice was flat and unemotive, as if no one but Dudley and the producer and his colleagues were listening.

'What are we to make of the commercial? Experts compute that by the time we reach the modest age of thirty we've seen about a million television commercials. But what influence – aesthetic, political, moral – do they have? With me is Mr Martin Prout, classical actor turned commercial personality. Martin Prout, the commercial is art as banality, true or false?'

Martin's faces appeared on the screens, blank, floating and ghastly. He seemed not to have heard the question, but stared off, eyebrows knitted, above the camera-line. Dudley's heart sank.

The producer shouted at his microphone, 'Whatever your name is, Trout, he's talking to you.'

The interviewer, looking confused, said, 'Well, the commercial as art is one issue, the commercial as *philosophy* is another, equally interesting. In your experience, Mr Prout, would you agree that in the late twentieth century the commercial is the paradigm of all other discourse?'

Martin's faces reappeared, briefly and silently, all turning from left to right, as if he had just discovered his whereabouts, and was slowly taking it in.

'You mean you don't agree?' the interviewer asked.

The producer shouted, 'We don't have time to rerun, we can cut, just get the mute to talk, will you? Ask him something he can understand. I don't want any of your faggot highbrow garbage.'

Martin said, 'Television has advantages. No one else exists.'

Four faces of the interviewer all talked wildly of the nihilism of commercials, an immense single sentence doomed never to have an end. In the observation room Dudley put his hands to his face. Once he would have relished such fluent theorizing, now he felt sickened.

Martin interrupted the interviewer. 'Adverts aren't interesting. Ask me about my childhood, ask me where I went to school.'

The producer had left his instruments and was pacing the astrocarpet, pawing the window. He wanted to know why he had been assigned an arts and media show by assholes at the network, he wanted to know why he had spent his life dying for other people. He knew, of course, that farce was the mode he operated best in.

Dudley sidled over to the vacated microphone and spoke at it in a soft voice.

'Martin. This is the voice of your conscience. You're doing well, very well. The man's a windbag. Pop it.' He was rewarded by the sight of four faces of the interviewer swivelling upwards in momentary surprise, and four hands clutching four left ears. He was amazed and delighted that he could do this.

'Get away from that microphone, douchebag,' the producer said, knuckling a cigarette into his mouth.

There were the screens, and there was the studio, and there was the observation room, and they appeared to Dudley in his uncertain and exhausted state three separate dimensions. He himself was partial and incomplete, and so was media reality; he was licensed for bad behaviour, as the insane are. Comments

169

made by Martin about the illusory nature of character came back to him without censure.

The interviewer went on, 'Leaving aside the philosophy of commercials, I want to pursue something else here. Let me try something out on you. Commercials tell you nothing about the product, they tell you everything about the consumers, what kind of headaches they have, dreams, tastes, ambitions, fears, what kind of underwear they prefer. So what I'm saying is, they hold up a sort of mirror. Yes?'

'You see yourself reflected in the camera's eye,' Martin said. 'That's what we were taught. That's when I was at Borstal. It's not called Borstal. Call it prison. Television sees only one thing at a time, not like stage. Not like pantomime with its rabbits and clowns. Why are we talking about this?'

Dudley, frowning, bent the microphone almost into his mouth and whispered, 'Engagement with nonchalance. I like it. But please Martin, I beg you, change the subject. What about feature films? What about the great classical roles?'

'Will you get away from that frigging microphone!' the producer shouted.

The interviewer veered on his stool, smiling falsely and warbling, 'Let's talk about you.' Confusion showed in his four faces. 'You're a celebrity now, sort of.'

Martin said, 'I know exactly who I am. Do you know who you are?'

'We of the late twentieth century', the interviewer went on, 'are witnessing a new phenomenon regarding commercials. What I'm saying is, first you had celebrities making commercials, now you have commercials turning people into celebrities. Know what I mean? You're one.'

Martin said, 'I don't know what you're talking about.'

In the observation room the producer screamed, 'Prison, the only reason we're interviewing the dork is prison! Talk prison, faggot-head!'

'Something I'd like to move on to,' the interviewer said, 'is your time in prison.' His faces were rigid, damp and florid on the four screens.

Dudley felt the whole scene sliding away from him; he said harshly into the microphone, 'Don't do it. Get out of this mess.'

Martin responded directly for the first time. 'I was in prison for several years. I learned to act there. It's in my records. Ask me what I went to prison for.'

'Can I ask what you went to prison for?'

'I killed a man.'

In the observation room the producer spat a cigarette from his mouth. Dudley gawped.

'Is this the truth?' the producer shouted. 'We heard different. We heard buggery. We heard sodomy. We heard small boys. We're unprepared for murder.' His face was wildly enthusiastic. Dudley turned in horror from Martin's faces on the screens.

'Martin,' he said into the microphone. 'Martin,' he pleaded. 'Please don't, not on television. It'll ruin us.'

'Killed a man?' the interviewer said, his four faces helpless.

The producer wrestled the microphone away from Dudley. 'Are you deaf?' he screamed into it. 'This is murder, we have to do something with this. Get in close!' Martin's eyes appeared in pairs, then his mouths.

'This man,' the mouths said. 'It was me or him. It could've been me. But it was him. I went to prison because I killed him. That's where I learned to act. It's all written down. I killed him with a razor.'

'We got one minute!' the producer shouted. 'I want blood!' He was back at the window, both hands in his hair, three-quarters demented. Dudley was inert behind a bank of instruments, remote as if he had been swept into a world in which he could not exist. At the window the producer was beating his head with the savagery of a clockwork toy. On four screens Martin fantasized about murder. A flick of a switch, a turn of a dial, the sliding of a lever seemed to have achieved all this.

Dudley suddenly lost his temper. 'Martin!' he shouted into the microphone. 'For God's sake, stop it! It's gone far enough.'

The interviewer was saying, 'You're that rare phenomenon, Mr Prout, murderer turned television star. Tell us more about the murder.'

'He was the opposite of me, but he was my double. There are people like that, they're what you should have been. We had this pact. Ask me about my friends.'

'Razor?'

'It was old. It had a funny handle.'

'I mean, you killed him with it?'

'It was him or me.'

'You argued? You had a fight?'

'He was asleep. We shared a room. A cell. In prison. He had his mouth open. He always had his mouth open, asleep or awake, he was the opposite of me.'

'Thirty seconds,' the producer screamed. 'I want carnage, I want major bleeding.'

'Martin!' Dudley shouted again, wrestling the microphone back towards him. 'What are you doing? What are you doing to me?'

'I want to get this, Mr Prout, he was your best friend, your only friend, but you killed him.'

'I hear his voice all the time. His mouth was open. I cut his mouth.'

'Christ, you mean, *the lips*? You mean you slashed his *lips*? The fleshy bits? Can you give us a description here?'

'Sometimes promises aren't said, they just exist. I put the razor inside his mouth.'

'We're out of time,' the producer moaned. 'We're shit out of time.'

Dudley sat shaking, tight-lipped and silent, and the day fell away from him, his search for Martin, his feelings of tenderness and loyalty, the excitement of television, until nothing remained but four strange faces on four screens which he rejected as the awakening dreamer shakes off a nightmare, with revulsion.

The clock hand on the screen began to glide again as the interviewer said in a rush, 'Mr Prout, I know this has been not easy. What I mean to say is, it's incredible. I mean, you did this, and here you are.'

'I suppose so.'

'I mean, all this is true.'

'It must be.'

'You don't know?'

'I'm tired of questions. I want something that can't be questioned. I'd like to travel.'

The producer had bent the microphone off the desk. It was in his hand. He screamed gibberish into it, anguish of a private nature. The screens showed the interviewer's four faces signing off, a rattled résumé of nothing that had happened, a prelude to a vanished or imaginary past, and then the farce was over and the screens were empty. Dudley stared at them as if they might yield a meaning, but it seemed to him that television possesses no memory, not even the memory of dream.

The producer strode around him, foaming, the remains of the microphone in his hand, and Dudley watched him, not listening but observing the low, discontinuous movements of his legs and the impaired flight of his arms. Eventually he made out some intelligible phrases. 'All my life,' the man was saying. 'I've said give me five and I'll be okay. I knew that if I could hang on my time would come.' He stopped and looked at Dudley, his eyes shining. 'You,' he said. 'You know nothing, you wouldn't know great television if it grabbed you by the nuts. *That!*' He pointed towards the window. '*That* was great television. After that I feel five years, ten years younger. After that I know I'm going to live for ever.' His face was flushed, his hair wild, his tracksuit twisted round him in folds as if it had been soaked and wrung out. He was ecstatic. His right hand pounded his heart.

Nothing could have disgusted Dudley more. 'I have to go,' he said. 'I'm not well.' As he went, out of the bright lights of the observation room into the dark corridor and down the unlit stairs, he could hear the producer shouting after him. 'Don't talk to me about your health! Your health? It doesn't interest me. Talk to me about ratings, about promotion, talk to me about the best years of my life . . .'

The concrete stairwell spiralled below him and he went down

173

into it with a wavering step, hands groping in front of him. There was one thing only in his mind: to get out of the building without seeing Martin. He did not trust himself to see Martin.

At the foot of the stairs was a lavatory, and he went in and stood looking bleakly at the surgical white tiles, the smeared mirror, the aluminium urinal with its melted wheel of disinfectant, gum wrapper and cigarette butt. Resting his forehead on the tiles he urinated for three whole minutes as if the last dregs of his body were leaking out of him, listening to the sounds of voices and footsteps in the lobby, a buffeting of doors, all fading into the gurgle of the drain, a trickle, the last echo of day when there is nothing of it left but regret. He thought perhaps he might cry, but as he stood in a deformed attitude zipping himself up he was halted by an unexpected click from the cubicle next to him, a pert insane noise like the turn of a key in an empty house. A footstep followed and someone came out and stood unseen round the blind side of the door. Slowly the door swung back with a wistful creak – a noise expressing more of change, of disappointment, anger and sorrow, than any number of midnight conversations – and Martin appeared, furtive and doom-laden, his ponytail adrift.

Their eyes met and there was a moment of silence when Dudley began to bite his lip. Then the urinals began to gush together. It was the moment for an outburst, a long excoriation, a detailed critical account of Martin's behaviour in New York, his irascibility, his sulks, his hostility, his inability to understand Dudley – but Dudley was not suited to such moments. He tugged at his zip and straightened up. His eyes blinked back tears. Martin had not moved at all, his face was that weird mask of oblivion.

'I know what you're going to say,' he said, his voice barely rising above the hiss of the plumbing.

Dudley waited.

'I never went to Borstal. It's the truth.'

Dudley nodded.

'I went to the asylum,' Martin said. He held out his arms like Lazarus emerging from the grave and Dudley moaned and

174

turned abruptly, pushed his way through the door into the lobby and fled, with a quickening, righteous step, down the street, not daring to look back.

27

It was midnight in the Village, hot, dark and festive; Bleecker Street was crowded with browsers, clubbers, kids on skateboards, shoppers and strollers – a bustle nostalgic for Bohemia. Among the bars and cafés, the late-night record marts, hair salons and leatherwear boutiques they shopped or sat on the sidewalks, shouting to passers-by and setting off chain reactions of laughter. Sometimes they glanced towards Martin who stood alone, at odds with the prevailing sociability, in the shadow between an Afghani restaurant and a store selling cabalistic silverware, staring across the road. In Joey Blue's All-Nite Unisex Hair Parlour Dudley was having his hair restyled. Martin could see him settling himself into a chair, swaddled up to the neck in a long white robe. He was passing a piece of paper to the girl, and indicating it, a picture of some sort, a desirable image.

He had trailed Dudley here down Eighth Avenue, the sidewalks almost deserted at that hour except for a few teetering whores and men with squat dogs on long leashes – those who seem to know only the dreariness of New York nights. By the time Dudley stood at the corner of Bleecker and MacDougal where the crowds began, Martin was already part of the street; he wore an army jacket and dark glasses and he carried in his pocket Dudley's lost razor. Perfectly erect, his hands bunched into his pockets like a small boy caught between self-consciousness and elation, he walked down the opposite side of the street from Dudley. His face had hardened so much over the last few days he looked much older.

Dudley walked in an almost infirm way, slowly, as if his feet hurt him, as if he bent under the heaviness of a life laying trails, depleted by the constant sacrifice of character to plot. He tiptoed gingerly into a shop called US Leathercraft.

After a while he appeared again, carrying a large shopping bag, and made his way to Chelsea Army Navy. No detail escaped Martin: he saw the bag, his walk, the way his head wagged up and down. He made no guesses, he knew instinctively Dudley's anxiety and frivolity, the slowness of his search and all his searches.

Over the next hour he followed him to East Village Leather, Belts and Buckles, Dave's, Outrider, SoHo Generation, Bleecker Boots and, finally, the Caffe Maggio.

It was getting late. Dudley went into the café wearing long white shorts, smiley T-shirt, basketball boots and baseball cap, and emerged fifteen minutes later clad head to foot in black leather – black leather boots; black leather trousers belted with a silver buckle; black leather vest; black leather motor-cycle jacket with bi-swing back, underarm footballs and silver studs; and black leather peaked cap. He posed for a moment on the sidewalk as if for Martin's benefit, looking left and right – the pantomimic gesture of the lost – and then he moved off into the crowds towards Joey Blue's, just another tall man with an awkward, heavy way of walking, his head rolling up and down as he looked at the front of his new jacket and his new boots. Martin followed. Gone were the days when Dudley bounced on his toes. Now he seemed hardly to be able to maintain a forward momentum. Martin watched him. Everything about Dudley, his slouch, his tired shoulders, his nodding head and ponderous arms suggested that he could not go much further. He had come too far. And it was not really fatigue slowing Dudley down, burdening him even after he had rid himself of his shopping bags. Martin knew what it was. It was guilt. In the chequerwork of street light and shadows Dudley was judged.

*

176

Martin leaned his back against the wall and watched. He was even more intently watchful than the Negroes who stood gawkily on the sidewalk behind their rugs, ivory ornaments and painted gourds, watching everything. This was how it had always been, waiting for a call from Proctor, and now it was the same, though the tables had been turned and the roles reversed. Like everything else, revenge has its own momentum.

In Joey Blue's, Dudley was tilted in his chair.

There was a noise down the street. Two old men came running slowly, with great effort, in the middle of the road, one after the other. Cars pulled over for them. Of all the passions only fury could account for their overwhelming effort; they were oblivious to everything but their rage.

In Joey Blue's Dudley swapped chairs and sat upright in front of a man plying an electric razor.

The first old man drew level with Martin and passed him, grey-faced and intent. Then the second came past, grotesque with the strain of his pursuit. The crashing of their feet and the faint explosions of their breath were the only sounds they made, and these died as they passed. The distance between them had not altered and did not seem likely to, they would run like that, in that frozen combination, out across America and plunge, one after the other, into the Pacific.

Dudley was sitting in his shroud with his back to the street, caressed and talkative, and soon the men disappeared and the scene resumed its bland bustle. At twelve thirty Dudley came down the steps from the salon on to the sidewalk and paused again – for who if not for Martin staring out of his shadow? Almost all of his hair had gone. A faint blond aura clung to his scalp. A pink-faced, baby-bird head sat diminutive on a tough-leathered body. Cautiously he put up a hand and a cab stopped. Martin began to move forward. The cab cruised slowly away, and Martin walked down Bleecker after it, as stark as a symbol, a grim reaper in T-shirt and jeans. The Negroes called to him as he passed, gesturing to their rugs and gourds, but he ignored them.

177

28

It was one thirty in the morning and the moment he had dreamed of for years, an entry into clubland and an inducement to mingle with the great and the notorious. He stood with his empty glass in the hot and lurid crush at one of the bars of the Gold Coast Muscle Club, looking round at dimly famous faces in the partying crowd and feeling awful. Partly he was drunk. Partly he was having some sort of breakdown.

Bella was standing a little way off, watching him with curiosity. In common with rest of the crowd she was wearing very little in the way of formal clothing: raggy, knicker-length, cut-off denims over white fishnets, and a clinging white lace blouse which only partially obscured the dark, mobile outlines of her breasts. She still had hair, but it had changed again, hanging in long, straight braids, Cleopatra-style. Dudley was under her spell more than ever, but even the scintillating progress of testosterone through his body could not alleviate his feelings of confusion and despair.

He took the drinks and went to stand with her at a balcony which overlooked a dance floor packed with writhing figures and saturated with confetti-pieces of coloured lights flung off a revolving globe high overhead. A nearby mezzanine housed a large screen splayed with black-and-white images from old B-movies – faces, automobiles, buildings, cities – versions of history loved equally by fashion designers and sociologists. Beyond that, although obscured by the effects of a laser display, were other levels containing other bars and other dance floors; and everywhere were staircases, escalators and elevators linking them together in a flickering constellation. It was as though a design by Piranesi (those dungeons, those staircases, archways and buttresses) had been realized in glass, chrome and mock marble by the architects of Trump Tower. There was an obligatory waterfall and vague foliage spilling out from unseen sources.

Dudley handed Bella her drink and began to explain to her, slowly, the paradox of spectacle. It seemed to him that the more spectacular the effects of a particular room, the more the viewer expects a greater spectacle still in the room beyond. This viewer asks himself: if such skill is evident *here*, what wonders are there just round the corner? It is a mistake ever to attempt a culmination of effects. How much more intelligent to collude with the viewer by suggesting the gratification of his senses elsewhere.

'In this room,' Dudley said, sweeping his glass in front of him, 'everything suggests a somewhere else. What else could account for so many different, so many ambiguous levels, so many staircases leading to who knows where, so many elevators and escalators? The architect is playing with our expectations, with our unreasonable and unappeasable desires. This is human nature after all, not to realize that there may be a nowhere.'

'Tell me one thing,' Bella said. 'Where's Psycho?'

'Martin?' Dudley said. He looked into his glass as into a fathomless pool. 'Martin couldn't make it. A slight indisposition.'

'What happened at Channel 155?'

'Channel 155?' Again the divination of his martini. 'Nothing happened. He was indisposed for that too. We couldn't make it.'

Bella shrugged. 'I don't care enough not to believe you.'

On the movie screen below a plane was taking off, unpeeling from its shadow on the runway. Dudley finished his drink and forced a smile.

These were moments he had dreamed of but he couldn't enjoy them, he was too unhappy. It was suddenly three o'clock and he was drunk on his feet, talking or pretending to talk to Bella and two other girls who appeared to be starlets of the stage or screen, he couldn't remember which. They were both petite, one blonde and the other brunette, and both sipped from their cocktail glasses with the same intent expression. Dudley had

179

not understood a word either of them had said. Noting in himself the babyish mannerisms of the very drunk – his thoughts tending to apprehend the obvious with the wild force of intuition, his wide eyes making delayed sorties after passing figures – he glanced over the balcony and saw on the screen a man with mad eyes holding a gun to the head of a teary blonde while the smooth-jawed hero dithered.

The brunette starlet said, 'Just some guy name of Trout or something. Midget. Looked queer.'

Dudley started, froze, and slowly put his glass up to his face.

'Bi,' the other starlet said. 'They're all bi now.'

'Killed some other guy.'

'They're violent. It's because they're confused.'

Bella raised an eyebrow. 'Where did you see this?' she asked.

'That show on 155. That dreadful show.'

Bella looked at Dudley. 'Well?' she said.

Dudley looked from Bella to the blonde to the brunette.

'Do you know this guy?' the blonde asked him.

Dudley removed his face from his glass. 'No,' he said, and coughed once. 'No, good God no. I don't know why you think that. I'm English, I come from England, I don't know people like that.' He turned to Bella, his face whiter than usual, as if to ask, 'What more can I do, I've denied him twice?' and then he said, 'Would you like to dance, perhaps it's time to dance.' Taking her elbow he led her away from the starlets down a glass staircase towards a dance floor.

At the bottom she said, 'You want to dance?'

He stopped. 'No, I don't think so. I think I want to curl up in the foetus position. Do you want to dance?'

'I don't dance. I do deals, I do blow, I don't dance.' They stood watching the dancers, the men moving their arms and legs in slow, disconnected revolutions, the women grinding through pelvic routines. Someone, their sex uncertain in the swirl of lights, was topless. There was everything in the party that Dudley could wish for, but he had no enthusiasm for it. After a while he became conscious that he was endeavouring to explain to Bella the theological function of whirling dervishes in Muslim fraternities. 'The expression of sexual and religious ecstasy are generally close,' he concluded and fell silent. Looking away, not knowing where to look, he saw on the movie screen a man and a woman kissing, he tall and stooped, and she svelte and submissive, dragging him down with a gloved arm.

Bella yawned and said, 'Think you can handle a little action, Dud?'

Wildly he imagined himself looming over her, her arm round his neck, her fingers in his cropped stubble. He nodded.

'We're done with this crowd. Let's go.'

'We're leaving?'

'Not exactly.'

'I am ready.'

They circled the dance floor, she leading, he following, and made their way into the shadowy recesses behind the DJ's podium where they came to a door marked *Members Only*.

'Okay?' Bella asked, turning.

He nodded. 'Very okay.' Although he did not know what waited behind the door he felt a twinge of pleasure at the condition of entrance.

'Feeling strong?'

He raised his eyebrows, puzzled. 'Strongish,' he said cautiously. Her face was very close to his, he could feel her breath on his face, a concoction of alcohol, tobacco and watermelon bubblegum. 'Why do you ask?' he asked. 'Do we have to break the door down?'

She held up a key, a narrow glint, bent and fitted it in the lock. Her breasts bumped his arm, a soft, quilted sensation, valedictory, and the door swung back. Fluorescent light blinded him and he dashed his hand to his face. But he did not ask where he was going; he did not cry aloud as he might have, 'How many more portals must I pass through before I reach my just destination?', he followed her quietly down a long, bright corridor carpeted with coarse matting, the walls decorated with framed posters of men and women with appallingly

181

misshapen arms holding huge weights above their glistening contorted faces. Who were they if not the damned? *Lasciate Ogni Speranza Voi Ch'entrate!*

'So this is where the Muscle bit of the Gold Coast Club is hidden away,' he said.

They reached the end of the corridor and turned into another, equally long. Here the posters were replaced by mirrors, and in them an athletic-looking moll was leading a ponderous male, as a bold child might lead a drugged bear, a short chain passed through the sensitive flesh of his nose. Noticeable were her stride, her swing, her profile, her beauty and her buttocks. Noticeable also were his apprehension, his fear, his anger, his guilt. These images were like framed states of desire displayed for choice. But there was no choice.

'I don't know if I mentioned this before,' Dudley said. 'But I'm worried about Martin. Terrified. I think he's going to kill himself, in fact I'm sure of it.'

'What happened at 155?'

'It was a mess, and then I walked out. I mean I left him there. I didn't tell him about this party.' He caught sight of himself in a mirror. 'In the interview he made up these stories about killing people, I don't know why. Perhaps because he's depressed enough to kill himself. I try to understand him but I can't. I feel very guilty.' The mirror showed the image of guilt, a mournful scowl.

Near the end of the corridor were two fire doors, and going through these, they heard the music for the first time, a vague pounding. Two doors on their left were marked *Hombres* and *Signorinas*, and in front of them was an unmarked door through which came the music, loud, metallic bangs and the slithery noises of uncoiling rope. They stood outside for a moment, Dudley wincing and running his hands across his cropped head, then Bella pushed open the door, the music roared, and they entered the gymnasium.

It was not big but, lined with mirrors, it looked infinite. Shiny equipment was multiplied in endless series, confusing the real and the illusory. In the middle of the room freestanding machines were shelved with banks of bullion-like weights on cords, bristling with seats, saddles, benches, handlebars and halters. Round the edges were rows of cardiovascular bicycles, Nexus rowing ergonometers, Powerjog running machines, Vertical PeckDecks, sit-up benches, leg-extenders and batteries of wall-bars hung like racks in an interrogation chamber with ropes, belts, loops of waxed cord, metal clips, elasticated bands and strong gloves.

It was like a miniature city built of puzzles and reduplicated *ad infinitum* on all sides.

'The Chapel Perilous,' Dudley said. 'I've been wondering what it would look like.' He looked very nervous.

Each machine had its martyr: they stretched on, squatted against, hung from, crouched under or sat behind their contraptions, each wearing that badge of shame and honour, the luminous latex body-stocking in pink, green and orange varieties, soaked a darker shade around the neck, the small of the back and the groin. Dudley flinched as a man next to him began to beat a punchball: *thocketa-thocketa-thocketa-thocketa*.

There was something odd about this gymnasium. One of the inmates, straddling a low-slung bench, appeared to be drinking from a bottle of liquor. Another, hanging upside down from a wall-bar, seemed to be smoking something. There was a peculiar smell.

They stepped back outside.

'Extremely interesting,' Dudley said. 'Do you know the word *quemadero*? A Spanish term denoting a place where heretics are tortured and burned.'

'We'll need to find you kit.'

'Kit?'

'You want to pump iron in those?'

Dudley coughed. 'I fear my iron-pumping days are over. It's also worth saying that I'm drunk, depressed and incapable.'

'Let me tell you about yourself. You are the great Dud, you hustle, you hassle, you kick ass. You're style king. You handle quantities of action. You were born to pump iron.'

183

'I was rather asthmatic as a child.'

'You're going all the way to the top, the sky's the limit, the world's your oyster.'

'I have this slight cardiovascular thing.' Dudley tapped his chest sadly. 'Dodgy ticker.'

'You're the all-time winner, you're top banana, you're hung like a horse. You want to strip down and sweat out. I'm trying to comfort you. You need comfort. If you die, you die, but if you're about to die, I have great qualifications in resuscitation, you wouldn't believe how good.'

There was a long pause while a pressure built inside his chest. He licked his lower lip. 'Do you think you'll be able to find anything my size?' he said.

It was not an orthodox weight-training session they were joining. Dudley, who knew nothing of orthodox weight-training sessions, concluded this when he saw the drinks bar set up on a leg-extender. Six-packs of beer were stacked in cool-bags under the bench-press. Bottles of liquor were wedged into the wall-bars. An upturned mirror on the floormat displayed a range of smokables and sniffables.

He looked around. Some people were working furiously at the machines, others relaxed with a drink, some lay on their backs smoking. It was as if by some mad logic the party in the Piranesian suite continued here, supercharged with the erotica of physical culture: the latex, the shiny chrome and mirrors, the music (one long rap with whiplash scratching and dustbin-lid drums), the crash of weights, squeak of pulleys, human snorts and grunts. The air was saturated with the intimate stink of sweat.

He was wearing magenta latex. Bella was dressed in a high-gloss tracksuit of brilliant green and bubblegum pink, her hair gathered in a bead-ratcheted coil at the back of her head. Without her spike-heeled shoes she appeared shorter than before, but more feline and powerful, rolling on the balls of her feet.

He accepted a smoke from a muscular woman encased in a

stretchsuit of blinding yellow who reached above her, took hold of a pair of handlebars and began a series of chin-ups, her apish arms rigid with muscle, her lean expressionless face glowing. Out of consideration he turned away and studied a poster in which a cartoon man stood dwarfish on distorted legs with a hugely stacked barbell resting across his impossible shoulders. This was labelled *Hack Squat Lunge. Anterior Deltoids*, he read. *Trapezius, Latissimus Dorsi, Erectors, Pectorals, Flexors, Abdominals, Gluteals*. At the sight of these incantations he knew he was among barbarians whose ways would be inexplicable to him and whose forms of sorrow and joy would be freakishly strange.

Callisthenics were being performed by men and women lined against wall-bars, their hips swivelling and thrusting, caryatids come to life and in torment or ecstasy. Next to them was a fire door marked *This door is alarmed*.

Bella went past and he said to her, 'Look, what I really want to do is talk about Martin.'

'Really?' she said.

'Really.'

'Get serious, will you? You need comfort. You need toning. This is the place.'

He was far out of his depth, no longer knowing what time it was, nor what he was doing there. He was aware of being drunk and reckless, but he felt, obscurely, that this was good for him, a trial by fire or forced metamorphosis from which he might emerge if not more like his dreams then less like his nightmares. He thought he understood now how people changed in crisis, in conflagration, with the willingness of the doomed; and he went over to the mirror on the floor, randomly selected a puce tablet with the letter V stamped on it and, with the greatest possible insouciance, swallowed it. Immediately he felt sure that he was going to die.

Then it was later, how much later he did not know. He had not died but he had been gradually cut off from himself and at the same time filled with an overwhelming sense of his own presence – his skin, his breathing, the movement of his eyes – until he felt like an underwater diver in his deep, sealed calm, moving weightlessly, as in a heavy tide, through the strangely harmonizing images of the gym.

It seemed that he was occupied at that moment watching Bella. She was mounting the PeckDeck and settling into a posture of seated crucifixion, legs akimbo, scowling dead ahead. She was squeezing her arms together in that slow, exaggerated handclap, and the great rack of weights behind her was rising and falling. As he watched, she disentangled herself from the machine and peeled off her tracksuit, producing the sudden colour clash of cyan sweatshirt and scarlet micro-shorts. She existed in slow motion: standing with her legs apart, bending to touch the side of her calves (gastrocenmiuses in her own language) – once, twice, three times – her breasts bumping heavily; then rotating from the fascia lata, swinging on the axis of her pelvis in a greased rhythm, heat and provocation radiating from her. His breathing intensified, like the sound of surf in his ears, the last noise a drowning man hears.

Later still it occurred to him that for some time he had done nothing but watch Bella, monitoring her progress round the room. He knew her squats, her V-ups and one-arm French presses, her lunges and leg-curls and all the ramifications of her body as it braced and crouched and stretched to the crash of chrome and slurp of rope. He knew every shade of expression on her glistening, stressful face. He knew how dark and gritted with hairs her armpits were when she raised her arms above her head. He knew with what slow, strenuous rhythm she ground her pelvis towards the man next to her as they touchd each other's toes. He even knew something of the background from which she stood out, the sighing and grunting and moaning, eyes protruding, veins bulging, shoulders jerking, hands slapping, heads nodding. Dudley was nodding his head too. He was part of the pattern.

186

Patterns within patterns. As soon as Bella finished on a machine, he took her place, and slipping on to the seat she had just vacated he felt, along with the raw warmth and slight dampness, a sort of bond with her, a confederacy. He watched as she stripped off another layer of clothing. She was down to a cut-off cotton T-shirt which ended with the underhang of her breasts and rose-pink bikini-bottoms slashed away at the sides. With aromatic oil she massaged her skin, her quadriceps and adductors, abdominals and pectorals, her wet, grappling hands disappearing beneath her T-shirt.

It did not upset hm that each time he ensconced himself on her abandoned seat he had to reduce the kilos on the machine before he could operate it; he marvelled at her physical power, at the rhythm of her strength. Such a rhythm he could only aspire to in vain. When she sauntered away from the rowing machine he stumbled towards it. When she slipped off the PeckDeck he hauled himself on to it. When she vaulted off the leg-extender he clambered crabwise over it. And all the time her reflections in the mirrors were gliding away, those gluteals undulating with a delicate, weighty swing, oddly suggestive of sorrow and loss; and on the PeckDeck (for the twentieth time) his arms were meeting in a clumsy, strained embrace of nothing. He couldn't keep up with her reflections, there were too many of them, from behind, from the sides, from above, from below: he saw too much and attained too little, and there was nothing in his head but those empty patterns of desire.

He didn't know what time it was but at some point he became aware that he was sane again. It seemed to him like the terrible, temporary lucidity of a dying man, and instantly his thoughts were fixed on Martin.

He was lying on his back on the Bench Press with the aluminium bar suspended an inch from his nose. Bella was leaning over him, an apparition with a powerful smell, lacy sweat decorating her abdominals which were on an exact level with his eyes.

187

That amused look.

She said, 'This is the game you wanted to play.'

'Yes,' he said. His legs were cold and he shivered.

She said, 'Kick ass, Dud. Start on fifty, lift ten and come down ten, and go again. This is the game. I give orders in that voice. You do it. You are Muscle King. You say very little.'

He struggled, let out a grunt of astonishment, and his knees hit his chest. The bar stayed where it was.

'Give it some.'

He heaved again, eyes popping.

'Go with the flow,' she said. 'You're under orders. You're the man. You're numero uno, top banana, premier personality of the televisual world. How much jargon do you need?'

He kicked and wriggled. The bar did not move. 'I can't,' he said in a gasp. 'I can't stop thinking about Martin.'

'Wait. Come down to forty.' She adjusted the machine, and he pushed again, his face seeming to leap out of his face as he strained. Slowly the bar moved away from his nose.

'Big man,' Bella said. 'Keep it going, big man. You've got it licked.'

Deep in his chest, soft and comic like the chimes of a cuckoo-clock, he heard a clicking noise, a gentle creak, possibly mortal.

'You're top man,' Bella was saying. 'Mr Strongarm, the man with the power, the man who makes it happen.'

'I'm not, you know,' Dudley said, with the last of his strength.

'Okay, now go down to thirty.' She bent forward to adjust the weight again, and Dudley, groaning and rolling his head, caught a glimpse of a shadowed, quivering breast, a giant shy anemone.

'Hit it,' she said.

'I can't,' Dudley said. 'I can't.'

'Don't think about anything. Nothing but yourself, think about how strong you are. You are the strongest man in the known world. You are number one Conan, the man with fire in his arms. Nothing can resist you.'

The bar rose once. Then twice. Dudley yelped as he sucked

in air, his breathing was an irregular series of yelps, as if he were a hound whom a larger animal had gored, leaving him to trail his spilling, jumbled coils of pink and grey intestines into some dark place to die. These were his thoughts, jumbled and lurid.

'I'm comforting you, Dud. Get comforted. You are the mover and groover, you shake it up, you give it some, you pump it up.'

'Stop,' Dudley gasped. 'Stop it.'

But Bella LaRose ignored him. 'Let's go again,' she said, readjusting the weight. 'Twenty on the clock. Come on, strong man. You're under orders. Do your stuff.'

If he turned his head through ninety degrees he would look into her navel, that dark, roseate bud of skin, and perhaps, looking into it, he would see a reflection of himself as he might have been. This seemed to be his only possibility of original success, a desperate and forlorn hope. He did not turn his head but heaved with a whinny at the aluminium bar.

'Twenty on the clock and you can do anything you want. There's no end to your strength, no end to your talents, you can make the whole city move.'

'No,' Dudley gasped as he pushed. 'Please don't.'

'You're going all the way, you're going straight to the top, to the big house on Long Island, to the penthouse suite on Central Park West, you're going into the record books. You're the best, you're the meanest, the slyest, the hardest. No one stands in your way. Okay, let's go again, ten on the clock.'

There was a long pain in his gut. He thought he was going to cry. Turning his head, he saw nothing but a blur of light and shade, the vague outline of Bella, legs apart, stern and damp, rotating at the hip, warmth radiating off her, her smell flooding him. 'You're under orders,' her voice said.

This was the game, it was all coming back to him, meanings of ordering and obeying, different mirrors giving different reflections of the same thing. A kind of bullying, a kind of desire. If only he could look into her navel and see himself altered. His arms were pieces of obsolete machinery, rusty

189

hinges locking. He gripped the aluminium bar and thrust it away, and again, and again, the pain burning him.

'Okay, finish up with zero, no weights, just the bar, lightweight aluminium bar, weighs nothing. This is the hardest, nothing is always the hardest. Okay? Pump it up, burn out. You've no idea how good this for you. Let's go.'

His anterior deltoids had frozen in a rictus, his swollen biceps set like concrete, they weighed more than all the kilo blocks on the machine put together and could not be lifted. Just the bar! The lightweight aluminium bar was stuck an inch from his nose and would not budge.

'Let's go, Dud. Nothing gets in your way, you always come out on top, you are the original hustler. You break other people. You use them and leave them broken. You know every trick. You can do it smiling. You are always going to get what you want, it's a law of the universe. You are the only important person alive.'

He could not move the bar. He began to cry.

'Martin,' he sobbed. 'Martin.'

Bella had left him, he was alone, lying flat on his back with his agonizing arms folded across his chest, weeping, as around him he heard the crash of machines and the incessant pounding of the music and the din of his own unquellable heart.

It was dawn. He was told this, he had no watch any more, and in the Piranesian room times of the day did not exist. On a stale, smoky mezzanine, Dudley, Bella and some of her friends were drinking from a jug of Bloody Mary. Bella had called this a pick-me-up. Dudley was finding it difficult lifting his glass to the level of his mouth.

Music still played, but no one was dancing. On the large screen a different movie was running, images of frontier landscape, brooding Indian women, cow-faced old-timers. Dudley could not stop yawning or shivering. He lounged at the table, eyes glazed, nerves frayed, spectral through layers of fug.

Bella was about to leave in order to prepare for a modelling

190

session. Within the hour she would be bald. Dudley had not been invited to the session, and even his imagination had deserted him.

Slowly he got to his feet.

Bella looked at him. 'Can I get you anything?' she asked. 'Like an ambulance maybe?' He shook his head and wandered off, hoping to find a lavatory. For several minutes he circled deserted dance floors and crept along the sides of bars. Figures like ghosts loitered on the peripheries of his vision, disturbingly inexact.

'Christ,' he muttered, and looking up he saw Martin, standing watching him from the foot of a glass staircase, a tilted shape more permanent than the rest. He veered suddenly sideways and stumbled, and when he had recovered his balance Martin was gone. The staircase swept down to nothing, as intended. Wildly he searched round it but found no trace of him. Had he ever been there, was it a trick of the conscience? He had no time to consider further; nausea took him, lifted him almost, and spotting a rest room on the far side of the mezzanine, he made for it at a lurching run, the one thought in his mind a memory of swallowing something, a small puce tablet, tasting of chalk and marked V for verity.

29

Finally it was all coming to an end.

In the Charles Chaplin suite of the large hotel whose name he had already forgotten – an Edwardian pasty-walled room panelled with stills of stars of the silent screen – Dudley tried to bring his cocktail glass to his mouth. Fifteens hours after his ordeal at the Gold Coast Club his hands were still shaking.

'I suppose he used to come here and complain about the food, so they named it after him,' he said to Bella. 'My mood is cynical, I am in a cynical mood, there's no need to point this out to me.' They were waiting together to see if Martin would turn up. Dudley thought he would not. Around them fabulously dressed men and women milled and conversed, and Dudley was outshone despite his best efforts. He was dressed in black silk socks, white Trowbridge and Eley shirt, Venturi dress trousers, white cummerbund and bow tie and maroon velvet evening jacket with the gaudy insignia of the Imperial Indian Croquet Club of Madras handstitched on a lapel – the principal reason he had bought it from a costume agency in Oxford. He felt and looked terrible. Finding it difficult to concentrate on the scene around him, he let his gaze wander over the pictures on the walls, and was dead with those great men and women, dreaming their dreams.

No one looked at him, they all looked at Bella LaRose, mainly at her head. Although the neckline of her gown was notably low and the slits up its sides were long and revealing, it was her head they looked at. Totally hairless, it sat like a bolus of polished jet on her neck. Dudley had looked forward to this moment all week, but now it had arrived he was unseduced, even frightened: with her stone-like skull Bella looked as if she inhabited a different world altogether. And now he realized that she always had.

Somewhere a string quartet was playing Haydn. Dudley's hand shook and champagne cocktail trickled down his chin.

'Advertisements,' he said bitterly. 'Adverts. Commercials. Will I never get away from them? Have you noticed the sponsors? Everything's got someone's name on it. Look at this cocktail stick, there's a telephone number on it, you wouldn't think they'd be able to fit it on. And the napkin that came with the canapés: something called Happy Munching Discount Experience. Did you see that sign by the door? The string quartet has been provided by a firm that makes radial tyres. Everywhere you look, adverts.'

'This is an advertisers' ceremony, Dud, what did you expect?'

He trembled and fell silent, and as he looked vacantly round the room for the fiftieth time a nearby crowd parted and Martin limped through towards them. For a moment he was unrecognizable, his face seemed to have hardened and aged – but it was clean and his hair was combed back into a ponytail and he wore a dinner jacket of a reasonable fit. It would not have been an exaggeration to say that he looked human, and the effect was unsettling. Dudley and he stood silently facing each other, then Dudley began to stammer, a string of confused and incomplete preliminaries, and Martin nodded, cutting him short.

'Martin. You look . . . well.'

Martin stared at him inexpressively. 'Never felt better,' he said.

'You look about to die of happiness,' Bella said.

'*You* look like crap,' Martin said to Dudley, and a waitress in an old-fashioned maid's uniform offered them more champagne cocktails, a label on her stiff white blouse wishing them a Happy Advertisers Awards Day, courtesy of Vacuum Joy. People were moving to the private John Barrymore Balcony Suite, and they went with them, Dudley and Martin proceeding with a formal awkwardness, absurdly aware of each other as only strangers are.

'You didn't think I'd come,' Martin said.

'I confess I didn't.'

'I didn't think I'd come either.'

'We agree, I think, about the momentum of things, the compulsion of events, the conspiracy of unwanted thoughts.'

Martin paused then said, 'You're a fool. But you're all right. I like you.' A muscle in his cheek jumped. 'It was my fault at that television place.'

Dudley looked amazed. 'No, no, *my* fault, my fault entirely. Terribly bad-tempered of me, inexcusable, irredeemably bad behaviour. I was about to apologize.' Fussing with his bow tie, his cummerbund, his jacket lapels, he seemed to melt with relief, suffused with the feeling of reconciliation. 'Let me apologize, I want to apologize.'

'It's okay,' Martin said in the same inexpressive manner.

'Please, I must, I have confessions, terrible confessions, I blame myself for everything. I'm only waiting for the opportunity to make amends.' He could not stop talking but apologized on and on, loquacious with the relief, the words flowing from him, and Martin looked away again.

He was still apologizing on the John Barrymore Balcony where they took their places among florid, tuxedoed men and svelte, old women admiring the sunset over the jagged skyline and, far below, the fountain in the octagonal entrance area lit up blood red by submerged lights and dedicated to the Fraternity of Humankind. And he apologized more as they made their way towards the Jefferson Banqueting Hall. From the balcony they saw the pennant of the World Advertising Council of America spread out like a call to arms behind the top table, and they looked down past huge crystal chandeliers at the pattern of dining tables containing the more intricate pattern of cutlery and glassware, sparks of light reflecting off it all as they descended the curving staircase into the hall.

They took their places among executives, admen and media personalities and Martin put on his headphones.

'Al Wollheim,' the man sitting next to Dudley said. He had thin, grizzled hair and long-lobed ears.

'Geoffrey Dudley.'

'I see you're sitting at Ed Slezinger's place.'

'The late Ed Slezinger.'

'Late?'

'Overdosed, poor man. They say he was a bigamist several times over.' Tired though he was Dudley was delighted to dispose of Mr Slezinger in this way.

'Allow me to introduce you to Kent Dodge.' Al Wollheim indicated the man sitting on Dudley's other side, a conventionally handsome and short-sighted graduate of Princeton University who never stopped polishing his glasses and who began immediately to talk to Al Wollheim about business, specifically the power relationships between the advertising agencies, the drink manufacturers and the communications conglomerates who had been involved in the launch of Quench. It seemed that Drink Inc. owned the British subsidiary Pilkingson Food PLC whose trading partner Barnet produced the drink, and

194

MultiMedia Communications leased the rights to produce its commercial to Ad Ventures who commissioned Fast Film to shoot the video.

'How interesting,' Dudley said. 'So we were working for the Americans all along?'

Apparently not. Kent Dodge instructed Dudley in the largely covert relationships of international finance.

'So the Japanese are our masters?'

'Who knows?' Al Wollheim said. 'Who cares?' His face was flushed already from drink.

'A conspiracy? How human.'

While Kent Dodge was carefully disputing this, Dudley looked round the hall. The noise of a free dinner was overwhelming but to him it was the noise of a dying empire, the crumbling to dissolution of a dynasty, the end of an era. He was finished in New York, already a spectator. The vista of tables extended to the staircases in solid layers of gaudy diners, and throughout the dinner small crowds of socialites wandered loudly among them, high-fiving and slandering their friends, and generally trying to outdo each other. The banquet was like a picnic become grotesquely aware of its own self-importance. Food seemed almost irrelevant to it. More important were the itinerant television cameramen who shouldered their equipment around the hall looking for the noteworthy. Incidents were continually staged for them, and they were aware of their power: even the bored semi-skilled stooge trailing a microphone boom behind appeared superior.

Dessert came and went, then brandies and cigars. Al Wollheim grew redder. Martin remained slouched in his seat listening to his headphones and staring into his glass of wine. There was a moment when Bella was leaning forward – speaking to a wide-mouthed executive from MultiMedia who knitted his eyebrows and nodded his head – and Dudley shamelessly stared at her, admiring the fluent buoyancy of her breasts in their velvet cups as she turned her head towards the top table. Flashbulbs popped somewhere, followed by his delayed reaction, like a dinosaur's, away and back again, and before he

195

realized it he was looking into Bella's eyes. There was nothing there that he could read, nothing for him, and he realized that as far as she was concerned he was already departing, as if at that moment he were saying goodbye to her, pushing back his chair, quitting the table and bowing out in a puff of cigar smoke. He saw himself in a long process of continuous exit, checking out of the hotel, leaving New York, flying back to England, vanishing from sight, fading from memory, becoming someone else who had perhaps been here once long ago but couldn't now remember what it had all really meant or how he had survived it.

Later, from the balcony where he stood alone, he watched the liveried waiters moving between tables, the busy camera crew and penguin-suited diners, and thought more about himself. There was a pause in the proceedings before the awards. Every two minutes his cigar went out. He was so tired, his eyes almost closed.

Below, in a brief, white blaze, a man was talking to a television camera, the lightman craning his light over him. This was the intimate, famous scene that had occupied him for years – but now that it had substance, he found that he himself had none. Advertisers were like him, he had thought, making nothing, transforming everything, weaving fantasies around original themes; but in the last day or two he had changed, he had reversed this process of elaboration and unwound himself like a ball of wool until the last skein of self-invention came off and he discovered that he had no original theme at all. He was finally empty, an empty man.

His cigar went out again, and he felt a finger in his cummerbund. Bella LaRose was talking to him, reflections of light off the top of her head winking at him.

'Oh dear,' he said.

'You look awful. Are you okay?'

He gestured at nothing. 'I'll survive. I'm a survivor. That's what I've learned about myself.'

'Worrying about Psycho?'

'Actually no. Should I be?'

'Just that he's disappeared again.'

He stared out over the hall sucking on his dead cigar. 'I've been a real shit to Martin,' he said. 'I want you to know that. I want you to know something else too. I like him. I'm going to make all this up to him. I don't know how, maybe we'll travel. He'd like to tour the States, get away from it all. Don't think this is some false testament of friendship, I'm thinking out loud, it's all genuine.'

'What if he wins this award? Don't you think about that?'

'He doesn't care about it, why should I?'

Below them preparations were being made for the award-giving, screens sliding down from the ceiling, a podium being set up near the top table.

'He still needs to be found.'

'I'll find him.'

'Need anything? Automatic weapon? Tranquillizer dart?'

He shook his head.

'Know what?'

'I doubt it. I don't know anything any more. I don't *want* to know anything.'

'You're okay. For a dork.'

He waved, it was as much as he could do. 'I'm going now. This is me going.'

He went.

Martin was standing at the urinals, elbows tense, shoulders stiff. Because he was so much smaller than the men standing next to him, he looked like a child. He had always looked like a child, though now his face was harder and older.

'It's time sir,' Dudley said in his policeman's voice. 'It'll be easier on yourself if you come quiet, sir.'

Two of the men at the urinals swivelled round, splashing their patent leather shoes, and for their benefit Dudley nodded at Martin who hadn't moved. One by one they went, leaving

Martin on his own. After a while, still facing the tiles, he said, 'What does this remind you of?'

'What does what remind me of?'

'All this.'

'I don't know. *Phantom of the Opera*? The Book of Job?'

'Shammings.'

'I might have guessed.'

'Skipping Chemistry. Lessons going on everywhere else, all over the school, and this is the only quiet place in the whole fucking building.'

Dudley picked up a card from a stand next to the wash-basins and read to himself: 'Hygiene by Hygiene Inc.'

Martin, still facing the tiles, said, 'Shammings. I'm standing under the window in the toilets, skipping Chemistry, and the door opens and Proctor comes in. He's not surprised to see me, he knew I'd be here, and he walks right up to me, until he's very close, and he touches my cheek once, very softly, and then he hits me hard with his other hand. The floor's wet. I can taste the blood in my mouth, metallic. In his pocket he has a compass and a tin of black shoe polish, I know this. There's twenty minutes before the bell rings for the end of the lesson. What do you think I feel?'

'I don't know,' Dudley said.

'I feel like I deserve it.'

Dudley put down the card. 'Martin. We don't have to stay here now if you don't want to. We can go. You've always said you wanted to go. Forget the awards, forget the fame and fortune.'

Turning, Martin walked towards him until he was very close. 'It's too late,' he said in a quiet voice. 'It's too late.'

'It's never too late – remember what that funny man used to say?'

Martin shook his head.

'I won't argue. See you at the table. Oh, and good luck.' Crossing his fingers and waving his hand in front of his face, Dudley backed out.

*

198

In a cubicle, elbows pressed to plastic walls, he removed Dudley's razor from his pocket, then sat in his shorts on the toilet seat, checking its working parts. The parts did not work. The dull Bakelite handle concealing the blade would not budge. His finger ends throbbed as he struggled with it. Eventually, with a crack, it ground free, and for the first time he saw the blade, rusted, bent and unusable. Stuff had lied, he had never shaved with this. 'Family heirloom actually,' he said in a furious undertone. But when he pressed it to the tiled wall, it gouged a slow line through a floral pattern and did not break. This incensed him. Sitting again, white-faced and breathing in short, shallow gasps, he bit his lip and put the blade suddenly into his thigh above his knee and forced it two inches across his leg, hissing as the blood came, a big squeezed roll with a beauty that surprised him, pulsing over his knee.

What more proof did he want? He pulled up his trousers and fastened them. The razor blade resisted for a moment then clacked back into the handle. Applause was already sounding in the hall as he left the lavatory and made his way back to his table.

The dinner had been rowdy but the award-giving was rowdier. Manners were dictated by an etiquette of hysteria which demanded constant emotional outbursts from the speakers, recipients of awards and the floor. For each award – and there seemed to be hundreds, from Best Ad to Costumes Technician of the Year – the format was the same: the announcement of the short-list (rapt respect from the audience); the viewing of the ads on giant screens (cries of enthusiasm); the slow disclosure of the award-winner (droll suspense or orgiastic emotion); the award-giving itself (blood-curdling screams, mistimed handshakes, lost footings, fumbled trophies, frantic waving and opportunistic kisses); and at last, and over and over, the speeches – speeches of gratitude, triumph, humility, self-righteousness, joy, anger, vindication, forgiveness, ecstasy and revenge, without exception culminating in the thanking of wives, husbands, lovers, mothers, fathers, sisters, brothers, colleagues, friends, accountants, God and pets — debts of gratitude so great as to seem insupportable.

Martin sat meticulously destroying the cardboard rosette which had been placed on the table to draw diners' attention to the donation of the cutlery by Monster Toy Design of Massachusetts. Occasionally he looked up at Dudley. When the moment arrived to announced the award for the best actor, Dudley smiled at him, winked and waved his crossed fingers at him again.

They began to show the six ads. The first promoted manure, a wistful comic performance. The second attempted a tricky narrative involving a high-rise construction engineer, an orangutang and a tube of new-formula adhesive. In the third a pale-faced man fell three thousand feet from an aeroplane whilst using a battery-operated shaver. As Martin's name was announced Dudley looked over to his seat and saw that he had gone. His eyes registered this, and then a second later, his brain. Martin's chair was empty, there was nothing left but Bella LaRose shrugging, bald and unconcerned. Dudley gawped.

'Hey,' Al Wollheim said, nudging him. 'This is your man. Didn't recognize him. Guy's so small in real life.' On screen, larger than life, Martin was demonstrating the familiar range of Method School expressions while a woman's fingers climbed his naked chest. But his chair was still empty.

Bella leaned across. 'Relax,' she said.

'Can't.'

His chair fell away as he backed abruptly from the table, and turned into the dark space, the massed tables, the incandescence of a spot above.

'Hey,' Al Wollheim said a moment later, but Dudley was gone.

The lavatory was deserted. He ran rubber-legged down empty corridors signposted to *Walt Whitman Parlour*, *Heinz Conference Room*, *Chrysler Concert Hall*, down to the entrance and out through slow electronic doors on to the pale arena where he stood panting, bathed in red light from the Fountain to Humankind. Water chugged in its trough, a cool sound. The thick material of the sky lay above. His heart was racing with the beauty of the evening and his nervousness, and he looked up to the balcony where they had stood earlier, and thought he saw a silhouette. Now he realized why. Why it was too late.

He stumbled inside and up stairs past shut doors. *Rest Room, Private, Laundry*. Almost immediately he was lost. From somewhere in the vast building came the faint noise of applause, and hearing it he felt cut off, not only from the banqueting hall, but from the rest of his life. Mirrors reflected him rushing down long, soft corridors, a fat man red in the face, slovenly in dripping shirt and fluttering bow tie, fleeing a fire or an assassin or his past. He thought his heart was going to burst with love.

Lurching to a halt, he ran the other way. *To the John Barrymore Balcony*. This was a dramatic entrance into another life altogether: he was running onstage like a messenger from a Shakespearian battlefield, a sweaty bit-player with half a line.

Gasping, he staggered up the staircase. Even the illusion of other people had vanished; there was nothing left but baby-blue carpeted stairs rising and falling in front of him, his panicky breathing, the wrong turns, the dark games of nightmare and, at the end of it all, the figure of Martin, already climbing the balcony rail. It occurred to him that he had foreseen everything that was about to happen, and he stopped suddenly with a noise like a short laugh, and turned sideways through french windows, shouting as he went, 'Don't jump, Martin! Don't jump!'

The John Barrymore Balcony was empty except for a shaft of light, some potted plants and a fringe of grey skyline. He bolted across it and ran round the rail, looking down. All was peaceful, except for him. He stopped running and crouched with his hands on his knees, fighting for breath. A mist hung on the tops of buildings, a long sleeve of cloud. Cool air streamed against him. Trembling in the minute of release after exertion, he lifted his face to feel the breeze, and a huge sigh broke from him. He blinked back the impulse to cry. The stars were hidden, and Manhattan was drawn more delicately than he had seen it before, its outlines softened as if the city receded from him. The heatwave had broken. Nostalgia afflicted him again.

He turned and Martin was waiting for him, a silhouette against the bright french windows, exact and unmistakable. Lost for words, Dudley panted and shook his head.

'Do I detect signs of exhaustion?' Martin said in Dudley's voice.

'Martin, thank God. Thank God you're all right.'

He limped into the light and his face was ravaged like an old man's.

'Worry not. Won't be for long.' The voice was sarcastic, how Dudley's voice used to be, and Dudley nodded.

'Go ahead, I deserve it. You don't have to tell me.'

'There's nothing to tell. It's all over.'

'You might be Advertising Actor of the Year by now.'

'I don't believe in it. That kind of crap. And if I don't believe in it, it doesn't exist.'

'I suppose not.'

'Neither do you. Neither do I. If I don't believe in it.'

'I know what you mean, it's been a depressing week. Over now.'

'Finished.'

'All over.'

There was a seat framed by pots of basil with a view of Central Park and the city around it, and Dudley went over to it and sat down. The park was a grey streak of mist lying in a steep-sided black dish. Clouds moved grandly above like repositories of all that might be known. Martin sat down next to him, hunched and stiff.

'This week', Dudley said after a while, 'has been a fiasco. I thought I was used to fiasco but I wasn't, this has been the one true fiasco of my life. Nothing I hoped for has happened. Nothing. Hardly an hour went by without some new calamity.

And all this . . .' He paused for effect. '. . . was my fault.' He paused again for Martin to disagree, but Martin was silent, bunched over with his hands in his pockets.

'I know this now. But what can I say? That I am a clown, a buffoon, that I've never been serious in my life? Everything I've done has been a little worse that what I did before, and it's gone on like this until it couldn't get any worse.

'When I came here I really thought I'd escaped. But "hell is here, nor am I out of it". Good God, the uses of literature. Do you know what I've learned? Life is a massive failure of the imagination, that's what I've learned. The exact opposite to what I thought before.'

The breeze was stronger, the sky darker. Clouds overhead massed black like soaked reflections of the city below. The tang of rain was in the air.

'One minute you were in your seat, the next you were gone and I imagined you lost, injured, dying, dead. The things we suddenly think, the worst things. It was like a revelation. For the last two or three days I've been wishing I could remember you at Shammings, I thought that without those memories we have no common ground. But we do have common ground, we've both been through hell in New York. We need to get out. Why don't we travel? You wanted to go across America, why don't we do that, drive across, all the way to the other coast. I can ring home for money. Forget New York, forget television and magazines and clubs and ceremonies, just get in a battered, overpowered old car, and take off. I like the sound of that, it has a certain circumscribing symmetry: the theme of discovery in a different key. I see us in Chattanooga, Tennessee, pulling up in front of one of those whitewashed, clapboard houses with a porch and antebellum furniture and the Stars and Stripes on a pole outside; I can see us sitting in a bar in downtown Tucson, Arizona, with Buds in our hands and the tumbleweed somersaulting past down Main Street; I can see us driving to the edge of the ocean in San Diego with the cicadas all around us and the palm trees and the warm breeze and the light on the water like gilt. Things build up their own momentum, you said so yourself, what's to stop us going all the way across until we get to the other side? A quest. It would be like a quest.'

He leaned forwards and gestured over Central Park and Martin said in a broken voice, 'It's too late, Geoffrey.' The razor was open in his hands, and he reached up and forward, and as he pulled back Dudley's head, his eyes were fixed in the direction of Dudley's failing gesture, a line racing beyond Central Park, over the landmass, across all America, rising and plunging to the Pacific.

THE MOON RISING

Steven Kelly

Having avoided all responsibility during his national service in the Italian army, Andreas Weissman returns home to the realities of life as apprentice to his uncle, a hotel night porter. It's a job that encourages reflection, and Andreas has time to ponder his love for Elisa, the beautiful and turbulent prostitute whose lust for life complemented his own emotional absence. 'You should live on the moon' she said to him once, 'because your mind is already there.'

While he pieces together the fragments of his past, the calm of his new routine is shattered by the arrival of a pugnacious businessman and his entourage of bodyguards and whores. And as the moon rises, and the night stretches out before them, it is clear that the lines of stress between the characters must fracture sooner or later...

Spare, almost ethereal, *The Moon Rising* is a powerful and deeply unsettling novel from an outstanding young writer.

'Kelly gives the "unfailing sense of being young" - and in love - with all the skill and precision of a true professional'
Penelope Fitzgerald

'A writer of unusual talents'
Sunday Times

Abacus Fiction

ISBN 0 349 10595 2
£5.99

THE DEAD HEART

Douglas Kennedy

That dumbshit map. I'd been seduced by it. Seduced by its
possibilities. That map had brought me here ... That map had
been a serious mistake.

The map in question is of Australia, stumbled across in a
second-hand bookshop by American journalist Nick Hawthorne, en
route to another dead-end hack job in Akron, Ohio. Seduced by all
that wilderness, all that *nothing*, Nick decides to put his midlife
crisis on hold and light out to the ultimate nowheresville - where a
chance encounter throws him into a sun-baked orgy of surf, sex and
swill, and a nightmare from which there is no escape.

'Pulls off that most difficult feat of being hilariously funny and
frightening at the same time'
Independent on Sunday

'Fluent and entertaining ... a highly accomplished début'
Sunday Telegraph

'A comic triumph, culminating in a high-temperature, high-tension
attempt at flight which has the reader sweating almost as much as the
character'
Time Out

Abacus Fiction

ISBN 0 349 10645 2
£5.99

☐ Complicity	Iain Banks	£6.99
☐ The Palace Thief	Ethan Canin	£6.99
☐ Generation X	Douglas Coupland	£7.99
☐ The Virgin Suicides	Jeffrey Eugenides	£6.99
☐ The Moon Rising	Steven Kelly	£5.99
☐ The Dead Heart	Douglas Kennedy	£5.99

Abacus now offers an exciting range of quality titles by both established and new authors which can be ordered from the following address:

> Little, Brown & Company (UK)
> P.O. Box 11,
> Falmouth,
> Cornwall TR10 9EN.

Alternatively you may fax your order to the above address.
Fax No. 0326 376423.

Payments can be made as follows: cheque, postal order (payable to Little, Brown and Company) or by credit cards, Visa/Access.
Do not send cash or currency. UK customers and B.F.P.O. please allow £1.00 for postage and packing for the first book, plus 50p for the second book, plus 30p for each additional book up to a maximum charge of £3.00 (7 books plus). Overseas customers including Ireland, please allow £2.00 for the first book plus £1.00 for the second book, plus 50p for each additional book.

NAME (Block Letters)_____

ADDRESS _____

_____

_____

☐ I enclose my remittance for £_____
☐ I wish to pay by Access/Visa Card

Number ⬚⬚⬚⬚⬚⬚⬚⬚⬚⬚⬚⬚⬚⬚⬚⬚

Card Expiry Date _____